T ... ge in alien su ... ight and a p ...

... with its reminders of man's past triumphs. One-time soldier, erstwhile poet, his own past is a dull mosaic of betrayal and compromise . . .

Lucy, torn by jealousy of his first wife, is in turn demanding and destructive . . .

For these two Hell can hold no surprises.

This brilliant novel is an absorbing study of the tangled relationships which beset men and women, of the strange complexity of their needs and desires.

'Perhaps Brian Glanville's finest book . . . satisfying and distinguished' – *The Sunday Times*

'Done with deftness and subtlety . . . beautifully realized' – *The Guardian*

*By the same author in Pan Books*

THE ARTIST TYPE

THE OLYMPIAN

# A CRY OF CRICKETS

BRIAN GLANVILLE

UNABRIDGED

PAN BOOKS LTD : LONDON

First published 1970 by Martin Secker & Warburg Ltd.
This edition published 1972 by Pan Books Ltd,
33 Tothill Street, London, SW1.

ISBN 0 330 02969 X



*Printed and bound in England by*
*Hazell Watson & Viney Ltd,*
*Aylesbury, Bucks*

# ONE

## I

I sit with a whisky on the terrace, contemplating the view. The view I detest. The view I once adored. No, I must be fair to myself; I never adored it. I saw its aesthetic qualities; that steep torrent of olive trees, pouring down the hill in a cascade of pale green. Very pale green. What I would now call *pallid* green, though I'm aware, oh yes, I'm quite aware, of the way the light changes. I have read my Huxley. I have spent hours and hours watching the bloody light change, for want of anything better to do, and I can talk of it as expertly as anyone. The hazed opacity of the early summer mornings. The sharp, limned, Japanese quality of mid-morning. The mirage, shaking gently in the heat haze, of the early afternoon. The blue shadows of the evening and finally, of course, *pièce de résistance*, the sunset, the inevitable, the obvious, crown of the whole thing, the light pinkening then darkening, throwing a slow cloak, thank God, across the limited perfection of it all, while the hideous cypresses loom on the hillside like enormous candles.

Christ, how I detest them, those vile, implacable, funeral-mute trees, and how appropriate they are in this context.

Beyond the hill, the city, the fat *cupole* and the striving *campanili*, jostling each other in the valley, those red domes and yellow towers, those green-and-white churches and those ochre palaces, tinged their evening pink, their tourist's pink. A tourist's city. A museum city. Claustrophobic. Stifling. At least one can breathe up here.

Lucy is down there somewhere; I don't know where. In her car – which is closer to her than I am. With Anna – eternally with Anna, who is almost as close to her as her car; drinking tea in Doney's, perhaps, tea made with tea bags – and talking. Or playing canasta – with Anna, again – at the Manfredini, or the Contini. She should be back soon. There are guests tonight, thank God.

Beside me the drink trolley; the whisky bottle, the water and the ice. The glass on my left in the socket of my basket chair, cold against my hand. It's my third. Or is it my second? I *think* my second. I have limited myself to three. Before the guests arrive. I've promised Lucy. And she's right. Perfectly right. One *has* been drinking too much. Quite inadvertently.

I am ... Ovid. The victim of a self-inflicted banishment; worse than an enforced banishment, because that is imposed from outside, and so can always be lifted from outside. Banished; not into barbarism but into civilization, an embalmed civilization; which again is worse. No wonder all those Victorians went mad, and threw their wives out of windows.

*God*, no, I would never throw Lucy out of a window, would I, darling?

I certainly hope not!

*Never!* It was the occupational disease of nineteenth-century Englishmen with sugary, consumptive wives who *deserved* to be defenestrated. But Lucy is *not* English, she is *not* consumptive . . .

And not sugary, Kevin-wevin?

And most *cer*tainly not sugary. If anything, I would call you astringent, darling. A Jamesian heroine, in decadent old Europe.

What does that mean, that I'm being corrupted? That you Englishmen are corrupting me?

I thought the boot was on the other foot by now.

You mean that I'm corrupting *you?* Isn't that killing?

Tableau: four of us on the terrace. Lucy, myself, and our two visitors from Cambridge. Chromatically perfect; the sky modulating from bands of livid red into a deepening blue. There's still just enough light to appreciate the villa itself; green vines, green shutters against the orange stucco. When they arrived, they were carried away, and so was I; quite genuinely. When someone sees it all for the first time, one sees it fresh, oneself, becomes transported again. 'You are *so* incredibly lucky to live here,' they said. Lucy was not yet back. And I said, 'Yes, we are. It's glorious, isn't it? Have you read Huxley on the light?' And pointed out the Signoria and the Ponte Vecchio and the Baptistery and Santa Croce.

'To be able to look at *this*,' they said, 'every day. One would *never* get tired of it.'

'And it's changing all the time,' I said. 'That's the fascination of it. From hour to hour. From moment to moment.'

'Marvellous.'

'Incredible.'

I wear my white alpaca suit, an I Zingari tie. Lucy, when she arrives, is wearing a plain green dress. She always dresses very simply, unpretentiously, *jeune fille*. She's just been to the hairdresser: that's why she's late. It makes her, as always, look severe. Severe but beautiful. The boys both wear suits of pale grey. Neil is very tall and blond and composed; a typical Etonian. Rupert is dark, with wavy hair; broader. How pleased I was to see them! How good it is to talk to them. And Lucy really seems to like them. They're both at King's. Ronnie Ogle sent them.

*Did* you read that memoir of Henry James visiting Cambridge? In some literary review? It's upstairs. I'll get it for you. *You* remember, Lucy? Punting down the Backs, and everything going wrong; the climax of it all when the pole comes down thwack on his bald head.

How priceless!

But *I* envy *you*. God, Cambridge! Though we *were* so much more frivolous than you. Lucy and I were there two years ago; I spoke about that with Ronnie. And they aren't, they *aren't*, building it up? It mustn't be allowed to lose that marvellous rural quality, and those lovely, subtle blues and greens.

Kevin's always talking about how much he misses Cambridge.

We'll swap with you, won't we, Neil?

*That's* the idea! We'll do a swap. You two can take over the villa, and Lucy and I will go to Cambridge.

Oh, Kevin, isn't that wild? Us studying at Cambridge! But I thought they didn't have co-eds there?

You'd go to Girton or to Newnham. And we should ride bicycles.

Like Dr Leavis.

*Are* you a Leavisite?

I'm afraid so, yes.

I *never* admired him. There was too much hatred, too much *pleasure* in destruction.

Oh, I don't know. There's Lawrence.

Yes, Lawrence. He lived *there*, you know. Do you see? That villa, over towards Fiesole. Throwing plates at Frieda, and quarrelling with everyone.

Did he throw Frieda out of the window?

No. She was too large.

Maybe she threw *him* out of the window, Kevin.

Ah, *that* could account for a lot.

Do *you* write?

Well . . .

Kevin's working on a novel.

Set in Florence?

Some of it in Florence, some of it takes place in the war.

That's when Kevin first came here, in the war.

Did you really?

I was a Grenadier. We captured Florence. With the Canadians. Pipe bands in the Piazza Signoria. The Florentines' eyes popped out of their heads.

And you liked it so much, you came back.

I liked it . . . and I came back.

Super.

To live the expatriate life.

Ah, but the expatriate life has changed; you've no idea

how it's changed. Until the war there were literally thousands of us, Americans and English.

What happened to them all?

Some died off; otherwise taxation has put an end to it. Now there's only us, isn't there, Lucy?

My arm around her; and she doesn't move away.

Us, and a few old English nannies, holding out in the tea rooms.

I love that, Kevin! A few old nannies in the tea rooms!

If you really want an idea of what it was like, go to the English graveyard, in the Piazzale Donatello.

So green, and such an un-English green. A dark green, death green, cypress green. Those damned candles again. All green and white; the white of the tombstones, cracking and buckling in the long grass. So foreign in the heavy heat, with the grasshopper noise all round one. Those pro-consuls and vice-consuls, those poets and aesthetes, commemorated and forgotten. I wander up and down the steep paths, nostalgic for their England, *my* England, which I have come here to preserve – and which they deserted, knowing it was there when they wanted it. Deserted it, to die here. But at least when they were here, they had each other. I shan't die here. And if I die here, I shall not be buried here.

But you're so perfectly placed up here, aren't you? I mean, this marvellous panorama, and whenever you get tired of looking at that – I never would – all those glorious things to see in the city.

Of course, one should have outside visitors more often. One does lose one's perspective. One forgets one's advantages.

Kevin doesn't go into town too often.

I can quite understand that. It's idyllic here.

Idyllic. Do you hear that, Kevin? Yeah, I guess it is. I guess it is idyllic.

No, I don't go into town often.

Into the tomb. Into the womb. Among the buzzing motor-scooters, attacking you like hornets from the front, the side, the rear. Where the cold soaks into your bones in winter, and that damp heat oppresses you in summer. I have seen the sights. I have looked at all the saints. All the maudlin, whey-faced Madonnas. All the plump, misshapen infants pulling at the breast. All the burghers disguised as apostles. All the cold cohorts of statuary. I have come, I have seen, and I have had enough. I prefer to stay here, where I can look down on it. I have restored the medieval concept of distance, which the motor-car has falsified. We are *not* in Florence, here. In a medieval sense, we are not even near to Florence. When Bocaccio moved out of Florence to escape the plague, he moved no farther than this. We are not obliged to live our lives there. To bow to the compulsion of the city, the twentieth-century disease.

Lucy is happy. How she loves to be admired. Changes and blossoms. She deserves to be admired. Laughing. Her laugh. I have never heard so much pain in a laugh. Invariably the same; seven beats, on the self-same note. Her laugh. The measure of my failure. I have failed to alleviate her laugh.

Yet these are the best times : in company. She's proud of me in company. And the worst times are when company disintegrates, the dreadful pauses, the slow death-throes of conviviality, the looking at watches, when one knows that very soon we'll be alone. What is it that happens then, what alchemy transforms us : her? And which is real? Us alone, or us in company? Which is the charade? *I* am the same. I'm surely the same. In company, I feel she loves me. Alone, I sometimes thinks she hates me. Am I socially admirable, in isolation despicable? Oh, God, he's looking at his watch.

Look, *stay* to dinner.

We'd love to, honestly, but we've got this invitation.

Well, *have* another drink.
No, honestly.
We insist, don't we, Lucy?
Kevin's awful hard to refuse.
And tomorrow you must both come to lunch.
Super.
One o'clock. And we shall talk about Cambridge.
Can't we talk about Florence?
Kevin doesn't like to talk about Florence. I don't know why.

My tomb, my prison, my exile within an exile.

Then you and I can talk about Florence while Rupert and Kevin talk about Cambridge. Then Rupert and I can swap.
Do you hear that, Kevin? They'll swap! Isn't that the end?

Her laugh.
And now, the four of us together. Down the three steps from the terrace. Along the gravel path. My head like a mountain peak in swirling mist. Up to the gate, the high metal door that closes us against the world.

Goodbye!
Goodbye!
It's been so nice!

I like Neil. There's something wry and detached about him.

We'll see you tomorrow, then.
Yes, super.
Okay! Tomorrow, then.

And the door closes. On what?

*Weren't* they nice?
Yeah, I liked them.

But something's happened. Some process of possession. Quite sudden; with the closing of the door.

And they obviously fell for *you*.

You think so? You think they liked me?

Darling, they were all over you.

That doesn't mean they liked me. It could be just their English way.

Walking ahead of me, back to the terrace. Just out of reach. I should like to touch her, to put my arm around her again, retrieve her physically. I should like to. Changed, utterly. How cold it is. A terrible coldness is born.

Kevin, you aren't taking another drink?

I frankly wasn't even thinking.

You remember your promise?

Of course I do.

I'm just so goddam sick of paying all those liquor bills.

I've told you, they should be paid out of my allowance.

Your allowance! That's good!

Looking down, over the terrace, into the bowl. Down the Lungarno, the lights like a regiment of gold bubbles.

Anna's right about those kinds of people.

So it was Anna.

They bum their way round Italy, off anyone who's fool enough to be taken in by them.

Anna hasn't met them.

She knows the kind. I don't want them here for lunch tomorrow.

Lucy, for God's sake.

Turning. Her face in the dark, across the terrace. Completely cold. No love in it. Possessed. Why? *Why* does she do these things?

You understand me, Kevin? If they come, I'll have Maria send them away.

I understand you.

No, I don't understand you. I shall never understand you. I have lived with you eight years, and in this mood I shall never begin to understand you.

We could ask Anna, as well.

Anna wouldn't want to come. Why should I ask Anna? Why should Anna have to listen to them sounding off?

We're worn thin. We've eroded one another, rubbed all the flesh away, the buffer of polite usage, until there's nothing left but bone and essence. Parody : of both of us.

So remember what I said about tomorrow, because I mean it.

Lucy, I don't know where they're staying!

Well, that's too bad. Because I'm telling Maria : don't let them in.

Lucy, this isn't you!

Or wasn't her. God knows. I've drunk so much.

It *is* me, Kevin.

It was not.

## 2

We are on the terrace again. All four of us; and Anna. But this time, in sunshine. And Anna has apologized. Characteristically. Slavic forebodings, then Slavic mutations. 'Anna likes them' – whispering. 'She says she'd no idea this was how they'd be.'

She was already here when they arrived. She's here so much. And I was still upstairs. In bed; I woke up late, I'd quite forgotten about them till Anna came, till I heard the door bell. Then I remembered and I thought oh, Christ, oh, *Christ*, and closed my eyes, till I heard Anna's voice, not theirs. Then lay there, wondering if I should go out. Somewhere. Wondering if she's forgotten. Because it wasn't her, it *wasn't* like her. It's always a whim, a passing impulse to hurt.

Anna's voice. So very hard and definite. Like a harsh, bright light, denying the possibilities of doubt. No shadow. She's devoted to Lucy; or so she says. And Lucy is devoted to her. She's said, 'I wouldn't stay here if it wasn't for Anna. Anna's the best friend I've ever had.' I wonder. I say nothing. We're polite to one another. What does she tell Lucy about me?

Should I go out now, go away until they've come and gone? But I've no energy, my head, when I sit up, rocks and spins. Or lie here till they've gone? I feel like Falstaff. Or – try to sleep. But the bell woke me, again.

Maria's steps out of the villa. Eight to cross the terrace. Fifteen to the door. At fourteen, the hiatus begins. Silent intercession. The sound of the door handle. Voices; *their* voices.

'Hallo!'

'Hallo!'

And then ... 'Hi! Wonderful to see you!'

It's all right, my *God*, it's all right!

'I don't know where Kevin is. I guess he's still asleep.'

Out of bed. One's face in the bathroom mirror. Eyes full of blood. Hair petrified. Every man his own Gorgon. Far, far more frightening than that dangling, dead thing in the *loggia*. Next, the habitual treatment, the fizzing of Alka-Seltzer, the splashing of cold water and Cologne.

The white suit sags in a heap, unwearable; I take out the beige, instead. Entrance: through the french windows, hand outstretched. '*How* nice to see you.' Which it is. They have no idea how nice. How colossal the relief.

'Did we disturb you?'

'Good God, no. I was reading: Palinurus. Do you know him?'

Or would have been, in other circumstances. He lies there by my bed, so perfect for my elegiac moods. I'm Palinurus. Or I'm Malcolm Lowry, sitting under the volcano, doomed; working on a masterpiece.

'Did you *know* Malcolm Lowry?'

'Good Heavens, yes. We used to watch cricket together, he adored cricket. He once told me it was the only thing he missed in Mexico.'

And introducing them to Anna.

'You've met Anna? Our fascinating White Russian.'

How crisp she looks. How crisply she looks at me.

'You make me sound like something in a circus. Anna, the fascinating White Russian.'

Her eyes pale blue and very quick. Ageless; or rather, an eternal sixty. Her hair's crisp, too; white and neat and very crisp. As crisp in her way as Lucy's mother, though hers is a different crispness, American, not European, not Byzantine; that's what I think of her, when I permit myself to think of her. Sometimes she puts her arm round Lucy.

'Are you a scientist or a humanitarian, young man?'

'Can't a scientist be a humanitarian?'

'Scientists have made the world the impossible place it is.'

'I'm merely a political scientist.'

'That's even worse. Ordinary scientists blow only people to pieces. You blow whole traditions to pieces.'

'I meant that I was reading history.'

'Modern history?'

'Till 1914.'

'Good. That was when Europe ceased to exist.'

'How about America, Anna?'

'I have told you before, darling. America has never existed. It remains an idea.'

'Do you agree with that, Lucy?'

'Oh, sure, I see what Anna means. America's just too big to have an identity.'

'I should have thought it had a pretty substantial one.'

'Power is not identity.'

'And Russia?'

'Russia *had* an identity. Now it has only a conformity. *Cosa vuole?*'

The same old song.

'So that's why you prefer Italy, Lucy?'

'I guess so. I came here to take a summer course, and I stayed.'

'Thank Heavens.'

My arm around her. She turns her head and smiles. I am aware of Anna.

## 3

On a summer course; and she stayed. On a summer day, obscenely hot, when the air seemed solid, immovable, piled in transparent blocks. Coming down the steps of the pepper-stoned Palazzo Antinori where I had been in the British Reading Room to keep cool, as in winter I kept warm; ploughing and plunging through the piles of *New Statesmans*, *Spectators*, *Observers*, *Guardians*, *Times*, full of familiar names, evoking a gallery of half-forgotten faces. The Antinori, where we'd colonized some corner of a foreign field. And seeing her rushing down the street towards me, quite terrified, hair flying, eyes dilated, hunted. That classic Florentine situation, gallant but predatory, infallible; let me save you from them, then come with *me*! From the two louts who were following her, laughing, resigned to making a game of it.

'Oh, will you please, *please* . . .'

'Why, are they chasing you?'

'Yes, for *blocks*!'

Tableau : an outstretched arm, stern countenance. '*Vattene!*' And they pulling up incredulous, reproachful, shrugging, as if I had betrayed my own sex. Once more, for good measure, *'Vattene!'* Both of them turning away then, up the street, bloodlessly routed.

'Gosh, I just don't know how to thank you.'

'You can thank me by allowing me to buy you a coffee.'

'That would be lovely.'

In the sprawled irrelevance of the Piazza della Repubblica, under a coloured sun-umbrella, at Gilli's. In winter it would have been the Tabby Cat, the old, superbly dingy Tabby Cat, down the Via della Vigna Nuova. She has a very pale skin, blonde hair. Her dress is blue, expensive; so is her diamond brooch. And she looks at me with total expectation, a readiness to be delighted.

'They just won't take no for an answer.'

'No, no, they've accepted defeat; it's all a charade. Everything in this country's a charade. They'd no real hope of success.'

'I wouldn't be so sure.'

'None at all. Whoever caught a woman by chasing her?'

'You've got a marvellous way of putting things. I could listen to you talk for ever, with that British accent.'

Infallible British accent.

'Are you a writer, or something?'

'Yes. *How* very clever of you.'

*Something.*

'Well, you had to be that; or maybe an actor.'

Which hurt, reminding me of Joan : 'You've spent your whole life over-acting in a third-rate melodrama.'

'And you?'

'Oh, I've been studying here. The course for *stranieri.*'

She is twenty-three. I am forty-one. She's from New York, but 'really from Pittsburgh'. Her parents, of course, are divorced; her father stayed in Pittsburgh. She is living at the Pensione Francia, which, like her dress, is expensive. I quote Auden to her, and admit that I know him. Or knew him.

'And Dylan Thomas? Did you know *him*?'

'God, yes! I was often drinking with him, in the Fitzroy Tavern and the French Pub.'

'And how was he? I'm dying to hear.'

'Like an enormous baby. Completely helpless and completely lovable.'

'And he drank himself to death.'

'Dylan did everything to excess: that was his secret. People are always saying, "Poor Dylan, how tragic he should die so young." Dylan *wanted* to die young! He would have liked to die younger! Good God, he was thirty-eight! By comparison with Shelley and Keats, that's middle-aged.'

'Go on! I love to hear you talk!'

But I am worrying. I have had three cognacs, she has had three *espresso* coffees, and it is time for us to think of going to dinner. But I have no money. I owe money at Camillo's, I owe money at Sostanza, I owe money at Zi Rosa. And if I don't have dinner with her it will break the thread, the splendid and inexorable progression; from rescue to coffee to dinner to bed. But when I pay the bill, she says: 'You've been so kind. You've got to let me ask you to dinner.' At Sabatini's, which I couldn't possibly afford. Where the brisk, deferential luxury oppresses me. Absurd, because this is what I'm used to. Or was used to. Or should be used to.

Wondering, as we ate and drank, whether I'd sleep with her that night, and thinking, probably not. American women are terribly pragmatic. If they're in town only for a day or two, pragmatically they won't resist. Or will make only token resistance. Otherwise one runs the dreadful risk of hearing, 'I want you to respect me.' At the sound of which, I reach for my revolver.

And Lucy is *very* baffling, her girlishness charming, yet at the same time, disconcerting. How innocent *is* she? How innocent is any American girl? The old myth of American innocence, when so many of them seem born knowing; and never to learn.

'And do *you* write poetry?'

'Yes.'

'I'd love to hear some. Could you recite me some?'

'I'll let you read some.'

And tell her I've lost my manuscript book. Is she a-sexual? Or experienced? It's hard to tell. Italian women seem sensual when they're cold, Englishwomen cold when they're sensual, American women aseptic when they're ... sometimes aseptic, sometimes lubricious. They want to command, yet to be taken by storm, to be overwhelmed, and yet to dominate.

I take Lucy's hand across the table, and she surrenders it trustingly, like a child. I stroke it, and her finger turns suddenly in the palm of my hand. She's not a child.

Afterwards we walk, arm in arm. Beneath the great green-and-white walls of Santa Maria Novella, up to the parapet of the Arno, where the dark obscures the sluggish khaki of the water. A cupola's lit up across the river; a perfect, plump rotundity, biscuit brown. Ah, the romantic Florentine summer night, made for visiting Americans. Beside me, I hear her sigh. And one may well sigh : the city is surpassing itself. Above San Miniato, the moon is trying to break through a thick, brown envelope of cloud. It swells and recedes, swells against it and recedes, as if trying vainly to be born. I point this out to her. She says, 'Kevin, you *are* a poet.' and then, 'It's so wonderful, I could stay in Florence for ever.'

Not I, I think, but I say nothing.

We walk, inevitably, across the Ponte Vecchio, lean over the parapet beside Cellini and look downriver past the Ponte Santa Trinita, which is still a wooden Bailey Bridge, rich with military associations, heat and pain and death; the stone heads still lie on the bottom of the river.

I have my arm around her. I try to kiss her. She laughs and says, 'You're getting like an Italian.' I don't try to kiss her again until I've walked her down the Lungarno to her *pensione*, and now she kisses me back, with her tongue, very earnestly and seriously, and looks at me afterwards with an expression so intense it hovers on the verge of pain, as if we're commemorating something. It's such a young look, so vulnerable, and it moves me.

She says, in a tone to match it, low and religious, 'You'll call me tomorrow, then?' and I promise I will. She has confused me. I feel, as I walk away, both predatory and protective. In the narrow chasms of the streets, one hears the cry of crickets. They have just had that strange, primeval festival in the Cascine, digging the poor little creatures out of the ground, and now they hang, invisibly high, outside the houses, in their tiny cages. *Crrreak!* they go. *Crrreak!* There's an awful pathos of hope in the noise, as if they expect to be heard, or released. *Crrreak!* A long, expectant pause, then *crrreak*! Varied by a sustained, frenetic *crrreak-crrreak-crrreak-crrreak*! by some cricket which has come to terms with its captivity, or has yet to realize that it can't escape. *Crrreak!*

I go through the Piazza Signoria, past the statues in their mute, frozen violence, past the deep, shadowed vault of the *loggia* where that green, implacable Perseus holds his Gorgon's head; and for once, I feel sorry for the Gorgon. As I leave the *piazza* at the farthest right-hand corner, I think I see Clovis enter from the left, squat as a tank, with his heavy, waddling, professorial walk. I raise a hand, but get no response. Perhaps it wasn't Clovis.

You know who I saw this morning? That Peter Clovis. On the Via Tornabuoni. He walked past like he didn't know me.

Peter Clovis is always walking past people as if he did not know them. It is in case they go past as if they did not know *him*.

Just listen to Anna! I think that's marvellous, Anna! Like he's afraid they won't know *him*!

The laugh. Up here, at least, one never sees Clovis. He's part of the Florentine thing, the banishment within a banishment. Perambulating conscience. When I was there, an exiled exile, we circled each other like two dogs, cut and were cut, each wary of the other.

Clovis? He's an American who's been here years and years. He's an art historian, I guess.

He says he is an art historian. Who has seen his history?

Who has seen my poetry? Clovis and I, both working towards the ultimate, irrefutable masterpiece which shall be our excuse, our justification. Palinurus: 'The only function of a writer is to produce a masterpiece.' An excuse for not writing. A *reason* for not writing.

*I* don't know what he's got against us.

Yes, she does.

I guess I've always been polite to him. We've asked him up here, but he's never come.

Peter Clovis. I admire and suspect his singleness of purpose.

Anna watches. How carefully she watches; like a cat a bird, a lizard a fly. How subtly she takes moral temperatures. How resourcefully she survives. But no, I mustn't think about Anna. It is far too dangerous.

Anna, *have* another drink before lunch.

We lunch in the dining-room. Like all the rooms, it's small and tiled and very cool. Maria serves us, in her aproned uniform; quietly, efficiently, almost reverently. There's Chianti, avocado pears, clear soup, fried chicken, salad. I eat what I can. I have not been eating well. Anna says, 'Florence is a village. All private life is public property.' With you, I think, chief broker. When Lucy looks at Anna, it's with such warmth; as a mother. But Anna doesn't look at Lucy like a daughter. I think I know why she resents me ... I must stop.

*Maria, ci può portare ancora pane? Questo qui mi sembra un po' secco.*

How well you speak Italian, Lucy!

Doesn't she? I have never been able to speak it the way she does.

Kevin, you have never been able to speak it at all.

Oh, Anna, he does speak some.

Of course he speaks some. After ten years, how could he not speak some?

Do you really not speak Italian, Kevin?

I under*stand* it very well, but I prefer French.

Kevin says he doesn't speak it because he doesn't like it.

Why ever not? It's so beautifully mellifluous.

Mellifluous? Pompous! Orotund! Bombastic!

Oh, Kevin!

I know what Kevin means. There's sometimes more sound to Italian than meaning: *vero*.

Exactly, Anna! It's a language for funeral orations and political demagogy! They don't even speak it among themselves, most of the time; they all speak dialect.

Sometimes, looking down into the pit, the crater, I seem to see little puffs of hot air rising, floating. Those clamouring voices, raised about nothing, soaring, billowing. Over the price of a dress or the result of a bicycle race. The hands waving like tendrils.

What keeps you here, then?

Lucy keeps me here, don't you darling?

I'm sick of keeping you here, Kevin. What do I get out of it? What do you give me?

What do I give her? Love, though she won't believe it. She can never believe she's loved. What could I have given her? I should like to have given her a son. Myself a son. It would have been so different if I'd had a son. 'I can't have children, Kevin.' Can't, or won't? 'It's dangerous for me.' Physically or psychologically? Would children have changed her, or destroyed her?

We sleep separately. We sleep together . . . at times of reconciliation. In those first days I made a note, one of my myriad notes, to be used in some unspecified future, to some unspecified purpose: 'She has known sex, but not experienced it.'

We weren't alone together, in a room, until the third night. Her room, in the *pensione*. I didn't want her to see mine. She said, then, 'No, Kevin, no, Kevin,' in a panic; a frightened animal, again. 'If you're going to be like this, Kevin, I can't let you up here.' And then, 'Just kissing. Okay, just kissing.'

And when I did take her, a week later, on her bed, in that room full of red plush and heavy furniture, her head was thrown back, she looked ecstatic; like an enraptured child. 'Oh, *o-oh*!' Her nails digging into my arm. 'Oh, Kevin, *Kevin*!'

Later on, in *my* bed, 'Kevin, you've taught me so much.'

Kevin, you've given me nothing.

'Kevin, I love you so much.'

*You've* never loved me, Kevin. I know damn well why you married me.

Joan, too. 'My dear Kevin, we all know perfectly well why you're marrying her.'

Which is a lie. Which has always been a bloody lie.

## 4

DID I MARRY HER FOR HER MONEY?

How often have I asked the question, dealt with it, utterly rejected it? Written it down, as I have written it now, now that they're all gone; Lucy and Anna to some exhibition in the Strozzi, Neil and Rupert to look at San Miniato. Down in our steep, cool, terrace garden, Italian green, under the shade of a fir tree, I write – and turn my face from the bloody olives.

I did not know she was rich when I picked her up. I did not know how rich she was, when we began our affair. I did not begin the affair with the intention of marrying her. It was she, not I, who first raised the subject of marriage.

She said, 'Kevin?'

We were in Siena; she had driven us there. We sat on the rim of the superb, sweeping, tilted Campo, so beautifully uncluttered, so different from the Signoria – with its nasty little plaque where they burned Savonarola.

'Kevin? We can't go on like this.'

And I, speciously, 'Like what?'

'Like we are.'

We'd had Chianti, then cognac. I was smoking a cigar. I was euphoric and a little drunk. 'Why not?'

'It's great fun for **you**, you're a man, but how do you think a woman feels? A woman needs a feeling of permanence.'

'Of course, my darling, of course I know what you mean.' My hand on her hand. My eye on the soaring magnificence of that tower. My thoughts on our own insignificance. 'Of course I know how you feel.'

'You can't know, Kevin. You're not a woman.'

Last week she said, 'Kevin, you're not a man.'

'If you're worried about supporting me, you don't have to, Kevin. I've got enough for both of us.'

'Perhaps that's *why* I have left things as they are.'

Was it why?

'What do you mean?'

'That I love you, but I am *not* anxious to be kept by you.'

At the time I said it, was it true? Analysis. There are two distinct propositions here. The first: I love you. The second: I do not want to be kept by you. Let us examine the first. I love you. Did I? How to recollect emotion in tranquillity. Or in tumult. At a distance, one does not recollect emotion. The poet's fraud. One falsifies it. One rewrites history like the Communists. I love you. I close my eyes and try to remember, seeing the Campo, the *palazzo*, her, smoother and younger. Anxious. Yes, in that moment I loved her. For her anxiety, her complete defencelessness. Her emotional dependence on me. And, perhaps, for the picture that she had of me. Something which Joan put so cruelly. 'Of course you'll love her; until she sees through your Byronic pose.'

My Byronic pose. A crippled athlete, physically strong. A crippled poet, morally ill. Better Byron than Hemingway, though; better to be a flamboyant aristocrat than a posturing tough. But I can admit this. That I sat there loving her, seeing myself as she did, needing her as she did me; a mutual need, and not an economic need. I'd lived precariously for years; I was ready to go on.

Did I, then, entertain the thought of comfort, ease, release? Yes, it was there, my eyes still shut, I feel it there, hovering, marginal, secondary. Is it corrupt to love a rich woman? We are all so conscious of our motives, now. We live in an age of self-disgust.

'Lucy, I think we must be careful.'

'Is this what you call being careful?' She laughs. 'I think that's real funny. We've been careful. Are you always as careful as this?'

'I mean careful about final commitment.'

As I must be careful, now.

'We are still exploring one another.'

'I don't want to be explored, Kevin. A woman needs security.'

Oh, God. One needed only that. Respect and security.

Respect me and give me security. Respect me and I will secure you. I press her hand and say, 'I know.'

She drives us back to Florence furiously, in silence, past the endless slopes of olives, the hill towns clinging to their cliffs like acrobats to ropes. It's beautiful and alien; and so is she. Did I love her on that drive? No. We were angry with each other. Which might simply be the obverse of love.

A few days later, she disappeared. No warning, just a note.

'I've decided to go home for the summer. Hope to be back around September. Don't cheat on me.'

Did I love her then? No, I detested her then, I went out and got drunk then, I plunged into a gulf of despair then; surely the other side of love?

Don't cheat on me.

Those four words lacerated me. Their cruelty, their arrogant insensitivity. I was determined to betray her: at the earliest chance. I contorted myself, trying to betray her, abased myself, humiliated myself, clambered off bodies which revolted me, once I'd used them. Then cabled to Joan: I LOVE YOU. COME AT ONCE.

And she came. My God, she came. How incredible it was to see her, in that smooth station with its stone canopies, getting out of the train, looking round uncertainly, older but *so* unchanged.

'Joan!'

'Kevin!'

Hugging her.

'*God*, this is wonderful!'

'Yes, isn't it?'

Still so English, so sturdy. Everything about her English and sturdy. Oh, how I hoped it would work.

'We ought to have done this before!'

'Yes, oughtn't we?'

Mother's coming on the seventeenth, Kevin.

I see.

I resign myself.

There's no need to sound like that about it, Kevin.

Like what?

You know what I mean. You know what happened last time she was here. The way you insulted her.

I did not insult her. There is simply a limit to provocation.

If that's the way you feel, Kevin, you'd better move out until she leaves.

Out of my own house?

It's *my* house, Kevin.

Yes : it's your house. How pleasant of you to remind me.

You don't have to be sarcastic Kevin. I can throw you out again, I mean it. And this time it won't be any use crawling back.

Not crawling back. I did not come crawling back.

You came crawling back, Kevin.

Turning. Away from her and from her voice. Her cruelty, which is really her mother's cruelty. Off the terrace, into the garden, my ears humming, not hearing. There are trees there, one can disappear. She never follows me.

Her bloody mother. Her bloody, steel-sprung, humourless, dehumanized mother. Who has been her ruination : and ours. Whom she came to Italy to escape. We have loathed each other from our first confrontation, and they have all been confrontations. Our first confrontation in the American Bar, on the corner of the Via Tornabuoni, where the vultures perched.

But we were cat and dog. A mutual, silent bristling, as we smiled at one another. Bitch, I thought. Adventurer, she retorted. We had been told about each other, and we'd read between the lines. 'You'll really love her, Kevin. She's got such vitality.' Which meant, dominating. 'She looks so young, you'd never take her for her age.' Meaning, she competes.

And of me, no doubt, she'd thought, what is he doing

there, without a villa, a man of his age, of his apparent attainments, and across me she had written: Failure. I looked at her and thought I saw the Bitch Goddess herself. Small, poisonous and neat. Extremely elegant. Obscenely well preserved. Completely self-contained. Snap, snap, snap; not a word, an effort, wasted. Not a pound of surplus flesh, not a hair out of place, not a superfluous smile.

'How *are* you, Kevin? We heard nothing but you all summer.'

All *will*. How much one understood now about Lucy, how sorry one felt for her father – two husbands ago – who came through Lucy's stories as a sentimental, dominated ass, the caricatured American husband, a jumped-up, self-made corporation lawyer, who'd jumped to *her*, but had the sense to jump away.

One was conscious of being charming ('Your *damned* charm, Kevin,' Joan said), conscious of her being charmed, conscious that it was all irrelevant. Charm is what she would expect of me; of an adventurer.

So she tried, of course, to stop the marriage; which she'd come to attend.

'Mother thinks maybe we ought to wait a little longer.'

'*Why?*'

'Well. You know. Till we're sure.'

'Till *we're* sure or till she is sure?'

'She means it for the best, Kevin. Don't forget I'm her only daughter.'

'The wedding is set for May 21st. I am marrying you on May 21st. If your mother wishes to be there, I shall be glad to see her. If she does not wish to be there, I shall marry you, in any case.'

'Don't hold it against her, Kevin. It's just that she loves me.'

There is no love in that woman. That woman has never loved anybody. When she comes, I shall be simply evanescent, there and not there, sleeping late, reading in the garden – a book is a very good defence against her. I shall leave her with Lucy, and with Anna. If she and I are cat and dog, then she and Anna are cat and cat. Kilkenny cats. If only they could swallow one another.

Meanwhile, I am aware of pain. The pain in my left side. Where the appendix would be, were the appendix on the left. I think of Lucy's mother, and I feel the pain. I shall say nothing to Lucy; she'd accuse me of dissimulation, believe that I was trying to gain cheap sympathy.

'If you've got a pain, go see the doctor, Kevin.' It is not as bad as that. It is not a pain worth taking to a doctor. It may have something to do with my wound, which was on the same side but in the back. The poet's wound! The wound that brought me Joan. How painfully simple life was, at the time of the wound. I mean, both painful *and* simple.

How simple the war itself was, in retrospect. Simple, if only one survived. What easy choices; between courage and cowardice, sacrifice and self-preservation. And there wasn't even a choice. One was too young for choice; one had been conditioned. One was Wilfred Owen, Siegfried Sassoon. Poets, like generals, begin a new war by fighting the old one. One read Keith Douglas and Alun Lewis, but tried to behave . . . like Byron.

How nostalgic one grows for one's primal innocence. For tangible enemies. For easy decisions. I put my hand to my side, and I fear death. But then I didn't fear death. Even in the Lazio, when we were surrounded and abandoned. It was too romantic to be real; a soldier's death, a young death, still seemed poetically right. Everything so clear: the prospect of execution concentrates the mind wonderfully. Clear enough already, in the sharp summer light. The green sweep of country around us, treacherously silent, now terraced and cultivated, now bucking and plunging in dark, boiling waves of trees. Each *paysage* with a double value, the aesthetic and the practical; as landscape and as cover.

There were eight of us, the remains of my platoon. Two of us wounded. Nothing to eat save what we could glean from the land and forage from the farms. Now and then a rising halo of smoke, a throbbing aeroplane, to remind us of what had happened to us. Time suspended. Fear suspended. Very beautiful.

It went on, in fact, for four days. Foraging and hiding. Strange, sudden bursts of action, when one was merely a bundle of reflex movement, feeling nothing, running, shouting, pulling triggers, till it was over, and we were away again.

The relief of my wound. Relief, still more than pain. Outside Cassino, a mortar fragment. Too shaken, at first, and numb, to feel anything but this drowsy satisfaction at an honourable release. One hadn't failed.

The rest . . . literature. That is to say, it had been written; or was being written. By Douglas and Keyes and Lewis. Army cots, cool hands, agony, mosquito nets, heat, the ether smell, Joan. *Her* cool hand. Love. Her kind face in my pain. Her kind smile. Her crisp, delectable voice.

And we were married. In England, in Shropshire, in our village, with a guard of honour. For four and a half years, while I tried farming and merchant banking and Kenya and a baby died and then I left her. With Rosemary; for Paris. Overnight, because I couldn't bring myself to tell her, to be there when it hurt her. I left a note telling her I wasn't worth her, and that she would have to forgive me. It was true; she *was* too good for me; her solidity, her strength, her very loyalty, made it worse to fail. We were still patient and nurse, the eternal nurse and the incurable patient; and I wanted to be well.

## 5

And Kevin?

Just the same, Mother.

Well, one wouldn't exactly expect him to change. Still hitting the bottle?

Much worse.

They don't tend to get any better, I'm afraid. I've had a little experience of alcoholics.

He's not that bad, yet, Mother. I wouldn't call him that. An alcoholic.

Oh, give him time.

It's still no life for me, Mother. Sometimes I think I live in this car. This car is my real home.

And you're going to let it go on like this?

What can I do? If I throw him out, he just crawls right back.

You don't have to *have* him back.

You don't know what he's like, Mother.

Oh, yes, I do, dear. I know exactly how that kind of man can play on your feelings.

Saying he'd kill himself.

You just have to call his bluff.

I don't think it was a bluff, Mother.

It's always a bluff, otherwise they wouldn't say it; they'd just do it.

And telling me he loves me.

Do you believe him?

Not any more. I've told him, what do you do to show you love me? Do you stop drinking? Do you settle down and write something? Do you try to make me happy? Mother, you saw all this coming.

It wasn't too hard. You were just so very young. You'd never met that kind of Englishman.

What'll I do, Mother?

I've told you, Lucy, you'll have to get away. Sell the villa and come home. That's the only way you'll ever lose him.

But I love it here.

You were just telling me how miserable you were.

I mean here in Florence. Right here in Tuscany. Look out of the window, Mother. Look around you at those hills. Look at that mountain on the left. Don't you see what I mean?

Well, you can make your mind up to it. As long as you stay here, you're never going to shake him.

The car. She has arrived; unless the plane crashed. Unless some kindly Providence has intervened. But people like that are usually invulnerable.

The key in the lock. Two voices. *Her* voice. Now Lucy's.

'Kevin!'

Do I conceal myself, or brave it out? I am invisible down here among the pines; they'll never come to look for me. No; one more whisky and I *shall* brave it out.

'Kevin!'

'*Here* I am!'

Drinking, rising, carrying my writing block and pencil, earnests of my assiduity, something to impress her work-warped, Puritan soul. What the hell's her bloody name? Barbara.

'*Bar*bara!'

'Kevin-nice-to-see-you.'

'*How* splendid! Did you have a good flight?'

'*Just* delightful. Still working on that novel?'

'I? Oh, yes. Still on the novel. We *must* give a party for you, while you're here, mustn't we, Lucy?'

'Oh, sure. Maybe on Sunday.'

'Well, that would be really lovely. And now I guess I'd better get myself unpacked.'

How do you think he's looking, Mother?

It shows a whole lot more. That mottled red around the cheekbones.

He seemed pleased to see you.

I know how pleased he was to see me.

My novel. God, she doesn't change. No, you bitch, not my novel, my investigation. Which would interest you, although one knows your views. Which conform with your shrunkenly inadequate life-view.

I have now reached stage two of the investigation. Not why did I first involve myself with your daughter, but why did I go back to your daughter? Joan, by the way, shares your opinion, though *her* life-view is so much larger. Still limited, but larger. But Joan is *parti pris*, and can be discounted.

And may I remind you of this. That your daughter wanted me back. That your daughter pursued me. That your daughter did not rest, gave me no peace, until she had me back. Something you would be delighted to ignore. And do ignore. I have no written evidence. I did not keep the notes your daughter slipped under the door of my *pensione* room. Literally dozens of them. 'Kevin, I don't know what I've done to make you treat me this way. You know I still love you and last summer you said you loved me, why has this changed?' She knew. She knew perfectly well. I had met force with force, and she had disintegrated. Joan was right. 'She's a bully. When you stand up to her, she capitulates.' As *you* are. As you would. As she would capitulate today, except that I find the battle no longer worth fighting. There are too many potential battles, with no end to the war. And I have fought my war, a real war; I have no interest in a mimic one.

I must retrace the past. Very carefully. Very honestly. Ready to condemn myself if necessary, because I was *not* guiltless, I acknowledge that; I can see that, from a certain point of view, it might be said that I betrayed Joan, that at the last, I made use of her. But there's the outwardness of things and the inwardness of things; the reality of motive and the imputation of motive. I did not betray Joan. I went back to Lucy, because her need was greater. And because I had seen that Joan and I were still wrong for one another. My fault was not in leaving her again, but in calling her back. That, I admit, was selfish. Yet to compound the error would have been worse. I was merely the first to see it; in due course, she'd have seen it, too. There was no need to send me back my book, my Wilfred Owen, with that damned inscription.

*All, all of a piece, thy life . . .*

My chase has *not* had a beast in view; or if it has, then only a domesticated beast. My wars have *not* brought nothing about. They have had something, a very small amount, to do with the fact that *we* have all been living here in Florence, and not the Gestapo. And my lovers were *not* all untrue. Quite the contrary. If anything, alas, it is I who have been untrue.

We spent that summer on a beach. In Calabria. Simply travelling farther and farther south until we found it. Living in a tiny stifling bedroom in a farmer's tiny cottage, with Sacred Hearts and family snapshots all over the walls and an outdoor privy: and laughing. My God, how much we laughed that summer. More than anything else, this is what I remember about it, the laughter. Laughing with the farmer and his nice, fat wife when we couldn't understand each other, and it never mattered. Laughing with Joan. Who healed me again, but couldn't cure me.

That's something Lucy and I have never done; laughed together. The difference between them; two kinds of laugh, two kinds of civilization. Lucy's laugh, pain and Joan's laugh, joy. One racked and wistful, the other so spontaneous. I can see Joan now on that splendid, rough beach. Robust and brown. Her light, curly hair bleached brighter by the sun, her eyes showing up a wonderful, refulgent grey in her tanned face, her teeth square and very white. Laughing at me. 'You *idiot*, Kevin!'

We swam a lot, we made love a lot, and though I swam – sometimes for miles, looking through a glass bucket – I'd no thought of Byron. My guru, if anyone, was Norman Douglas; it was him I thought of, striding up mountain tracks, through thick Calabrian forests, him, with his peppery omniscience, suspecting everything and missing nothing.

Did I love Joan, then? Yes. Very much. I look back on it now as a parenthesis; one of the happiest periods of my life. But it was unreal, and it was transient. Unreal, in that it obscured reality. It was brought about, like rainbows or whirlwinds, by a peculiar concatentation of circumstances. The sun, the sea, the isolation. The time we'd spent away from one another. The wound I'd had from Lucy. But it could not last. In fact it should have ended then, with the holiday. Which, in a sense, was a holiday from ourselves.

I even wrote poetry; the first I'd written since the war, when I was published in *Penguin New Writing*. I wrote about the colours of the sea.

*Changed by the sea, that wine-dark incorruptible,*
*A metamorphosis, now blue, now green.*

Which is all that I can now remember of it. No one published it. I was going to be a poet, then; we both believed it, just as we'd believed it once before. 'That's lovely, Kevin.' I agreed with her. In the sunshine, everything was lovely and enchanted.

And she was painting; seascapes. Which were 'lovely', too; very vivid, almost lurid, with thick, bright whorls of colour. It was something new; she'd begun to paint in England and in Florence, we were agreed, she would paint and go to the Academy, I would write poetry. We'd have enough to live on, till we were famous. Till then, if necessary, we could give English lessons.

But the moment of truth arrived. In the Via della Vigna Nuova, less than a week after we were back. Lucy, emerging from the Tabby Cat, where she'd doubtless been seeking me. Our eyes meeting : 'Kevin !' And I was away, down a sidestreet, making a grand detour round to the Lungarno. What object was there in recriminations?

The beat of her heels, pursuing me. And telling Joan.

'You'll have to face her some time, Kevin.'

'It would be useless and distressing.'

'If you don't, she'll think you're afraid of her.'

'I'm not afraid of her.'

But the Serpent had entered Eden. As I imagined then, though it looks different, now. Now, I can call it something else : reality.

'Kevin; she's a rich, spoiled American girl, and she'll go on pursuing you until she gets her own way or until you convince her that she can't.'

I said, 'There is absolutely *no* use my talking to her. *Nothing* will be achieved. She will *not* take no.'

'But until you face her, Kevin, she'll think you're running away from her.'

Did I love Lucy then? No. Or rather, I would prefer to put it like this : my love was in abeyance. I said to Joan, 'I have an idea. Why don't *you* see her?' And she looked at me. She didn't answer, but she looked at me. With a smile that I knew, but had forgotten. If I analyse, which I didn't, then, I didn't want to, I would say it was one of amused pity. That smile, I can see it now, was the dividing line. The end of our idyll. Throwing us back into our old roles, which we didn't want to play; nurse and patient.

Yet what I asked of her was reasonable enough. She *could* have talked to Lucy. Explained to her quite frankly about me, and what had happened, with a better chance than I of convincing her.

I talk as if this were what I wanted. Joan, rather than Lucy. Let me say this; that that was what I wanted, then. Rightly or wrongly. Or thought I did. Some clever Freudian, snatcher of sticks to beat the dog, might say I didn't; which was why I wouldn't talk to Lucy. Perhaps the truth is this : that I loved them both and needed them both. That neither was enough for me, alone, but both together would have been ideal. The *ménage à trois* which would be man's natural state, were women more accommodating.

Our cocktail party. Or rather, *her* cocktail party. For which she has put on her social armour; diamonds, new-blued hair, and a dress which is probably Dior. Inviolable. Cocktail noises, cocktail voices. Lifting from the terrace, into the purpling dusk. I am a host. I enjoy being a host. I enjoy the people here. Or most of them. Anna is here; she and Barbara smile and keep their distance. Smile and smile. Our friends. O'Kelly who is *so* nice and was once a concert pianist. Robert Clyde, retired from the Civil Service, who knows *so* much about eighteenth-century furniture. Giordano Marinari, who has the antique shop on the Lungarno Serristori; Titti Scarambone, carrying her poodle.

I see Lucy look at me – that look of pride. And I am proud of her. So elegant and so vivacious. So *young*. She is perpetually young, which will keep *me* young. Our eyes meet and she smiles at me, then turns and says something to her mother. Who nods casually and turns away, damn her. Now she is talking to Anna.

I think your daughter is pleased to have you here, Mrs Harrison. She looks much happier, tonight.

Lucy and I have always got on well together, Anna.

I too have always got on well with her.

She's a very likeable girl.

Who needs friends.

Yes, she's told me what a good friend you've been to her.

She has no better friend than me.

That's wonderful. But then she's never wanted friends.

She needs friends who will help her in her difficulties.

I guess that's what friends are for.

Have you seen the change in her, how thin she has become?

I'm Lucy's mother, Anna. There isn't much about her that I miss.

And you know *why* this is, why she should be so nervous?

I think I understand my own child.

Robert! *How* are the researches?

They progress, they progress. I've reached what I call Chippendale's irascible period. When he felt he could safely be rude to aristocratic customers. How's the novel?

Coming on. Definitely coming on.

Did you know that the Vicini have let their *palazzo* in Arezzo for two million a month?

To Americans, Anna?

To Americans. *Va senza dire.* To an oil millionaire from Dallas.

*Figurati.*

So now Gianni can spend next winter in New York with his boyfriend, while Lucia goes to the Paris collections.

*Godono una fortuna da morire.*

Kevin : don't drink too much.

And we must *really* start that literary review. In English *and* Italian. You and I and Giordano.

We must.

I even have a title for it. *Bellosguardo!*

*Indovinato.*

Now, what are you all talking about? Can I join in, or is it some kind of conspiracy?

*Una congiura senza di te non sarebbe congiura.*

Doesn't he say charming things? I hope he means them!

The laugh.

We were talking about our literary review, darling.

Oh, that again.

Wait and see, Lucy. We shall surprise you.

I hope you do.

The laugh.

Hi, Anna! They're talking about that old literary review.

Which you, of course, will be expected to support.

That's right. I hadn't thought of that.

*Allora, pensa.*

They won't get it out of me, Anna.

*Speriamo di no.*

Are you enjoying your party, Barbara?

I'm loving every minute of it. Kevin, I had a little idea.

Really? What was it?

I don't know how you'd feel about it. Just an idea. You're always talking about how much you miss England.

I miss *an* England. I miss *my* England.

And how much you hate it here.

With reservations.

Well, this is just something off the top of my head, Kevin. Something that came to me this minute. What would you say about living in England permanently?

But Lucy would never leave Florence.

I know that.

Then what *do* you mean?

I mean living in England. On a really good allowance. It was only an idea.

Which you've discussed with Lucy?

Lucy doesn't know about it.

No, I thought not.

If it doesn't appeal to you, let's just forget about it.

There are certain people, though it may astonish you, who cannot be bought. It may astound you still more to hear that I am one of them.

It was an idea; that's all.

I hear the three of them outside at coffee, Lucy and her two malevolent spirits. Poisoning her against me, each for her own purposes. With calumny. With innuendo. Though they hate each other, they will plot against me. I shall tell Lucy about last night. I shall insist her mother leave the villa. Her vile, materialistic witch of a mother, whom even *she* will see, this time, in a true light.

I hear my name; pronounced by Anna. Which she does, always, with a flick of contempt, a taking up with tweezers. While Barbara, the bitch, gives it an overtone of ridicule. To her, I am negligible, because I have not made myself rich.

If I go to the green shutters, I can see them and remain invisible. Smug, white, conspiring heads, on either side of Lucy's. The whisky is in my wardrobe; my fine, carved rustic, Tuscan wardrobe. I shall drink this one glass.

Possibly two. To support the fact that I have been insulted in the grossest way, and must *temporarily* bear it, for this is the last time she will come here. This time, she has over-reached herself, and Lucy will see it.

Is this my first, or my second? I shall compromise. Just half a glass.

I can hear them.

'But Kevin has no feeling for Florence.'

Anna.

'I can understand that. What I can't understand is why he stays. Or maybe I can.' *Her.*

'I don't think Kevin means all he says, Mother.'

'I hope not, dear.'

Bitch! I shall not endure this in my home. I shall drown them out. I shall obscure their filthy calumny. Downstairs, barefoot, on tiptoe, to the sitting-room. Where I put three records on the gramophone: Mozart's Clarinet Concerto, Beethoven's Fifth, and the New World Symphony. The good drives out the bad. Full volume then, locking the door, escape upstairs, again. Drown them out and drive them out.

Through the lattices, I watch them. Their heads turn. They have stopped talking. Protest registered. Music hath charms to soothe the savage tongue. Lucy is shouting: towards the sitting-room, where she thinks I am, but can't see through the shutters. Her mouth moves: 'Kevin!' I hear nothing. Only the music, which trivializes gossip. Anna and Barbara gape like fish. Lucy is shouting again. Now rising. I shall explain and apologize to her, later. When they have left us alone. Now she stalks into the house. Bang, bang, bang! on the sitting-room door. Where I am not to be found. Now I can hear her.

'Kevin, will you stop that? Kevin! I'm warning you, Kevin!'

Warning me of what? Oh, Lucy, I'm doing this for *you* as well as me! To protect your ears from poison.

Now she's out on the terrace, again. So agitated and up-set, explaining to the evil spirits, who stand on either side, feigning to comfort her. Anna's arm around her shoulder.

Barbara staring balefully at Anna. Who drops her arm. *I* am her mother.

The majesty of those violins!

Lucy runs into the villa again. I must put an end to this. One more whisky; and the rest for them. Fling open the casement. Raise the whisky bottle; over their malevolent white heads. I now baptize you in the name of Johnny Walker. Oh, God, this is priceless, this is wonderful! Now they look up. Look up, look up!

'You . . . two . . . old . . . *bitches*!'

# TWO

## I

*A small room on the top floor of the Pensione Oltrarno.*

*It has a floor of red tiles, whitewashed walls, and it is furnished with extreme simplicity. Along the wall opposite the door there runs a bed, its backboard in the far right-hand corner. At right angles to the bed stands a large, square, ugly wardrobe, a mirror on its single door. Facing the wardrobe, is a tall, plain, wooden chest of deep drawers, beside which, in the left-hand corner near the foot of the bed, there's a washbasin stand, of wood and dull grey marble, on which stands a white jug in a white basin. In the centre of the room, a small wooden table and a chair. Beside the bed, a narrower, lower, heavy, polished table on which stands an exiguous lamp, an empty whisky bottle, an empty glass, and a little pile of books, among them Palinurus's* The Unquiet Grave, *The Collected Poems of Dylan Thomas, a biography of Wilfred Owen, novels by Huxley, Waugh and Durrell.*

*There are two windows. One, in the left wall by the door, large and square, looks on to the flat roof, the railed balcony of the next* palazzo. *The other, near the foot of the bed, looks over the brown tiled roofs and high towards Bellosguardo, to the thick wooded slope, deep green in the pinkening evening light, the towers and villas guarded by stiff regiments of firs and the inevitable cypresses. Farther to the left is seen the exquisite plump brown cupola of Santo Spirito, beside it, an austere consort, its tall stone campanile.*

*In the bed, a man is lying, his broad, bare, freckled back turned to the room, his blond curly head obscured in the pillow. The rest of him is covered by a sheet. From time to time, the sheet, the body beneath it, twitches, like a whale harpooned. It seems, though the pillow deadens noise, that the man is crying, and when eventually he lifts his head, blinking, it's clear that he is; the noise of a sob is unequivocal. As if this made pretence seem futile, the man rolls over on his back and continues, sporadically, to weep.*

*He is in his middle forties, his face an actor's face, full, Dickensian, with something of the quick, sly, vagabond quality of a time when the stage was less respectable. His skin is rough and ruddy, red-blotched about the cheekbones, his eyes large and grey, his nose straight, solid and blunt, lending the face a mild obtuseness. Thus, his tears could be an actor's tears; he seems somehow aware, even as he cries, of the way he's crying.*

*It is* KEVIN.

*Outside the room there's the sound of one of the small, stiff, straight, metal door handles being turned, of a door creaking open, slow steps across the passage, and at last, a hesitant knock.* KEVIN *does not answer. He seems, indeed, not even to register the knock.*

*The knock is repeated. Gentle, still, but a double knock, and this time,* KEVIN *stops crying, lies rigid in the bed, while his eyes turn towards the door. Still, he does not answer. Indeed, he closes his eyes in an expression of weary disdain, as if seeking, in sleep, escape from the intrusion.*

*Once more, the knock. This time,* KEVIN *opens his eyes, turns his head, and calls out irritably.*

KEVIN: Oh, come in, come in!

*At this, the door knob turns, the door slowly opens, and in the doorway, diffident, appears a* GIRL. *She is tall and sturdily built, her full white arms bare, her hair long and blonde, her eyes grey, alert, her nose, short and curved, gives her a faintly bird-like aspect. There's a generosity implied both by her face and the contours of her body.*

THE GIRL, *her accent is American*: There's ... nothing wrong? I'm in the room across the way. I thought I heard noises.

KEVIN *sits up, the sheet still round him, staring straight ahead.*

KEVIN, *without expression* : There is nothing wrong.

THE GIRL : Well, I guess I'm sorry for intruding.

*Her hand still on the door handle, she begins to withdraw. At this,* KEVIN'S *head turns towards her and, seeing her, his expression grows suddenly animated, as suddenly alarmed.*

KEVIN : No, don't go! I'm extremely rude and you're extremely kind. One's so unused to kindness.

THE GIRL *pauses, looking at him with a surprised pity. And as if he'd received, from somewhere, a sudden charge of energy,* KEVIN *grows bright and effusive, full of a febrile gallantry.*

KEVIN : Look, do sit down! Throw those books off the chair. What a ridiculous way to meet! I'm Kevin Darnley.

THE GIRL, *mildly bemused* : I'm Ruth Chevalier.

KEVIN : How do you do?

*Moving to the wooden table in the centre of the room, she carefully takes a pile of books off the chair, places it on the table, and sits down.*

KEVIN : How nice to meet a nice American!

RUTH : Oh, we exist.

KEVIN : Of course you do! I was simply thinking of ... certain recent experiences.

RUTH : With Americans?

KEVIN : Yes.

RUTH : That's too bad.

KEVIN, *with manic jocularity* : No, no! *That* is the beauty of life! It's self-regulating! After the bad experience, the good one.

RUTH : Well, thank you. I hope the bad one wasn't too bad.

KEVIN : It was appalling! It was catastrophic! It could quite easily have been fatal!

RUTH : You seem so cheerful about it.

KEVIN : *That* is because it is past! At the moment you entered this room, it became history!

RUTH *smiles, half flattered, half astonished.*

RUTH : You could always be wrong about me.

KEVIN : I am *not* wrong about you. You are obviously beautiful and obviously kind.

RUTH, *with a smile of intense pleasure* : How do you know I'm not just inquisitive?

KEVIN : *All* women are inquisitive! (*He laughs, to mitigate the words.*) No, no, it was kindness that brought you in here, not curiosity.

RUTH : It could have been both.

KEVIN, *with a histrionic burst of laughter* : Of course it could! But it wasn't. A little *less* than kin and *more* than kind.

RUTH : Aren't your kin kind to you?

KEVIN : My *God*, no! They have cast me out of Eden! I have been banished!

RUTH : Why?

KEVIN : For pouring whisky over my wife's mother.

RUTH : That sounds a pretty wild thing to do.

KEVIN : It was the only thing *left* to do. (*More histrionic still.*) I said, "You bitch. You malevolent, domineering, materialistic bitch! There's no hope for you in your present incarnation. I hereby baptize you in the name of Johnny Walker." I anointed her : and I left.

RUTH : I guess there was nothing else to do. I mean, poetically.

KEVIN, *with joy* : Ex*act*ly! Not only a kind American, but an American with a sense of the appropriate!

RUTH : Is that uncommon, too?

KEVIN, *with an apologetic laugh* : *I'm* sorry. You see, my wife's American. My *mother*-in-law is American.

RUTH : And they're . . . still in Eden?

KEVIN, *with an outward sweep of the right arm* : Up there! If you look out of the window, you can *see* it! Our villa. Or rather, *her* villa. Which was frequently made clear to me.

RUTH, *looking at the books on the table* : You read a lot of poetry. I guess that isn't surprising.

KEVIN : Why not?

RUTH : The way you talk.

KEVIN : And you? What do *you* do? Stop! I shall *tell* you what you do. You are at Bryn Mawr.

RUTH : Vassar.

KEVIN : Vassar, then. My wife was at Bryn Mawr. And you are taking the summer course for foreigners at the University.

RUTH : Right.

KEVIN : And you would like to stay in Florence for ever.

RUTH : Right again. Wouldn't you?

KEVIN : Good *Hea*vens, no! I wish to God I could go back to England tomorrow!

RUTH : With so much beauty?

KEVIN : The beauty of the *past*; the *squalor* of the present.

RUTH : It's still beauty.

KEVIN : An oppressive beauty. An insidious beauty. A museum beauty.

RUTH : Don't you like visiting museums?

KEVIN : I like to visit them, *not* live in them.

RUTH, *regarding him, perplexed and cogitating* : So why don't you leave?

KEVIN, *for the first time losing impetus* : There are certain reasons. (*Reviving.*) But I *warn* you of Florence! Of the lure of Florence. Of the dangers of Florence. Get away, before it's too late! Run home, break the spell! Go back to the skyscrapers and the soda fountains!

RUTH : Must I?

KEVIN : At least they're alive. At least they're safe.

RUTH : Is this what happened to you? You fell under the spell?

KEVIN : Yes – and no. It's what happened to my wife. She came here when she was as young as you are. Which would be . . . twenty-one?

RUTH : Right.

KEVIN : There's no soil to grow in, here. Not for us. Not for Anglo-Saxons. We wilt in the shadow of the past.

RUTH : That's lovely!

KEVIN : Even a hundred years ago. Browning and the rest

of them. The Anglo-American colony. That was only top-soil. There was no striking root.

RUTH : Well, you really depress me.

KEVIN, *once more hysterically cheerful* : Do I? How unforgivable of me! You come in so sweet and sympathetic, and all I do is hector you. God!

RUTH : Oh, that's okay. You do it so nicely.

KEVIN : *And* I must apologize for my revolting nudity. (*He gives an uneasy laugh.*) *Could* you hand me my corduroy trousers? They should be somewhere by the stove.

RUTH *stands up, locating the black metal four-legged stove, to the right of the table. Draped across it, as though torn off haphazardly and flung there, lies a pair of khaki corduroys. She picks them up.*

RUTH : These?

KEVIN, *with hearty bravado* : Yes. Just throw them at me!

RUTH : They look like they're used to being thrown.

*Carefully, she extracts a trouser leg which has been turned inside-out.*

KEVIN, *with a burst of laughter*: *Isn't* that perfect? The European male asking the American woman for his trousers!

RUTH : *handing him the corduroys* : You've certainly got a great sense of metaphor.

KEVIN : God!

*He pulls the trousers under the sheet, and wriggles into them like a contortionist. Having put them on, he flings off the sheet and tries, equally dramatically, to swing out of bed. But with his feet on the floor, weakness overcomes him. He sits, dazed, on the edge of the bed, head in hands, while* RUTH *comes over to him in concern.*

RUTH : Maybe you shouldn't have got up.

KEVIN, *feebly* : I shall be *per*fectly all right in a minute. I can swim five miles at a time.

RUTH : Can I get you anything?

KEVIN : In that chest of drawers. The second down. Beneath the shirts. There *should* be a half-bottle of whisky.

RUTH *goes to the chest, pulls open one of the heavy,*

*wooden drawers, rummages inside it, then pushes it back again, shaking her head.*

RUTH : No luck. Just two empty ones.

KEVIN, *in despair* : *God*, I was certain!

RUTH : Shall I go out and get some?

KEVIN : No, no.

RUTH : I guess they sell it in the café below.

KEVIN *looks up at her with abject gratitude.*

KEVIN : Would you? Really? You *are* sweet and kind. Look here, I'll give you ...

*He puts his right hand into the back pocket of his corduroys, then leaves it there, his face frozen with dismay.*

RUTH : That's okay. I've got enough.

*She moves towards the door.*

KEVIN, *anxiously* : I'll pay you as soon as you get back.

RUTH : Don't worry.

*She moves briskly and easily out of the room, closing the door as she goes.* KEVIN, *on the bed, begins to weep again.*

## 2

So the poor sap's back again. Hiyah must have thrown him out. I saw him on the Lungarno as I turned off the Ponte Santa Trinità, wearing an open-necked white shirt, buttoned at the sleeves, *all' inglese*. He saw me, too, because he dashed down a side alley and didn't emerge again until he thought I'd gone. But I hadn't; *tanto maligno*! I'd turned a corner myself, down to Borgo San Frediano, then stepped back quickly, to see if he'd come out.

He had. He looked around as if he were afraid of my following him, then disappeared through the *portone* of the Pensione Oltrarno. That *studentesco* rabbit warren. I guess I can understand how he feels, and why he shouldn't want to see me, of all people. The dumb witness.

I suppose, if you felt that way about it, you could say he had it coming to him. That's what Joan said, the last time it happened. But as far as I'm concerned, it's all past history, a whole lot more remote than anything that happened here under the Medici, and much less relevant than the Massaccious, which I was on the way to the Carmine to see, when I saw *him*. I think I can understand why he should have left Joan, though he did it in the worst possible way, but why he went back to Hiyah, I shall *never* know. If ever there was a mean little bitch; and hollow as a drum. Joan always said it was a matter of money, pure and simple – which it obviously suited her to believe – but I certainly can't see any other reason. One used to meet so many like her, over there. All will and no cunt. Now he'll probably sit out the winter in the Oltrarno waiting for her to relent and have him up the hill again, like the last time. Whatever he's bought, he's paid a hell of a price.

In the Carmine, I forgot all about him. Going there is always like a kind of pilgrimage; through all the noise and the *vita popolana* of San Frediano, into that vast, bleak *piazza* with the church rising out of it on the far side like a sea monster. Rough and rugged like the *quartiere* itself, no patience with things like a façade, which is one of the reasons I like it. And inside, the colossal vault, quiet as a tomb and dark as a black cat in a coal cellar. With just that one, precious little corner. A monk or two, flitting by like bats. Then, in the corner, the *affreschi*, which are simply ... there. A miracle, if you believe in miracles. Belonging to nothing else, just to themselves; and changing everything. Those sad, marvellously modelled faces. Berenson wasn't wrong about *them*; they *haven't* anything to do with technique, in any basic sense. They spring out of the mind, and the paint brush just follows along, doing what it's told. I look at them in search of something new, and the problem is I always *find* something new, some new track, some new possibility. Yet the *how* it's done – I don't mean things like egg-yolk and temperament – in a sense is part of the *why*.

Two American girl tourists tiptoe up the steps to the chapel and whisper reverently over their guide books. I suddenly find myself thinking of Lucy again. 'Taking courses.' Jesus Christ, the barrenness of it all. The vacuum we've created; into which we try to suck *Kultur*, other people's culture, which came out of another kind of consciousness and was never meant for us. For the *cafone* college girls and the *professorini* pouring out of the universities with nothing in the world to fend with but their arrogance, their research grants and their PhDs.

But then we're only the West at its worst, only a distorting mirror of what Europe's done to itself. With our frantic energy, our perpetual, mindless motion, we're simply taking the process to its logical conclusion; and Europe's importing it right back again. The only hope, if there's any hope at all, is to go back to the original springs of creativity, which are to be found here. If you're lucky. If you dig long enough. Just as the springs of what happened here were once to be found in Athens. All of which, to most people, just sounds eccentric, because art history has gone the way of everything else. It's gone into the market place. It went into the market place the day Berenson started authenticating phoney pictures for Duveen, and it pitched its tent there definitely the day he came up with the Amico di Sandro. Though it would have happened anyway. So the only thing left for an art historian to be is a kind of spiritual archaeologist.

When I started this whole thing, I was going to call it *Toward A New Aesthetic*, but what one's really looking for is the old aesthetic which we lost and which *they*, of course, never formulated; something concrete and specific enough to work in present-day conditions; and change them. I even thought of calling it, *Beyond Tactile Values!* When I think of those, I think of Berenson stroking the ass of that bronze pig at the bottom of his staricase. Tactile values are just another way of saying, 'I like it', the same as 'life-enhancement'; and there's nowhere you can go from there. Where you make some sort of start is with the general acceptance that this place, those two hundred years, *were* life-enhancing. Then you start asking why, and you can only find out by looking, looking and looking, then going back to look again till it begins to get through to you.

The trouble, of course, is what the old Florence gives the new Florence takes away. You're involved in one constant battle against the torpor of the place and the loneliness of it, the way it throws you on your own, the way any serious activity seems to crumble to pieces before it's halfway through. And so, after fifteen years, I have ... nothing. A mountain of notes and a handful of essays; my opus. And have reached the point where I can accept that I may never have anything. The final revenge of Florence on the *forestiere*.

Coming out of the cool, back into the Carmine, the heat hits you like a blowtorch, the square's like a desert without an oasis.

Loneliness. I hope for his sake she takes Kevin back before the winter, or he'll have a double loneliness to face, his own and what Florence puts on him; and he could well go under.

## 3

Peter Clovis. One had forgotten that he lived round here. In that mausoleum of a flat with its drapes and busts and gloomy paintings. How curiously young he still looks. How curiously smooth and ageless. As if he'd somehow embalmed himself. Which, in a way, I suppose one does, if one lives in a tomb like Florence. At the moment, I can*not* face him. I can't face anyone except my sweet, lovely Ruth. Least of all anyone from *that* period, which I am still elucidating, anyone as involved in it and as *un*involved, as remote and hypercritical, as Clovis. Who sees me, I am perfectly sure, as flotsam, a sort of Conradian beachcomber. Despite our various affinities, our definite resemblances.

*Hypocrite Peter, mon semblable, mon frère.* You are *not* so different from me as you would like to think, even if your private income is bigger; or you spend it more circumspectly.

That winter, he was teaching Joan to paint, or rather, helping her to find a teacher, after the Accademia rejected her. I know practically nothing about painting, but I was still sure that Joan's wasn't very good. It was full of enthusiasm, which was something she had always had, with lots of strong, bright colour and rather Cézanne-ish shapes; Cézanne being one of the few modern painters Clovis would recognize. Painting seems to have come to an end of him somewhere about the death of Tintoretto. He was very non-committal but he did encourage her, I think because he liked Joan and saw that she *needed* to paint, just as, when we were married, she'd needed to collect china and to skate and to embroider.

Seeing Clovis brings it all so very sharply back again. We were at dinner with him, the night before she left for England. Which she should never have done. Which, I am still convinced, she did to test me. Dinner by candlelight. The three of us, and a friend of his, some man who owned a gallery, foxy and Florentine, who didn't speak a word of English, so that much of the conversation had to be in Italian, which I couldn't follow. And resented Joan, who could, and always seemed to take such a pride in chattering away in that inflated language.

A splendid, *heavy* meal, I remember, which Clovis had cooked himself, huge *bistecche fiorentine* done over a charcoal grill, and masses of splendid Chianti which he had brought in from the country. The faces: looming in the candlelight like faces in Renaissance portraits. Joan's, square and very happy, very animated, the candle-shadows showing up those jutting cheekbones. Clovis', square, too, very strong, Germanic, smiling – it was unusual to see him smile. He was an awfully *good* host. And the friend, his eyes darting about when we were speaking English, as if he suspected we were talking about him. Our last supper ...

I argued with Clovis about Florence. Or rather, we argued about some things and agreed on others. Such as the Florentines. Their utter callousness. Beneath the café good-fellowship and the pavement charm. Their total materialism. Which I am finding now – as I found before – as I walk about Florence, skirting the American Bar, where all the vultures gather. When they see me in the streets, they pretend they don't. They'll gladly drink my drinks, in Bellosguardo, but here in the city I become invisible, there's nothing to be gained from me, there might even, God help them, be something to lose. By speaking to me. By offending Lucy. But they're never flagrantly rude, because they know the day may come when I'll be *back* again, dispensing drinks on the hill. As for Anna, she goes past me with an icy righteousness, as if I were Antichrist. She'd burn me in the Signoria, if she could; and the others would stand and watch. How well I know them.

Ruth doesn't, though, she's still deceived by them, she separates them from the *pappagalli* who follow her in the streets, but I tell her that they're fundamentally the same. As Clovis said that night, 'They're *all* after something; especially from the foreigners.' And even his Florentine friend agreed. Very sadly, as Italians will, when something critical is said about them. Yes, they'll say, it's true, then go on as before. Like a confession in church.

Clovis said, 'It's no use trying to impose Anglo-Saxon expectations; the structure just isn't built to bear that kind of weight. What they *have* got is a kind of awareness we haven't; it's what's left over to them from something that was once a whole lot bigger. Something that, in England and America, we've never had.'

I said, '*I* can't see what it gives them. It simply smothers them. They aren't any better for it. They don't behave any better; if anything, it seems to make them behave worse. They don't create anything for themselves.'

'Well,' he said, 'who does?' and I replied, 'All I'm saying is that Florence isn't a city, it's a tomb, a museum, anything you like, but not a city. If Forster wrote that book today, he'd call it *A Tomb With a View*.'

'It's got a landscape,' he said, and we argued about *that* for ten minutes, but how can one explain landscape to somebody who's never seen England?

Joan used to say he was attractive. So he is, I suppose, in an abstract sort of way, like the sculpture he admires; for admiration, rather than for use. Women don't seem to interest him. How lucky.

My Ruth. God, how she reminds me of Lucy; then. Or is it that she reminds me of myself then, that she gives me back those years? She's as responsive and as eager as Lucy was, but she's a bigger girl, a more physical girl. She won't let me sleep with her, yet. I run my hand over her breasts. She has glorious big breasts, which I adore to shape under the palm of my hand. She shuts her eyes then shakes her head and says, 'No, *no-o-o*,' with this half-smile on her lovely face, and I kiss her fine, broad throat.

She has saved me.

That evening, when she came back, she not only brought a bottle of whisky, she brought two enormous roast-beef *panini*, a bag of plums and a bag of oranges. I said, 'Good God! Bundles for Britain!' and she said, 'I thought maybe you were hungry,' which I was, terribly hungry, I hadn't eaten for two days, partly because I felt so wretched I was quite inert, without the will to do anything but lie in bed and drink, and partly because I have so little money that I can't afford even the Oltrarno dining-room.

I was so touched by what she'd done, it was unbearable, and I drank a lot of whisky, she drank some, and we talked for Heaven knows how long. Of course she's been disappointed in love, which is one of the reasons why she's come to Florence, and of course she's over-reacted to it, everything Italian is bathed in that pink, romantic haze, and everything American is crass and abominable. *I* sympathized with her and *she* sympathized with me. She said, 'It must be pretty tough, suddenly being thrown right on your own, like this.'

I told her, 'Poets can live for years alone!' which brought us on to Auden and how one used to sit at his feet before the war. She's got Lucy *and* Joan about her; the earthiness and the mutual interests that I always had with Joan, and that marvellous, *fresh* quality Lucy had when I first met her. In a way, it's made my investigation easier by bringing things so sharply back to life, and in another way it's confused everything; there are too many parallels, too many similarities. Just what is in the present, and what was in the past?

I have phoned her twice. It was three days before I phoned her the first time, three days was the minimum limit I had set myself. I fought with myself to keep it, praying that she would phone *me*, that every time that loud bell jangled in the hall downstairs, it would be for me.

The first time I tried, she answered the phone herself. I had thought very hard about exactly how I would address her, and had decided on cheerfulness, on treating the whole thing as a joke, rather than a drama. I said, '*Lucy!*' as gaily as I could; and she put the phone down. The second time was two days later; the day I eventually met Ruth, and this time she didn't answer it herself; it was Maria.

I said, '*Maria. Sono il Signore. C'è la Signora*?' She told me, after a very significant pause, '*No, signore, mi dispiace,*' and when I asked when she'd be back, said in the same uncertain, embarrassed tone that she didn't know. Obviously she'd had orders. So I shall wait until I know her mother's gone, there's nothing to be done till then, and she should be leaving this weekend. Though when *she* goes, Anna will take over, filling Lucy with hate against me, feathering her own greasy, stuffy, repellent nest; that nest of overstuffed furniture, closed windows, Czarist relics and sickly ikons. She is, of course, a great churchwoman, which one has always found so different from being religious.

If only I could find the strength not to approach her at all; I *know* this is the quickest way back to her. I write to her almost every day, but none of the letters have I sent. At least one thing is clear to me, something which makes my investigation academic. My pain, the pain I feel, is love. (Strangely, my physical pain seems to have gone.) What else can it possibly be? It's spontaneous, induced, horribly organic, it wells up irresistibly inside me, and it cripples me. As long as she is here, I cannot leave Florence. Perhaps I should change my room, to some other where I can't see the villa. *Her* villa. I stand and watch it by the hour, just as I used to do the last time. If I had the money, I would buy binoculars. Ruth has never seen me watching. She's so discreet and thoughtful, something else I love about her, and she always knocks at the door. Giving me time to turn away from the window, dissimulate, pretending to be brushing my hair, looking in a drawer, reading a book.

Today, in the letter that I didn't send, I wrote : 'We have a mutual need, Lucy. I acknowledge my need for you, why can you not acknowledge your need for me? Which goes far beyond the crass consideration of who is "keeping" whom.

'We are the victims of our education. You have been brought up to respect wealth, I to despise it; and to take it for granted. If you had no money, I would still love you. If we lived here, in this extraordinary, primitive, uncomfortable *pensione*, instead of at the villa, I should still be perfectly happy. But at the moment, neither of us is happy; any more than I should be happy were *I* alone at the villa, and you down here : or anywhere.

'I know you feel disappointed in me. Don't you think I'm disappointed in myself? I have *not* written the poetry that you wanted me to write; that *I* wanted to write. Which would have justified to you my economic dependence and turned me, at last, from a parasite into a prize. I have not even written the novel which I've been cogitating so long, as a *faute de mieux*. Or rather, I have made a hundred false starts, thrown a hundred crumpled sheets of paper away. Do you think I don't want to write poetry? Do you think I don't want to get on with my damned novel? "The inability of the writer to do that which he most wishes to do is the symptom of a deep inner conflict." This is the standard I pin to my wilting mast.

'But you believe too much in salvation through works. You have all been processed, indoctrinated, with the Puritanism that you got from us, but in a so much more virulent form. I have, in fact, been cheated, though I don't expect you to see that. There used to be a place for *écrivains faillis*, especially here in Florence, in all those gracious villas. We put our art into our life and we were patrons, audiences.

We created a climate – in which other people's talents could flourish. We have been destroyed, made irrelevant, by two wars and by the iron functionalism of our heartless age. *Ora pro nobis.*

'Yet you are still, intermittently, proud of me, when I stand up and sing in public, just as I am *always* proud of you.

'Joan told me once – the day she found out I was marrying you and leaving her – that I was hiding from life. In that sense, the sense of living outside our own countries, we both of us are; something else we have in common, something else which makes us need one another.

'Yet I reject this "hiding" theory; it's too facile and shallow. After all, what is "life" and what is "hiding"? Is life any less real, as opposed to hectic, in Bellosguardo than it is in London or New York? You took me to New York once, and I found it quite unreal. *Sur*real. The skyscrapers spring straight out of some futuristic dream, symbols, not buildings; the whole city moves in a strange, hypnotic hum; one seems to exist behind plate glass in an aquarium. Nothing to touch or apprehend. What was "real" about all that? What, for that matter, is reality? After two thousand years, no one, so far as I know, has come up with an answer. Surely one has a better chance of isolating it, whatever it is, in quiet contemplation, rather than in all that febrile, meaningless activity, dancing to someone else's tune?

'Was I more "real" in the war than I am now, when life certainly *seemed* more real – much sharper, much more immediate – defined by the imminence of death? Was I?'

You must have known – continuing my investigation, which has become, now, my escape, my solace – you must have known that Joan had gone. Because that very evening, you came to my room. My old room, in my old *pensione.* Instead of the quick scuffle of a note under the door, your knock, which I recognized at once, a treble knock, more of a tap, very light. And lay barely breathing on the bed, heart thundering, wondering whether I should answer.

In that protracted moment, everything was decided, as

I knew it must be. What would have happened if I *hadn't* answered? The door was unlocked. Would you have come in anyway, to see if I were there? I don't think so. I credit you with more delicacy. You would have reasoned that I must either be out, or unwilling to see you.

*If that moment were repeated, would I still answer you?*

The question is unfair, as all such questions are unfair. Dead moments are irretrievable, unique, conditioned by their past and their present, never by their future. Besides, this is not the moment to ask, and answer, now that I'm down in the pit again, 'in adamantine chains and penal fire'. These things are always relative. A month ago, the answer would have been quite different from now. A month later, it might be different again. Once the moment has gone, it can never again simply be itself. Between you and Joan, I chose for the second time; and chose you.

You turned the door handle slowly, almost timidly, and I watched it hypnotized, as in a ghost story. In the doorway, you looked so fragile and defenceless. You said, 'Kevin?' and I cried out, 'Darling!' and sprang from the bed, across to you, embracing you; then we were making love.

You said, 'Does this mean you're coming back to me, Kevin?' and I said, 'Yes, darling, yes!' It was what I felt, it was what I wanted, it *sang* through me then, it burst out spontaneously, without reflection or calculation of any kind. What could have been truer than that? Isn't it at these very times that truth emerges? When it's caught unawares?

Lying beside you there, of course I loved you. When I came into you then and saw again, after so long, that intense, joyful, unguarded look on your face, how could I help but love you? I say, after so long, but oh, how long is it now since I've seen that look? Months? Years? So long, I can't even remember.

I moved out of the *pensione* before Joan came back; we'd been discreetly living next door to each other. Into *your pensione* which, I suppose, was the first surrender, because we both knew I couldn't afford it, alone.

Was I wrong? To move out as if I were fleeing from her? To leave a letter, rather than confronting her? But what was the point? Any more than there would have been any point in confronting *you*, before there had been a sea-change; and then it was no longer a confrontation. Quarrels are so useless, so irrelevant.

How Joan despised me; and how unfairly. Never accepting that I was thinking of her, not just of me, that I didn't want to hurt either of us more than was inevitable.

All, all of a piece, thy life.

When it's been anything *but* a piece. It's been, it still is, an absurd, impossible mosaic, in which each new fragment seem to be fitted by a capricious artist. I know now – and I knew then, in that moment – that I could not have lived with Joan. After all, we'd tried when we were young; what reason was there but my need, *her* need, to think we'd changed? That's what I told her in my letter; that I adored her and admired her but that I realized now, as she would soon have done, that we still weren't right for one another. I still do admire her; I wish she admired me. But admiration isn't enough.

## 4

I wish you weren't going, Mother.

I wish you were coming *with* me, dear.

I can't leave Florence, Mother.

He knows that, dear. He relies on it.

Mother, I've told you, it's finished. He could be a million miles away.

Isn't that what you said the last time?

Last time I let him blackmail me. That won't happen again. Why would I want him back? When he's home, he might as well not be here. He sits around reading, and he drinks. If I want company, I have to go into the kitchen. He could have done things for me, Mother. He could have done so much for me.

Not Kevin, dear. That's what he made you think. That's how he's always got by. On undelivered promises.

You're right, Mother, I can see that now, but it takes an awful long time. You keep hoping. You get moments when you think, maybe things are going to get better. Maybe they'll go back to being what they once were.

Or what you thought they were.

They were fine at the beginning, Mother. They were just fine until we got up here.

What I was saying to him was come on, save me, discover me, help me discover myself. And he heard that, he knew I was saying it, he said yes, everything he did said yes, and when he finished with me that first time I respected him, I hated him but I respected him, and I couldn't rest until I got him back, life wasn't worth living till I got him back. And then, when I did, was when it began. Or when it ended. When I found out the lies, when I saw through the disguises. The more I cut away, the less I found, till at the end I was left with nothing, a great big hole in the middle of a lot of borrowed attitudes, borrowed culture, borrowed quotations. Nothing was his. Except his body, and his face, which I'd loved so much, but couldn't now, because I saw the weakness in them, the way his eyes flickered away from mine because he *knew* I saw it. That's how he found his way back up here, through weakness. Through sinking so damn low that you either had to let him drown or pull him out again. I pulled him out. But this time if I pull him out, I know he'd pull me right back in with him.

## 5

This morning, my allowance came. Which is neither large enough nor small enough. Not large enough for one to live a life of ease, not small enough to force one into a new life altogether.

As I passed tiny Signora Cetti – they are all so tiny, here

– in the bleak front hall, the centre of this strange labyrinth, with its red tiles and stone floors and dim lights and gurgling lavatories and unexpected staircases and strange, rich smells and china basins, I said, '*Oggi pago, signora!*' and she dropped a little curtsy and said, '*Va bene, Signor Kevin!*' in that delightful way of hers, as if it really didn't matter, as though she were more pleased for me than for herself. How nice they all are here, how much they understand, though nothing needs to be said. Just a look, just a nod. I can tell they're pleased about Ruth and me, just as they were pleased about Dagmar and me, the last time; pleased, as they'd see it, that there's someone to look after me. They hate to see people solitary; like all Italians, they regard solitude and isolation as an affliction.

It was one of those mornings that I loathe, heavy and thick, the dull air hanging over the river like smoke, wiping out the mountains to the south which are one of the compensations. On the other side of the Lungarno, I met the Consul, whom I *so* admire. He was wounded in Italy, too, and it's left him with a right arm that hangs at his side, poor devil, like a wind-sock. He's terribly shy and I embarrass him, I know. 'Are you all right?' he asked me, looking up at me from under his thick eyebrows. 'Is everything all right?' Which is his way of saying that he knows it isn't, and of expressing sympathy.

I say, 'Of course, Consul, perfectly all right,' and he nods as if he's relieved I should say so, that I should understand what he means. He trusts me not to pour troubles in his lap. 'Not much of a day,' he says, he nods again, then we are both off. He is my England, I am his England. We understand each other. We are survivors.

At the bank, they were very affable, as usual, *buon giorno, eccolo* and lots of *pregos*, with just that little, lingering irony behind it all, which they think I don't detect. When the money was in my pocket, I felt my customary strange mixture of delight and disgust, a sort of guilty satisfaction, glad to have it there, but worried by what it represents; by the feeling that I'm being bought off. For a moment I thought I'd like to go straight up to the Arno and chuck it in, note by note into that filthy, bilious stream, oozing along like syrup out of a spilled bottle; and actually made my way there, striding fast and free.

But the way lies through the Piazza della Repubblica, and there I sat down outside the Giubbe Rosse, ordering a cognac and a packet of cigars, and the temptation passed. After all they owe me *something*; a great deal more than this.

After the cognac I had another, then another, and decided in the end to ring up Lucy, my darling Lucy, because this is *all* so ridiculous; if we could only meet just for five minutes ...

Inside the café, I bought the *gettone*, and the voice that answered, '*Pronto,*' was Maria's. She said, again, '*La Signora non c'è,*' but I wasn't going to have that, I said, '*Si, c'è, sono sicuro che c'è; c'è, la Signora,*' till she put the phone down and I heard her walk away. I heard her voice calling, '*Signora!*' Till at last there were steps again, Maria's steps, though; I recognized them. She said, '*Non c'è, la Signora, mi dispiace, signore,*' and that was that. That was when things became vague.

More cognac. A restaurant, where I ordered, but ate nothing. Bars. I fell asleep in one of them. And finally a night-club near the Tornabuoni, a shoddy little basement place where I'd sworn I'd never go again. An appalling orchestra in bright blue dinner-jackets, heavy *soubrettes*, bottles arriving which I knew I hadn't asked for. And, the last straw, getting the bill, a gigantic bill, an iniquitous bill, arguing with the head waiter till the manager came, arguing with the manager, and then, out of all patience, hitting the manager, who staggered back with such a look of astonishment that I laugh, remembering it. Whereupon the waiters came buzzing like bees, slapping and flapping, flicking at me with their napkins. I think I knocked one or two of them down, but there were dozens of them, and I ended out in the street. My money had gone; every note of it.

## 6

He called again this morning, Anna.

Surely you did not speak to him?

I certainly didn't. I had Maria tell him I was out. But I wish he'd stop calling. It makes me nervous. I don't like to pick up the telephone, any more.

You could get the police to talk to him.

I guess I could. Maybe he'll stop when he finds he can't get through to me. He did the last time. Right now he's so persistent.

Naturally. He was most comfortable up here. Down there, he isn't comfortable at all. *Cosa vuoi?*

He's only got himself to blame.

*Certo*. Shall we play canasta?

Okay. Maybe for once I won't lose to you.

## 7

KEVIN's *room at the Pensione Oltrarno. The early hours of the morning.*

KEVIN *stands at his washbasin, regarding himself unhappily in its oval, tilting wood-framed mirror. The face he sees is cut and discoloured, the right eye all but closed in a swollen, dolorous wink. He is dabbing at it, with a flannel.*

*There is a soft knock at the door.* KEVIN *glances in that direction, but does not reply.*

RUTH'S VOICE : It's *me*. Can I come in?

KEVIN, *hesitates, sighs, then answers wearily*: Yes, I suppose so.

RUTH *enters the room, her long, blonde hair tied behind her head with a purple ribbon. Over a sleeveless nightdress she wears a pink and white wrap. She seems only half-awake, she is almost yawning; her face, surprised from sleep, devoid of make-up, looks peculiarly soft and child-like.*

RUTH: Are you okay? You made such a noise.

*Seeing* KEVIN's *maltreated face, her expression changes to an alert anxiety.*

RUTH: Whatever happened?

KEVIN: I had an argument. In a nightclub. With some waiters.

RUTH: For Heaven's sake! Let me fetch something.

*She goes quickly out of the room.* KEVIN, *as though at once released and deeply relieved, drops the flannel and sinks, half reclining, onto the bed.* RUTH *comes briskly back into the room, carrying a box of tissues, a tube of ointment, a small bottle of lotion.*

KEVIN, *weakly*: You're much too nice to me.

RUTH *sits down beside him on the edge of the bed, and begins to dab capably at his face.*

KEVIN, *with a small, wry laugh*: Oh, God. You suddenly remind me of Joan.

RUTH: Your first wife?

KEVIN: Yes.

RUTH: I see. Well, maybe you just bring out the nurse in women.

KEVIN: Joan *was* a nurse.

RUTH: Then perhaps you just naturally gravitate to born nurses.

KEVIN: Are you a born nurse?

RUTH, *still dabbing at his face*: I'm beginning to feel like one.

KEVIN, *putting a hand on her breast*: Then I should never let them discharge me from hospital.

RUTH, removing his hand: Patients don't do that to nurses.

KEVIN: An aberration. Forgive me, Nurse.

RUTH: Okay, but watch it.

*For a while, they are silent. The treatment seems to have given* KEVIN, *who now has his eyes closed, inner as well as outer solace. At last* RUTH *ceases her dabbing, and screws the cap on the bottle.*

RUTH: Okay, I guess you'll live. Do you get into a lot of fist fights?

KEVIN, *in a hollow voice, his eyes still closed* : No.
RUTH : I'm glad to hear it.
KEVIN : There are simply times when this city becomes too much for me. Its meannesses. Its cynical materialism.
RUTH, *smiling warmly down at him, almost like a mother at a child* : Oh, come, now!
KEVIN, *bleakly* : And I have lost my allowance.
RUTH, *shocked* : All of it?
KEVIN, *sepulchrally* : All of it. In the fight. Stolen.
RUTH : And you can't do anything about it?
KEVIN : I can do nothing about it. I was drunk. It was I who began it all by hitting the bloody manager. It is their word against mine. I should probably lose my *permesso di soggiorno.*
RUTH : But that's terrible!
KEVIN, *quite deflated* : Yes. Yes, it is terrible.

*He puts his hands over his face.* RUTH *bends over him, her own face suffused with pity.*

RUTH : Don't worry. I can help you out.

KEVIN *convulsively shakes his head. He seems to be crying.* RUTH *puts her hand over his and continues to look at him until, with sudden desperation, he reaches up, pulls her head down to his, and they kiss. When* KEVIN'S *head moves down to* RUTH'S *breasts and, with the same, desperate need, he starts to kiss them, she doesn't resist.*

## 8

He done got himself another gal. High, wide and handsome. Blonde, too; *figurati.* Another American, but quite an improvement on Hiyah.

Well, I'm pleased for him; maybe she'll stay on and warm his winter. He's so cheerful at the moment, he's actually acknowledging me. In fact the last time I saw them together, in Piazze della Signoria, he even asked me over to have coffee. She's from California, the fresh air and seaspray state, and I guess she's never met Kevin's kind of animal before; a handsome, fancy-pants Englishman who can still roar up a bit of rhetoric. What's always puzzled me is how he ever keeps them after they've seen through the window-dressing, which must happen pretty early.

Joan used to say that this was part of it; she once told me, 'It's *because* he's so weak that they stay with him. They all think they can make something of him, and he trades on it, but it's like filling a bottomless pit. I know. I fell for it twice.'

I feel a little sorry for the new one. She seems a nice, bright kid, something better than all the little, homogenized *scolarini* they've been sending us these last few years; but no doubt she'll be able to take the whole thing home and put it to work as part of her great Yurropean Experience. I guess after all this time Kevin would ferment pretty well inside a susceptible young girl.

We got into another of those utterly futile discussions about Florence which I remember he used to start when he was still with Joan; he's still so obtuse about the place one wants to put him on the first train leaving town. And it's a bore to get dragged into justifying your own position to somebody so frivolous. Because that's what he is; you just can't take him seriously. He's got that English, dilettante, let's-not-commit-ourselves thing real badly. Joan had it, too – it was one of the things that would have fouled up her painting, even if she'd had talent – though not as severely.

What Kevin sees is just the negative side of Florence, which God knows exists; one's fighting it every day. But even this he sees superficially, *da turista*. While she, the girl, Ruth, is right at the other end of the spectrum; the open-eyed, open-mouthed stage, which at least presupposes some grasp of what it's got to offer. Initially. After which, it leaves you alone and lets you get on with it, to hack out of it what you can.

She and I talked quite a lot; about Fra Angelico and Donatello and Siena and the Medici Tombs, and I guess I shocked her by telling her my views on Berenson.

I asked her, 'Are you making the pilgrimage, then?' and her face lit up like a true believer's and she said she hadn't been yet but she was going: had *I* been? And I said, well, yes, I *had* been once, and she got more excited still, poor child; what had I thought of I Tatti and hadn't I found him wonderful? I said, 'The villa's remarkable, yes.'

'And him?' she said.

I said that I'd found him very old, a tiny old man in a white jacket with a white beard, *tutto bianco*, including his ministering angel, all in white, too, as angels should be – and with very white hair. He was wondering aloud why people hated him so much, hated an old man so much – as if age should be some sort of protection – why did the Middle-European critics hate him so?

I told her I thought he'd done a lot of original and valuable work, but it was flawed, and Kevin burst in with one of those great, hammy gestures of his, I guess he felt he'd been kept out of the conversation long enough, and said, 'Of course it's flawed; he was corrupt.'

She got quite angry then, it was rather charming, she said, 'He was *not* corrupt, Kevin,' and to me, 'Do *you* think he was corrupt?' and I just shrugged and smiled, because I was damned if I was going to stand up and be counted with Kevin. Who went off into a technicoloured fantasy about how *he'd* met Berenson, and they'd argued about the attribution of a Tiziano which Kevin said had been in his family for generations. I think the poor devil's reached a point where he himself couldn't tell the difference between fact and fantasy.

He has a curious attitude towards me, he seems to need my approval, God knows why, it's a little pathetic. Maybe it has something to do with the Joan thing, though I seemed to notice it before that. As for her, she looked at me like I was part of the *gita turistica*, a kind of fascinating curiosity; look, fifteen years out of America, and it can still walk on its hind legs! She said, 'And you're *never* going back? See? There you are, Kevin! I don't blame you. I wish *I* never had to go back.'

Which began this whole, futile discussion about living in Florence. Kevin said, 'But you've got a specific reason for living here,' as if this exonerated me.

Yet I know I'd stay here, anyway. With all the day-to-day annoyances. The small-time chicanery. It's still home; Jesus, far more than New Canaan ever was or could be. And it's still, in some strange way, central. Not in the way that little, jumping Sicilian cracker of a mayor's trying to make it, putting on those blown-up international conferences in the Palazzo Vecchio. You can't use the past as crudely as that, it just goes sour on you. But in what it's kept alive in the middle of our total anarchy, our hopelessly fragmented consciousness. In which art turns in on itself, we have paintings 'about painting', *porco Dio*! and what must surely be the last mad, mindless heresy: that what matters isn't the painting at all, but the act of painting, itself.

We got on to all this, as well, when Kevin told her what I was doing; or his version of what I'm doing.

She said, 'But don't you think art always has to find new forms?'

I said, 'Of course it has to find new forms, but it should move towards them organically. Today they've become an end in themselves. Form shouldn't dictate content. Now, as often as not, the form *is* the content. The artist swallows himself whole then says, "Come and admire me."'

So I didn't like Pop painting?

No, I didn't.

And I didn't care for Action painting?

No, it seemed to me like a baby playing with its own excrement.

'*Ab*solutely,' said Kevin; who at least has something left, the tail end of that English literary tradition which gives you so many literary references and so few places to go with them. Still, there's nothing like a well-turned quotation to hook a visiting female fish. Even if she runs away with you *and* the hook, like Lucy did.

## 9

It is all no more than an armistice. An idyll, an episode, a parenthesis. I know it, and I ache sometimes when I think about it; yet for the moment, it has healed me. *She* has healed me. With her belief in me. Not simply her abstract belief in my opinions and my possibilities. It's physical, as well; I see and feel it when she lies there, so joyfully and joyously naked, on my absurdly narrow little bed, her eyes closed, smiling.

How fine her body is. It's the paradigm of her; full and strong and generous. I kiss her breasts, her thighs, I run my lips over the golden hairs on her arms, I sink my tongue in her deep navel, like a bee at a flower. She regenerates me. Now, when I look up at the hill, I am anaesthetized, pain hangs in abeyance, inhabiting the past and the future. And yet I'm aware of it, waiting to spring. Just as I know that my 'reality', to use that maddening word again, is Lucy; as I am hers.

She will naturally know all about us. The basilisk, Anna, has seen us in the streets more than once, but in Florence, nothing's secret. As Clovis says, 'They not only know who, when and where, but how many times.' The beauty and the poignancy of it all is the very fact we both *know* it's transient. The limitation that gives perfection.

We're eternally looking at things. Or rather, she is looking at things while I, who accompany her, am looking at *her*, admiring her admiration. Yesterday, we went to San Marco, where I hadn't been for years; those peaceful, perfect cloisters, with their rhythmic elegance. If I were a monk, I think I'd have been reconciled even to these tenebrous stone cells, as cold as caves. And upstairs, in front of Fra Angelico's 'Last Supper', it came back to me when I *had* been here before. It was with Joan. We'd stood, as Ruth and I were standing now, and she'd said, 'The *kindness* in those faces.' Looking at them now, I hear her say it again;

those saintly disciples, two of them, especially; old men with an old man's innocence – not an old man's frenzy – unspoiled, a marvellous, peasant goodness, an openness to wonder which we've all lost.

I point it out to Ruth, and she takes my hand, squeezes it, smiles at me with, oh, so much love, and that same, sweet openness. Perhaps it isn't wholly lost. I don't deserve her.

I live in one fear only; that one day we shall turn a corner and meet Lucy. So far, I haven't set eyes on her. Florence is so small it must surely happen. It's as though we both have extra-sensory perception of one another, and pick up the signals in time.

So while Ruth is discovering Florence, I am rediscovering it. Reluctantly. Because the irony of it all afflicts me and depresses me. The massive dead weight (dead in every sense) of its gaudy past, bearing down upon its trivial present. How they irritate me, the Florentines, when they behave as if they're guardians of a tradition, when they have nothing to do with the tradition: monkeys dancing round a dead lion.

Now and again, we meet Peter Clovis. We turn the corner of a gallery corridor, climb the staircase of a monastery, go into the gloom of a church, and there he is. Always well dressed. Always wearing a good silk suit. Looking. Preparing this extraordinary treatise, which of course will never get written, just as nothing, in Florence, can any longer be created. Like Joan's pathetic paintings; she was sure there was 'something in the air', here. *Into my heart an air that kills.* For it does. It's a dead, cold, killing air, blowing from the tomb.

I felt it above all in the sacristy of the Medici Chapel, among those marble inhumanities, those white implacabilities, neither man nor woman. While Ruth, beside me, said, 'Aren't they majestic? Don't you love them?' and I took her arm, her *warm*, bare arm, and said, 'No, I love *you.*' She laughed her sweet, pleased laugh, but she's enraptured by them, she must have seen them a dozen times.

And then Clovis appeared, smiling his smile, which seems to say two things: that he knows more than you do, and that you amuse him. Ruth adores him. She says, 'Oh, but he's sheer Henry James. He comes from an America that doesn't exist any more. I wish we had more of him at home.' And she's right; he *is* Jamesian. Not American, but Florentine-American, with that austere Jamesian perfectionism; and a breath of the tomb about him.

Ruth says, 'The courage it must have taken, throwing everything up, leaving everything behind, just so he could come and study with Professor Borghi.' I told her, 'It's not courage, it's inertia. One comes for all sorts of reasons, but one always stays for the same one.'

She won't have it, of course. *Si la jeunesse savait.* Their strength is that they don't. So there, in that moonscape of sepulchres, the two of them talked about Michelangelo's draughtsmanship, and how his sculpture was indistinguishable, graphically, from his painting. She listens to him with such eagerness, her eyes smiling, her lips a little apart, as if she were taking in knowledge through her skin. Her eyes are grey, her lips are broad but not full.

She is reacting. As Lucy was reacting, and is still reacting. And I am part of that reaction. From the American Way of Life. The virtue of Florence, being that it is so radically not America. And my virtue, that I am not American. America produces these girls, warm and giving and idealistic, and having produced them, cannot nourish them. Yet neither can we. They expect far, far too much from us. How could Florence ever give Lucy – or, for that matter, Ruth – everything she lacks, everything she hasn't found? How could I? They swamp one with the vastness of their expectations. When Lucy says, 'You've given me nothing!' what she means is, 'You haven't given me everything!' Now that I am calm, I shall write her a letter to tell her that. To say that the burden is impossible – for anyone. That when she accuses me, she is really, by extension, indicting Europe.

The implicit, unspoken American-European bargain. That they provide the wealth, and we the sustenance. The bargain which Lucy feels – implicitly – I haven't kept. Which nobody could ever keep.

Again one thinks how strange it is to call life here unreal, when what it is is far *too* real, far too intense. We are characters in an endless closet drama, unprotected by the 'intensity' of real life, which simply represents escape from ourselves in meaningless motion. As soldiers escape from themselves in war; as *I* escaped from myself in war, which is surely why one looks back on it with such absurd nostalgia.

I dread Ruth going. When she goes, it will be much, much worse than before. She says she'll stay, that she'll try to find a job, but we both know she won't stay. She's too healthy and vital for Florence; Florence preys on the maimed. And when she goes, it will be winter. The *tramontana* in the streets and the endless, insidious rain in one's face. Where now it's full summer, and the city's an oven, the Florentines gone to the sea, the ugly tourists pouring out of ugly charabancs behind the Signoria, their cameras clicking like rifles. God, how I should love to be by the sea!

We've managed, in fact, just one day of it. By bus to Viareggio, where the beach was an insufferable ant-heap, a cacophony of obscenely fat mothers screeching at their indulged children, of *panini* sellers in yachting caps trumpeting their wares; deckchair jammed against deckchair, umbrellas bristling everywhere like great, bilious fungi.

We escaped into the sea. She's like me, she adores swimming; and she swims superbly. I love to see her swim, her hair gone dark and sleek in the water, her absolute Amazon detachment as she moves, her legs churning up a spray, her strong arms flailing. She swims faster than I; it was humiliating. To see her out there ahead of me, inexorably going on, made me ache for her.

At last she turned on her back and floated. When I caught her up, her eyes were closed, her face was turned raptly to the sun. What repose she has!

I said, 'My God, you swim well!' She said. 'You don't swim badly yourself; for your age,' and I ducked her, she pulled away from me, and for a while we wrestled in the water, laughing the whole time, her glorious flesh slippery and resilient under my fingers. Till at last I put my hands over her breasts and she was still, both of us still laughing, panting. I said, 'Ruth, you are completely adorable,' and she turned in my arms and kissed me.

She's a summer creature, unimaginable in winter.

## 10

I ran across Ruth, *l'amorina di Kevin,* on her way up to see the frescoes at the Fortezze. She asked me would I go with her; Kevin wouldn't – which didn't exactly surprise me. He'd said it was too hot.

'Well,' I said, 'I think he has a point; it *is* too hot. Now look here, why don't you let me make you coffee at my place, then, when it cools down a little, maybe we can go. It's quite a walk.'

So she said that would be wonderful, and how much she liked having me by to interpret things for her.

She hadn't been to my apartment before, and she liked it; she wandered around the *salotto* looking at things; the chandelier and the Florentine *cinquecento* tapestry that looks Gobelins but ain't, and the little Beccafumi and the possible Garofalo that Longhi thought was genuine and Borghi didn't, and those *settecentesco veneziano* chairs that I had re-covered with contemporary material I found right here in Florence. She suddenly cried out, 'I can *see* why you stay here, you've built yourself a nest!'

I said, 'Is that how you see it? I'd never thought of it like that. I've spent all these years feathering my nest!'

'Oh,' she said, 'I *wish* I could be like you! Really find myself a purpose here, and *never* go back!'

I told her, 'Well, I think it's a purpose. A lot of people would probably tell you it's a blind alley, and that I'm just a kind of hermit crab.'

'Oh, you're *not*!' she said. She seems quite torn about

going back home, though how much of it is Florence and how much Kevin, I wouldn't know. She asked things like, 'Wasn't it hard for you at first, to cut off? Don't you ever feel any pull? Kevin keeps telling me I'm reacting from the States, and after that there'll be a reaction against Florence.'

I said, 'There probably will. You have to bring Florence into focus.' But I know what she means when she talks about a pull. This strange, centrifugal thing that people seem to feel, tugging them back into the middle of things; or what they take to be the middle. It's a kind of guilt, I guess, like a captain who doesn't go down with his ship. Personally, I never objected to the weather; I just didn't care for the ship.

When I brought the coffee, she got to talking about Kevin. She said, 'He sometimes irritates you, doesn't he?' with an embarrassed kind of smile, as if she were a little ashamed about not feeling the same way. I said, 'I don't really know him too well,' and this amused her, she said, 'In some ways you seem so much more English than he does. He thinks you disapprove of the way he left Joan.' I said, 'I don't think it was delicately done. Aside from that, it just wasn't any of my business.'

Then she began asking me about Joan, what was she like, what had I thought of her. And looking at her, all bursting with sap, I suddenly found myself thinking of something Joan had once said. 'Kevin's like Humpty Dumpty in the nursery rhyme. "All the King's horses and all the King's men couldn't put Humpty together again.' I suppose they kept trying quite a long while before they realized he was always going to fall apart.'

I guess I must have smiled, because Ruth said, 'He amuses you, doesn't he?' No, I said, he didn't amuse me, but she said she could see how he might amuse people who didn't really know him. From certain angles, he did look a little absurd, but there was so much there, so much goodness, so much understanding and insight. I'd never seen it myself, but I didn't say anything.

She said she had the feeling he was ashamed of how he'd behaved to Joan, but that he'd been frightened of hurting her, he didn't know how to handle it. He'd simply realized that it just couldn't work, and he'd tried to disentangle it as best he could. I didn't answer that. I told her that I had liked Joan, that she had a lot of qualities, she was intelligent and practical and very warm, but I didn't think she had too much imagination.

She latched right on to that. 'That was the trouble! Kevin never felt there was a total rapport between them.' I asked her whether he thought there was a total rapport between him and Lucy, and she got very worried. She said, 'I wish you'd tell me about Lucy. He seems so confused about her.'

'Have you ever met her?' I asked.

'No!' she said, 'but please tell me! Please! I swear I'll never repeat a word of it.'

'Well,' I said, 'to be perfectly frank, I've never liked her. It's probably not her fault, but she's always struck me as a mean little number. Shallow and spoiled.'

'Oh,' she said, 'I was so afraid of that! Kevin won't admit it, he's so loyal to her. And if I leave him, she's all he'll have!'

'I may be wrong,' I said. 'I've met her very seldom. There may be things in her I don't appreciate.'

'No,' she said. 'I'm *sure* you're not wrong!' The poor girl was really distressed. 'She's treated him so cruelly, and if he ever gets back up there, the whole thing will start all over.'

Which of course it would. I wished there were something I could say to console her, but there wasn't; I just can't see Kevin as anything but a beat-up limousine on its way to the junk yard. An Englishman is like an American; when he hits bottom, he seems to stay there, where an Italian can bounce right back on top again.

When it had cooled a little, we started off for the *fortezze*, up the Costa San Giorgio, which is just in back of my apartment, then up the Via San Leonardo, which is one hell of a climb. Still, the higher you get, the better the view you have of the city. The light by now was soft yet very clear, and when it's like that, it gives Florence the look of a mirage, it all seems to be floating down there in the valley, the trees and *cupole* and *campanili*, like a beautiful hallucination that will disappear at any moment.

Over towards Bellosguardo, the light did the same kind of thing for the trees, a marvellous gradation through the grey-green olives on the lower slopes, to the deep, thick, solid, almost tangible green of the firs and pines and cypresses, higher up.

Ruth pointed up there and said, 'That's where Kevin lived.' I said, 'I know, I've been up there, once.'

I remembered it horribly well. It was a cocktail party, where they seemed to have gotten together the scourings of the Tornabuoni; that awful, crumbling sub-society that gets its hooks on a foreigner when he first hits town, to see what it can use him for. In my case, I guess they found it wasn't much; anyhow, I unhooked myself just as quick as I could. Lucy seemed to have fallen into the clutches of the one I called the Battleship Potemkin, poor girl. One of the worst of them, a perfectly dreadful parasite.

Most of the rest of them seemed to be there that day as well; the Poodle Lady with her frightful dog and the usual half a pot of rouge on each cheek, the *finocchio* who runs that home-made antique shop on the Lungarno, one or two of the impoverished local nobility who hang around the rich tourists, waiting for crumbs. I got the impression that it was Lucy *che tirava mosche*, that they came buzzing round her, rather than him, but that he realized there wasn't any getting rid of them, and he was making the best of it, weaving in and out like a high-grade waiter.

As for Hiyah, she looked happy enough among them; as far as I could tell, she took all of them at face value. She doesn't appear to have any real direction of her own, just impulses that she rides to the limit. She reminds me of one of those snakes that seem to be all stomach, while she seems to be all will. The snake doesn't seem to mind what it swallows, and she doesn't seem to know what she wants; it's all a question of just getting it.

Ruth said, 'That villa's like some kind of shrine to him. I don't know; some kind of refuge. Sometimes I see him looking up at it with this yearning. I know he's still in love with her.'

I said, 'With her; or the house?'

She said, 'It's not as simple as that. They're bound up together, somehow. Like one stands for the other.'

In Via San Leonardo, she kept saying, 'Isn't it beautiful? Isn't it exquisite?' and it was; those great, stone, solid walls dwarfing the little road, reducing it almost to a tunnel, everything pale grey and pale green, the grey walls, the pale green foliage dangling over them.

She told me, 'Kevin says he hates it because it's closed.'

'Does he?' I said. 'I've never thought of it that way.'

'He said it makes him long for fields and cows and trees and hedges.'

'For England?' I said, and she laughed, she said, 'It certainly sounds like it.' She's a delightful girl, and seeing Florence with her is delightful. There's always a special joy in being with someone who's responding to it for the first time; maybe, too, because it reassures me!

The *fortezze*, I confessed to her, I don't like. No doubt it was all necessary; no doubt the *affreschi* would have crumbled into pieces if they'd been left on their own on the altar walls, instead of being so skilfully and painlessly conjured off. Yet there's something about it I dislike. An element of rape. A particularly sinister and direct intrusion of the present into the past. In the cold rooms, on those bleak walls, the *affreschi* have somehow lost their life, their true, organic being; like jungle beasts in captivity.

Am I just being sentimental? After all, one sees them better than before, those golds and blues are so much clearer, the Madonna-faces still more inhumanly ethereal. One comes hard up against the Berenson theory that religion was peripheral to the artefact, that the artists were there, and just painted what they knew they had to. That may have been so in early Christian days, when they hired who they could, but I still don't think you can disentangle a Renaissance artist from his age.

As we passed from one room, one secular cell, into the next, there, *misericordia,* were the Nunbergs. Pale as dough and heavy as lead. She saw us first, whispered to him and pointed at us, in that unfailingly elephantine way of hers that just kills everything around her like a blight. They're usually in Florence for the summer, but up to now I hadn't seen them.

He said, 'Hi, Peter!' in a friendly enough way. He's like one of those big, sloppy, cheerful dogs that jump all over you when they're soaking wet. She watches over his talent, if that's what it is, like a mother over her daughter's virginity, and if you don't subscribe to the myth, then Heaven help you. In fact Heaven help *him* if she ever stops believing, which must get more and more difficult every year now he's over fifty and the world still ain't listened to his message.

They're neither of them exactly pretty. He looks like a giant sheep, and she, with those heavy features and that scraped-behind-the-head hairstyle I suppose, if you were being kind, you might call patrician.

She asked Ruth, 'And what are *you* doing here?' again with this insinuating undertone, that just sets my teeth on edge. Ruth said, 'Oh, just looking at Florence,' to which *she* said, 'And do you like it?' as if it somehow belonged to them. When Ruth said she did, she nodded with the same, damned patronizing smile.

She said, 'Well, we've been living here for more than fifteen years.' Ruth said wasn't that wonderful – she has excellent manners – and Mrs Nunberg managed to get into her next few sentences that her husband was a com*poser* who taught at the University of Whatever-the-Hell, which she was very defensive about, I was amused to see – and of course he'd only agreed to take on the job because they gave him so much freedom in planning his courses.

After all of which, inevitably, it was why don't you

come round and hear his music, some time, which Ruth said she'd love to; then thank God we got away.

Ruth said she thought he was sweet but his wife was kind of prickly, which was fair enough. He's basically a nice, kind, simple guy, but he should never have gotten himself involved in the arts. Ruth asked me how I liked his music, and I told her. I said, 'Kevin's not the only one who's hiding here.'

She asked me, 'Do you blame people for hiding, Peter?'

'No,' I said, 'I suppose some people would say I'm hiding, myself, and perhaps in a way I am.'

She looked at me and said, 'But not like Kevin.'

'No,' I said, 'not like Kevin.'

## 11

You think that's what it is, Anna? That he's started an affair with this girl?

They are always being seen together.

Someone ought to warn her.

If she cannot see for herself, *peccato*.

He can still be very persuasive.

But not for very long. *Ad ogni modo*, you might find it useful.

It really settles one thing, I can tell you. I'll never have him back here, now. How can he keep on telling me he loves me, then go right off and do this?

Did you ever believe him?

No, I didn't believe him. And this has proved it. This proves how right I was. He never did love me.

Kevin loves only Kevin.

That's right, I guess.

It may even be he does this to make you jealous.

You think so? Yeah, that could be true. The only thing is, I'm all on my own here, now. First Kevin goes, then right after that, Mother goes. I've got nobody.

You have me, *carissima*.

I know I have, but you're not here, Anna.

I could be; if you wanted me to be.

Could you? Could you really? That would be wonderful, Anna.

I don't miss what he is. How could you miss what he is? I miss what he used to be. Or what I thought he *could* be. Which was why I kept him here so long, I guess. Why I took him back that time. Because that's the crazy thing, you never quite give up hope. You have this feeling that one day things will change, they'll go back to being what they were. Or what you thought they were. When I heard about this girl, it enraged me. I was really amazed at how I felt. I had to tell myself, this is ridiculous. He's nothing to me, now.

The trouble is, when he's away like this and I don't see him, I don't remember him like he is, I remember him like he *was*. Why doesn't he leave Florence? Why the hell doesn't he go?

## 12

Autumn, now. One knows it by the calendar, not by the mutation of the trees, the metamorphosis of leaves from green into a spectrum of yellows, reds and golds. At home I would walk, walk, walk, looking endlessly at trees, horse chestnuts and oaks and elms and beeches. On over the wet, giving ground, kicking my way through thick, dark, yielding leaf-piles. Rugger weather. God, how I used to love it! Sharp rain in your face, the ball coming hard into your stomach, and running, running till you sobbed, in that marvellous air.

If one had known about that time. Known enough to cherish it, known that it was going to be unique, borrowed, unrepeatable. What use in going back now? Simply to open old wounds, spark off a useless yearning, make living here more difficult than ever. Yet how I'd love to go back with Ruth, and show her things. Like fields and hills; those astonishing, thick knolls of bushy trees. Live trees, real trees, that change with the seasons.

And Ruth has said she must go. She cries when she tells me, but she goes on saying so. She was going to go last week, but I made her change her mind. Now she's leaving *next* week – unless I can stop her – and so it will go on; until she does go. Leaving me in winter, when it's worst. And I've no right to keep her, for I can offer her nothing.

Today, we walked round and round the Boboli Gardens, debating and deciding, I begging her to stay and knowing she should go, she saying she should go, yet wanting to stay.

We're quite often in the Boboli, at her instigation rather than mine, though it *is* one of the few places in the city with the advantages of space and privacy; unless one wants to go miles downriver to that dreadful dank Cascine, with its dusty, mosquito-ridden walks; it has all the vulgarity of a public park and none of its spatial attributes. The Boboli, of course, have elegance and majesty, even if one doesn't like Italian gardens, which I never have; that evil tendency, again, to tame, enclose and domesticate everything. How Nature frightens them! Their instinct, whenever they see anything grand or wild, is to fillet and diminish it.

But here, there are things one can admire. The vertiginous sweep of that hill, down to the amphitheatre, exciting as one of those green, swooping hills in Devon. And the amphitheatre itself, where Ruth and I have sat so often on the white steps and talked, like two spectators of an invisible event; the drama taking place, for once, not in the arena, but on the terracing.

How much we've talked! How much we've told each other! Enough to fabricate the stuff of a hundred dramas! There they go across the grass, beneath us; parents, brothers, wives, lovers, mistresses. I think, again, of Joan:

'You're not a failed writer, Kevin, you're a failed actor. Your whole life consists of postures. You've no idea yourself, now, which of them are real.'

Through everything Ruth says comes that unvarying, inner theme of all American women : disappointment. Am I really so selfish in wanting her to stay? To the question, what have I to offer her, I put the question, what has America? Poor girl, she left to get away from some married man, with whom it 'didn't work out', and here she is with another married man.

'Why does it always have to be married men?' Her *cri de coeur*. And I : 'Because you're still trying to grow.'

'Is that the only way to grow? By getting into situations where I know I'll be hurt?' Her eyes full of a pleading pain that overwhelms me. She wants an answer, but what answer can I give?

'Am I always going to be this way, Kevin?'

I say, 'Life's always hard for people who won't compromise.'

'And if I go home,' she says, 'I'll have to compromise. I know it. I feel it. I can't grow there, Kevin, there's no *richness* there.'

But here, in Europe, we have richness. The richness of a rich, rotting past, the thick compost of decaying forest giants.

I can't sit still, I have to move. I rise, taking her hand, and we climb down from the amphitheatre, up the steep hill, disappearing at last into the dark labyrinth of trees, those wretched, narrow paths, again, still hand in hand. She says to me, 'It's so much easier for a woman to compromise than a man. She only has to close her eyes and let things happen to her. Marriage, children, and that's it. A whole, fresh set of problems. Enough to stop you thinking for the rest of your life.'

Which suddenly made me think of Lucy, who, in her own peculiar way, has *not* compromised, who at least is still looking.

Ruth said, then, 'I *want* children, of course I want children, but not as an escape. Not just because I'm too damn cowardly to go on looking.'

A great wave of love for her came surging up in me, then, and I had to kiss her, to hold her against me; I pulled her down on to one of those stone benches and I went on kissing her, I put my hand on her wonderful big breast, I wanted to give her so much, and she was giving *me* so much, she had such hope and youth and courage in her, she recharged me.

When she broke away from me, she said, 'This doesn't solve anything.'

I said, 'For God's sake, Ruth, don't go. Please stay with me. Stay with me this winter,' but she shook her head convulsively, and turned away. She said, 'The longer it goes on, the worse it gets. For both of us.'

'But we haven't reached the end,' I said. 'We've so much more to give each other.'

She shook her head, again, and stood up. She said, 'We're taking from each other, not giving.'

## 13

*The front gate of the Villa dei Pini, Bellosguardo. Mid-afternoon. It is a metal gate, painted pale green, with a smaller door set in the middle. Over the top of the gate one can see the higher branches of the pine trees which give the villa its name. Away from the gate, a road winds away into the valley. From its parapet there is a view, over olive-slopes, of Florence, dulled today by a rain-laden air which softens the outline of trees, blurs the contours of domes.*

*Round the corner, climbing easily and steadily, comes* RUTH. *She wears a gay, shiny yellow plastic raincoat, broadly checked in pale blue. Seeing the gate of the villa, she turns away to the parapet and stands there for a few moments, looking out over the city, as if committing it to memory. Then, with a brief, regretful shake of the head, she goes to the gate and, after a hesitation, presses the bell. From within comes the sound of footsteps.* RUTH*'s stance and expression grow, as they approach, increasingly tense. Then the gate is opened by* MARIA, *wearing her maid's black dress and white apron; a dark, grave woman in her middle forties.*

MARIA : *Buona sera. Desidera?*

RUTH : *uncertainly* : Signora Darnley?

MARIA : *Lei chi è?*

RUTH : Ruth Chevalier.

MARIA, *stepping aside* : *S'accomodi. Ora vado a vedere.*

RUTH *enters the garden, followed by* MARIA, *who walks briskly by her, up to and across the terrace, through the french windows, and into the house.* RUTH *stands between the gate and the terrace steps, watching the half-open window with a wary apprehension. At last,* LUCY *appears in the doorway. She is wearing her hair, like* RUTH*'s, girlishly long and straight, but in her case, it throws into sharp, contrasted relief the worn pallor of a face which has neither the expectancy of youth nor the experience of age. She looks short of both food and sleep. In the doorway she pauses, looking at* RUTH, *wearily suspicious, almost, it seems, as if affronted by such physical exuberance. The hiatus is tense and pregnant.*

LUCY, *at length, in a low, hostile voice* : Who are you?

RUTH : I'm Ruth Chevalier.

LUCY : Who sent you here?

*She now leaves the doorway, and comes out on to the terrace, pausing while still a few yards away from* RUTH.

RUTH : Nobody did.

LUCY, *with a sudden throbbing of hysteria* : You came about Kevin.

RUTH, *diffidently* : Yes, I did.

LUCY, *her voice, now uncontained, rising abruptly to a high recriminatory shout* : You've been living with him, and now you've got the goddam impertinence to come up here to my villa? I don't want to see you! (*She advances towards* RUTH.) Get out! Get the hell out!

RUTH, *though pale with dismay, stands her ground.*

RUTH : *Please!* Please *listen* to me!

LUCY : I don't want to listen to you! Why the hell should I listen to you? You think I can't guess what you want to say? You think I haven't heard every damn thing he's told you a thousand times? I'm planning to divorce him, did you know that? And *you're* going to be in it!

*With immense difficulty, as if she were struggling to contain a torrent of feeling,* RUTH *calms herself, to reply.*

RUTH : All right. If you want to do that, then I accept it. I can't stop you. But please hear me.

*Her desperation, the sheer, anguished force of the plea, seem to break through to* LUCY, *who subsides into a quieter though still vibrant antipathy.*

LUCY : Say it and go, then.

RUTH, *with great intensity* : Kevin loves you.

LUCY, *bitterly incredulous* : Is that what you came up here to tell me? Just that?

RUTH : Mostly that.

LUCY, *with a manic laugh* : Isn't that great? He loves me! So he sends his mistress up here to tell me!

RUTH : He didn't send me.

LUCY : I don't believe that. Of course he did. He's using you like he's using everybody else. This is his way of getting me to take him back again, and it isn't going to work.

RUTH : I swear to you; Kevin doesn't know. He wouldn't do a thing like that.

LUCY : Wouldn't he? Would you like me to tell you some of the things he's done, so he could stay up here? How he pretended that his wound was hurting him? How he told me a doctor in Rome said he only had a year to live, and when I called the doctor, it was all a lie? How he threatened to kill himself?

RUTH, *gravely* : He *will* kill himself.

LUCY : He's told you that as well, has he?

RUTH : No, he hasn't told me so. I just know it. If I leave him and you won't have him back, he'll kill himself.

LUCY: So that's what it is. He's said he'll kill himself if *you* leave him.

RUTH: I tell you, he *hasn't*!

LUCY: Well, anyway, he's made you believe it. Kevin's very subtle. Kevin's very clever. I've known him a lot longer than you have. Don't forget that.

RUTH: Mrs Darnley, I *am* leaving. I'm leaving on Saturday. Kevin knows it.

LUCY: I see! So now you're turning him over to *me*! Well, I don't want him. You can tell him that.

RUTH: I guess he knows that, too.

LUCY: Then that's fine. If he knows it, he won't go back to bothering me. If he knows it, he won't start right in calling me, again. If he knows it, maybe he'll even leave Florence.

RUTH: No, he won't. He won't ever, as long as you're here.

LUCY: Then if you care so damn much for him, why are *you* going? If you're so worried about him, why don't you stay?

RUTH, *in deep distress*: I can't stay.

LUCY: Of course you can't stay. Why should you stay? How long does it take to use up all there is of Kevin? A month? When he was younger, it took a little longer.

RUTH: Please don't!

LUCY: So you come up here and dump the responsibility back on *me*. While you slip off home to the States and tell yourself you've done everything you could. You've made the big sacrifice. You've given him up.

RUTH, *her head bowed; almost inaudible*: No. It's not that.

LUCY: It's exactly that. And don't go away with the idea that you're the first. Ask him about the Danish girl, the one he had the last time I threw him out. Kevin exploits young girls. He always has done. He needs them to kid himself he's still alive. Did he tell you how fresh you were? Did he tell you what vitality you have? Kevin's line hasn't changed in years. When you slept with him the first time, did he go through that bit about 'my America, my new-found land'?

RUTH, *in tears*: For God's sake don't go on.
LUCY: I don't want to go on. Kevin bores me. He disgusts me.
RUTH, *now raising her head to look at* LUCY: Haven't you anything left for him?
LUCY: Why do you ask me that? Why don't you ask if he's got anything left for *me*? I've told you what I've got left for him. Disgust.
RUTH, *with humility*: I guess I have no right to call you on it.
LUCY: You had no right even to come here. You don't know how lucky you are, leaving Florence with a few illusions about him.
RUTH: I don't think I have any illusions. If I had illusions, I wouldn't be going. I just know he loves you, and if he's got any life left, it's right here.
LUCY: I have my own life to live right here. What he's left of it.

## 14

Last night, I had Ruth round to see me. Looking very pretty, very distressed; and soaked. She's going, which I was delighted to hear, though I didn't directly say so. And she'd just been to see Lucy, up at Bellosguardo, which must have been enough to distress anybody.

I asked her, 'What on *earth* did you do that for?' She shook her head and sighed as if she couldn't tell me, herself. I made her take off her raincoat, sat her down in a chair, and gave her a cognac. She was very pale, and she seemed almost to be in a state of shock. I let her come round, and after a time she said, 'I don't know what's going to happen to him, now,' and out it all came.

I told her nothing would happen to him. After a little while, when she thought he'd served a long enough sentence and she'd got around to needing something to sharpen her claws on, Hiyah would twitch that rope and haul him back up the hill, again.

She said, 'Now that I've met her, I can't bear to think of it. She hates him so much. She's so little and cruel and destructive.'

'She's all of those,' I said, and Ruth burst right out, 'Why did he *marry* her? Oh, I know what you think, but it couldn't have been just that. She *must* have been different.'

'Well,' I said, 'she was certainly younger. That particular breed of cat doesn't improve with age.'

'Was she pretty?' she asked.

'I didn't think so,' I told her. 'But maybe other people did.'

'I ought to stay,' she kept saying, 'I should stay with him.'

'Don't delude yourself, my dear,' I said, 'there's absolutely nothing you or anybody else can do with Kevin. You'd just be pulled right in with him.'

'You'd just let him flounder, then,' she said. 'Is that what you're saying?'

'No,' I said, 'I'm just saying that he's beyond any help you or I can give him; and people like that are dangerous.'

Then she came up with what was really the trouble; she's afraid he'll kill himself, she'd told Hiyah and Hiyah didn't care, in fact Hiyah thought he was using it as blackmail; which presumably means she must have heard it, before.

I did what I could to reassure the poor child. I said, 'I'm certain he won't,' which I am, if only for the reason that dead men don't kill themselves. Or, if you like to look at it another way, Kevin's whole life ever since I've known him has been a business of whittling himself away by inches, and I don't see why he should suddenly do something drastic, now.

'Please will you promise me something?' she said. 'Please, please will you keep an eye on him? Especially in these weeks after I've gone, especially through the winter. He's afraid of the winter. And he's got such a lot of respect for you.'

I said well, I'd do what I could, and she was so grateful it embarrassed me, because what *can* I do?

infinite stone stairs. We were a *cortège*, and the taxi was a hearse, though all the way to the station I was insanely euphoric, for my sake as much as hers.

She was to catch the boat from Naples; we'd made gallows jokes that it would be full of blue-haired ladies who'd been 'doing' Europe and mistaking Florence for Venice, ordering gondolas to go on the Arno, but it didn't amuse her now. When she looked at me I could scarcely bear the misery in her face, the self-reproach; the guilt at going. On the station, she looked at me and said, 'I'm sorry, Kevin.'

I said, 'Sorry! God! Sorry for what? You've saved me! You've regenerated me!' I could scarcely look back at her, at all that sweet melancholy. When she got on the train and stood there in the window, I wanted to turn and run at once, but I didn't, I made myself stay, capering about like a comedian, saying things like, 'You will *write* the moment you get to America!' at which she nodded, still without a smile; I might have been sending her into exile.

I said, '*Smile!* For Heaven's *sake* let me remember you with a smile!' and she produced the absolute parody of a smile, her usual, riveting smile; the merest grimace.

Then the train began to move, and just as her smile was not a smile, so when she said, 'Goodbye,' one didn't hear the word, she merely formed it; and I ran crazily beside the train for a while, then waved madly till, thank God, it had turned the corner, she still at her window.

So it stays as a memory of something perfect, perfect because it is complete. All that rubbish about 'love is not love, that alters when it alteration finds'. The most poignant, unblemished love exists when there's no time for alteration, when you retain this intense, pristine image of each other.

So the train carried her away – with Pluto in the driver's cab – and I knew quite well we should never see one another again, precisely *because* it had been so perfect.

On the way back to the Oltrarno, I had a cognac. Which I needed. While she was with me, I had drunk so little,

I had felt no need for it, and I'd promised her not to drink hard when she'd gone.

Is this what should have happened with Lucy and me? Or even with Joan? But Lucy wanted me to marry her. The canker was *there*. Her conditioning. Impossible to conceive of a love without marriage: in terms of anything but exploitation. And when we did part, that first time, it was bitterly, on my side. On her side, provisionally.

Then, Joan. If we'd never met again, after Naples. What an exquisite memory! Her beautiful, healing kindness. The boat out to Capri; everything, that day, gold and blue. Her spontaneity towards me. Her body, seen for the first time, stretched out on the rock, brown and strong and firm. And the mad walk in the dusk, for miles and miles, climbing and climbing, till we reached Hadrian's Villa and stumbled about among the ruins, laughing like children, falling like children, and then, at last, making love.

But I was too romantic, then, far too young to think of love in anything but terms of permanence. For which I am not designed. For which so few people, surely, are designed.

And so I plan my days in comprehensive detail. My room is particularly sad. I try to spend the least possible time in it, because when I am there, I am too vulnerable. If it were larger, it would be so much easier to live in, there's too much about it of the prison cell, but I can't afford a larger room – I can scarcely afford this one. Perhaps I should change it, though, for another, where I can't look up the hill. Yet I should still be here, not there, and in a sense, it gives me comfort, now, to look, to know the villa's there, that she's there.

Again, I have promised myself I shan't phone her yet, or send her any letters, else she'll think I've turned to her just because Ruth has gone, when in fact I turned to Ruth, marvellous though she was, because Lucy had turned away from *me*.

I can cope, more or less, with the day; it's the evenings that are so difficult, when the black dog leaps on my shoulders; the evenings when there is nowhere to go and the room, in pale lamplight, closes in on me, when the wind in the stove crackles away like the malign parody of a country-house fire, when the ugliness of drawers and chairs and wardrobe oppresses one so.

By day, I have the cosy blue plush of the British Reading Room. I smile at the toothy smile of the woman in the anteroom, then stride into the room itself, purposeful and composed, in search of the latest newspapers and the last reviews, of my corner on the sofa, a weather eye open for my adversaries, above all of the fat, white woman with flesh like bled veal, malign behind thick spectacles, who will occupy the whole sofa, if she can.

How we glare at one another! She from the sofa, I from the table of newspapers, which she's ransacked and spread arrogantly about her. Don't glower at *me*, you bitch, I tell her, wordlessly.

In my sofa corner, time is suspended, place annihilated. Or rather, both are recreated. Whatever I read, I see names I know, triggers of the past; people with whom I was at school, at Cambridge, in the Army. Old friends, old enemies; most disturbing of all, old lovers. My God, this is where one 'alteration finds'! Opening *The Times* or the *Tatler*, to see a face one used to see young and blooming on a pillow, now seamed and disappointed, with the youth gone out of it. Would *they* think that, if they saw a picture of me? Perhaps they would. I don't examine myself down here, where in Bellosguardo I would look in mirrors as critically as an actor, at teeth, eyes, hairline, wrinkles; my watch on the frontier, against the guerrilla raids of middle age.

I look at these photographs, and I think of deb dances with their chaste exchanges, and May Balls and punts on the Backs and roaring down country lanes in the dicky of a sports car; and those mad leaves in the middle of the war. Getting drunk in the Café Anglais – one was always drunk or getting drunk – waking up in bed with somebody in Jermyn Street or the King's Road or Heaven knows where.

Or of hunt balls at our house, with that high, confident

babbling, the band playing *Sir Roger de Coverley*, and Father looking down from the gallery, a glass of champagne in one hand and a cigar in the other, like a brooding deity. Bacchus or Jehovah? How much of what he censured in me was what he'd conquered in himself? And Mother, dancing with each of us in turn, Roger and Tom and me, looking so terribly young and so frighteningly austere.

I look through the obituary columns with a fearful joy, so frightened of seeing a name I know and yet, when I see one, aware of the *frisson: J'ai vécu!* Brother officers shot obscurely in Cyprus or Malaya. Should I have stayed in the Army? How often have I asked myself. Again, it simplifies life so much, even in peacetime; the context of an institution, each day decided for you, the luxury of not reasoning why, the indulgence of cultivating small gardens of verses; to end, perhaps, as a General Wavell, publishing a bland anthology of other people's poetry.

I very nearly stayed, very nearly went back, but I wanted to be free to do . . . something. Which I still might do. Which I knew the Army wouldn't let me do. Besides, I had given enough of my life to the Army.

In the literary weeklies, I see names where my name should be, reviews I should have written. The names of people I drank with in the beer-and-raincoat Forties, in the French Pub and up at the Colony Room. Changed, changed utterly; a terrible complacency is born.

Reading them, I am keeping in touch with them. I am vexed and amused and pleased and put out. From Bellosguardo, I would sometimes correspond with them, but not from down here. Here, I merely compose letters in my head. I contemplate articles. Florence, Now. The romantic myth exposed for ever. Poetry: The Need for a Synthesis. Between the Eliot-Auden Cerebrations, and Dylan's Lyricism. I am beginning to make notes.

## 16

It is perfectly obvious he sent her here.

Well, that's what I told her, but she wouldn't admit it.

Naturally. She would have orders to deny it.

I guess you're right. Only at the time I thought she seemed pretty honest.

*In modo suo.*

But I certainly told her. I told her I wasn't going to have her dumping Kevin in *my* lap, now she'd had all she could take.

*Hai detto bene.*

I'm not having college girls coming up here and lecturing me about Kevin. They have a month of him, I've had ten years of him. Telling me she's afraid he'll kill himself.

Which certainly he made her say. *Che vigliacco.*

Well, it isn't going to work, Anna. I'm not going to be blackmailed that way.

*Meno male.*

And now I've got you here, I don't feel so lonely any more. I don't feel so vulnerable. He can't play on that, now.

It is my duty to look after you.

You really do, Anna. You're like a mother. I mean, a mother I get on with.

Not a mother, *carissima*; a friend. You must be protected – from other people and from your own generosity.

Well, it certainly isn't any use being generous to Kevin.

*Inutilissimo.*

Where are we going tonight, Anna? The Rimbaldi, is it?

No, to the Azzini. Simonetta Rimbaldi has left for Rome, though actually for Venice, where she will meet Luigi Maroso, who is supposed to be in Paris.

Anna, you're wonderful! Supposed to be in Paris! That's so killing!

## 17

They still treat me so kindly here; like a convalescent, which perhaps I am.

There are very few people in the dining-room. The summer students have migrated back to their campuses; we have only a few painters and a scattering of spinsters. One looks and waits for the newcomers, the transients; our eyes are always on the door. I am looking, I suppose, for another Ruth, though I know it to be an impossibility. Lightning won't strike twice. Before each meal we shiver round the stove and chat about nothing. Or rather, Miss Roach and myself discuss her ailments and the weather. Miss Roach, who is one of the last frail, peripheral bastions of Anglo-Florence, who gives lessons, who complains constantly, poor thing, about her failing health, and yet, in her absolute Englishness, reminds me so piercingly of England; prototypical English spinster.

'How are you, Miss Roach?'

'Oh, *not* too bad.' Her voice loops up and down. 'My *knee's* been aching, again.' Her head cocked to one side, her mouth set in a little snarl.

And John, the painter from Texas, whom I like but to whose handsome taciturnity I have nothing to say. Whose manners are good in that curious, withdrawn way some Americans' manners are, mere reflex actions, designed to save themselves from trouble.

How quiet it is, with just the few of us here. Every word is heard, every stirring of the stove, every pouring of wine or water. I owe them money, but they've been so nice. I shall pay them the moment my allowance comes, the first thing I shall do. I shall walk implacably, straight from the bank to the *pensione*, not stopping for so much as a coffee or a newspaper.

I am drinking more, but drinking very carefully. Nothing on any account before ten o'clock, and then only one:

a small one. Assiduously measured – I've scratched a mark on the glass. After which, nothing till midday, except in unusual circumstances. That is to say, as an incentive bonus, when I've been working. and then only on a specific basis of productivity, calculated either by the hour or by the page.

Besides, I have to make it last; I've only one bottle intact, and I can only afford a couple more. It's awfully good discipline, but what one can't predict are the hazards. Thus, the other day – Monday? Tuesday? God knows – when I succumbed at last and telephoned Lucy, my finger trembling so much in the dial that I had to stop and start again, stop and start again. It was Anna who answered. Anna! I put down the phone without speaking. As if the effort of phoning at all weren't enough, as if it didn't take days for me to reach the point of being capable of it! And she will *always* answer that phone, now, I know it. She has deputed herself watchdog. A watchdog bitch.

After this, I awarded myself three glasses.

The following day, I wrote a letter. Knowing, with every word I put down, that it was bound to be read by Anna. So that it took me three full hours to finish, during which I drank half a bottle. And I asked for no favours. I did not ask to be taken back. Merely to see her. To meet her, and to speak to her. I suggested the Tabby Cat, which has associations for both of us. I named an hour at which I should be there. And there I went, arriving fifteeen minutes early, waiting for more than two hours, perfectly aware, when she was half an hour late, that she would not be coming.

On my way back, I saw Peter Clovis. And walked past him. How could I possibly have spoken to him?

## 18

I don't know why it is, but Kevin's cutting me, again. Which doesn't bother me so much as it puzzles me. Is there something I've done? Or that I haven't done? Am I supposed to have had him round? Or has he just gotten himself into this state since Ruth left? I don't know. I'd been meaning to call him, after what I'd promised her, but I never got around to it. Now, I guess, this lets me out, and I'm not sorry.

It was at the top of the Tornabuoni; I was on my way to Armando's gallery, and when I got there I mentioned it to him; Armando had met him once up at my apartment. He shrugged and said, *'Un bambino,'* which I suppose is true. He has the Florentines' contempt for oddball foreigners. I told him how Ruth had gone, and he said, *'Precisamente. Un bambino che ha perso la bambinaia.'* A child that's lost its nurse.

That afternoon, he was in one of his piss-and-vinegar moods, taking on the world, going from the kind of *stranieri* who light on Florence to how perfectly impossible it was to get anything done here because of the way the Florentines were, themselves.

I agreed with him. It's perfectly true. Nothing sails straight into port, it always has to be steered through the narrows, and if you're wise, you keep an eye on the pilot. Armando's as prolix as any of them, but he's honest: and he's got that luminous Florentine intelligence. He's one of five or six one's found here, over the years, out of which I guess one's thrown together some kind of a society; or the closest I'll ever get to one.

He said, 'And your friend is married to that American idiot up at Bellosguardo?' I said he was, but she'd thrown him out, and he nodded to himself and said, 'Then everything's explained. He moves out, La Krutkova moves in.'

It seems that the Battleship Potemkin had been around and told him she was staying with an American woman in Bellosguardo who might be interested in buying some paintings. Armando had got the point and said that he was quite prepared to sell paintings to Americans from Bellosguardo as well as to anyone else, and that he reckoned his gallery was well enough known for them to find their way there.

'With types like that,' he said, 'I don't involve myself.' But if Anna's moved in, I guess Kevin's going to have a tougher job getting back.

## 19

I like having her here, and yet there's some things that bother me. Maybe it's just I haven't got used to her, yet; like the way she touches me at times, the way she sometimes kisses me. It's something I'd noticed before, but before she wasn't staying with me so it wasn't that obvious. I don't think she means anything by it, I don't think she even knows she's doing it, but sometimes it can be kind of creepy.

And then there's moments when I feel she's surrounding me. What she thinks we should do, what she thinks I should wear. She's very insistent about what I wear. Today when I put on that blouse I bought in Rome, the purple silk, frilled one, she came right up to me and said, 'Darling, that is how I want you to look,' then threw her arms round me and kissed me on the lips, which was embarrassing. And yet I like her liking my clothes, I like her taking an interest in me, not just a critical one, like Mother, nothing right, everything wrong.

This is a crazy thought. Maybe what I need is Kevin *and* Anna. One balancing the other where, on their own, they're not enough, either one of them. Except of course that they'd fight all the time; Anna can't tolerate him. She knows what he's put me through. And now this girl's gone home, he's starting in to try and get back up here.

Last Thursday there was a letter. When Maria gave it to me and I recognised his handwriting, my hand shook, I dropped it on the floor, and Anna picked it up. I said, 'You open it, Anna, it's from Kevin. I just can't open it.'

She took it and said, 'You must be spared these things,' then she opened up the stove and pushed it right in. It was a relief at the time, but afterwards I got around to wondering what he'd said, even though I knew what he must have said, the same old lies about missing me and needing me. I told Anna while we were playing canasta that evening after dinner – we always play it and she always wins, and when she doesn't I have this feeling that she's letting *me* win – I said, 'It's worrying me, Anna.'

She told me I just had to forget about him, it could be a little painful at first like getting rid of some old habit, but the longer I spun it out the worse it was going to be; for him as well as me. She talks a lot of sense; she's seen and done so much in her life. But it's like it was the last time. When you're so used to having a man around, you're going to need one; even if it was someone like Kevin, who isn't enough of a man.

Another thing worrying me is the way they gossip in Florence. The next thing, they'll start talking about me and Anna.

But we surely do keep busy. There's a cocktail party most nights, cards or tea in the afternoons, a lot of exhibitions to see right now, and I'm having a couple of new dresses made. All this, and the shopping to do, the villa to run. Anna's helping me a lot with that; she even cooked a meal the other night, a Russian dish, it was fabulous. And she has these contacts all over; we're getting wine and oil now from a *fattoria* she knows. It's a little more expensive, but it's really worth it.

She thinks I'm too easy on the servants, and they take advantage of me. Yesterday she told Maria that the villa wasn't being properly cleaned. She said, to me, 'They're lazy, like all Italian servants. They clean the rooms they know you'll be using, and leave the rest of the place filthy.'

She certainly makes a difference.

## 20

I have written again. Twice. And there is still no answer. Daily, I await the post. I'm usually in the hall when the *padrona* comes singing up the stairs with it.

*'Lettere per me?'* I ask, laughing like Pagliacci, and she, *'Niente per Lei, Signor Kevin, niente per Lei!'* laughing too and wagging her finger. We've made a ritual joke of it, though God knows it's no joke to me.

But I have had a letter from Ruth; the *padrona* gave me that with great joy, convinced it was the one I was expecting. A letter from seven thousand miles away. Missing me and apologizing to me. She'll never forget our time together; it's taught her so much and it's meant so much. She thinks so often of me here in Florence, and she hopes I won't be lonely, she hopes I'll soon be back up the hill, because she knows that's where I really want to be.

Futile and useless. Useless and futile. What can I possibly write back to her? Nothing. It has all been completed. But God, how I miss *her*; my lifeline.

I have been reduced even to phoning again. Russian Roulette; five chambers loaded with Anna and the other blank. Reserved, at the best for Lucy, if not, at least for Maria. But this time it was Anna once more, and I shall wait a week now, existing, till then, as best I may.

At least I have sleeping pills now, prescribed by a doctor who told me I seemed *molto nervoso*. Most perceptive of him. They help me through the nights, they reduce the days, and they save me money on alcohol. They sit benignly by my bed, yellow in a little brown glass bottle. Lethe.

My allowance came. I had made definitive plans for it. I kept part of my promise, returning straight to the *pensione*, stopping once to buy only one bottle of whisky. I met the *padrona* as I entered the hall, and immediately gave her ten thousand lire. I intend to pay her the rest in the next few days, as soon as I have taken my bearings.

Meanwhile, I have a new and rigid dispensation. This first bottle of whisky went too quickly; in a day. In future, each must last at least four days; preferably a week, which is my undeclared target.

I am contemplating a visit to Lucy. The problem is

Anna; if she weren't there, I think I should certainly make it. But her malevolent presence changes the whole situation; it means that I can't go straight to Lucy. If Anna were present when I came, the impact would simply be deflected. Her presence would hang about us like a fog.

What happened that last time was that we simply ran into each other, the first time we'd seen each other since I'd left, met quite by chance in the Piazza del Duomo. I said, '*Lucy!*' I was delighted to see her. She said, 'Hi, Kevin,' in that expressionless way she has when she's nervous, and I bore her off to a café in the Repubblica, I simply wouldn't let her refuse, then insisted that she come with me to lunch. I said, 'With *no* ulterior motive, *no* possible developments. We have simply met, and we are happy to see each other.'

It was the most marvellous lunch we'd ever had together, and I moved back into the villa that evening. If I met her now – alone, without Anna – I'm sure the same thing would happen again. It's simply, as I said to her then, that we need these times away from one another. To appreciate each other. All marriages need them.

I've contemplated going up there in any case, Anna or no, and insisting I see Lucy on her own. But she might, under Anna's influence, refuse, and besides, it would still be different, that extra factor, snarling the equation.

I did actually start walking there the other day, a sort of dummy run. Up that long, narrow, noisy street to the Porta Romana, where the cars buzz in and out of that superb great arch like venomous little anachronisms, up the gradient of the Via Ugo Foscolo, till I was on the road to Bellosguardo, looking out over that implacably familiar view, with all its picturesque aridity; pines, firs, vines, olives, cypresses.

I was about halfway there when I decided not to go on, because the nearer I went, the more melancholic I grew, as if some force were pushing me away and back. Childe

Harold to the Dark Tower came. In that condition, it was quite useless to proceed; one needed gaiety and exuberance. So I went back. And I wrote her another letter.

## 21

This time when Kevin's letter came Anna wasn't here, and I opened it. First off, I didn't want to, I let it lie there on the table, just looking at the envelope, written in his handwriting which is so good, very clearly formed, not like Kevin at all. When I knew him first, it was the kind of writing I expected him to have, but now it doesn't seem to belong to him.

I even thought of doing what Anna did, throw it into the stove, and I picked it up, I was going to do it, but then I changed my mind, I don't know what made me change it. I sat there holding the envelope a long time, and maybe if there hadn't been this knife on the table, that Maria must have left from breakfast, I wouldn't ever have opened it. But it was there and I slit it open, I pulled out the letter and unfolded it, and then I got so nervous my stomach was just palpitating, it was like being on a ship in a storm, I saw, 'My Darling Lucy' at the top, but after that, my eyes just danced about the page, picking up a word here or a phrase there, 'love you' and 'indispensable' and 'need for one another', but I couldn't concentrate, I just couldn't make myself go right ahead and read it. In fact I never did go clear through it from beginning to end, I just felt too jumpy and upset, I read a bit here and a bit there till there wasn't any left, because that way it was somehow less worrying.

It was only the same old stuff, of course, but he's got a way of putting it, he always has had, either on paper or when he talks, and in some ways it's even more persuasive on paper, because when he isn't there you've only got the arguments and the way he puts them, which is very clever, he's not there so's you can see through him, see his eyes move away from you, see what all that drinking's done to his face.

On paper he always has an answer to everything, like this time about the girl he'd been having an affair with, Ruth. Would you believe it, he'd even twisted it around to show it proved how he loved me; he'd never have got involved with her if he hadn't been so broken up about me; there just had to be somebody or he would have gone crazy. And stuff about his standing at his window and looking up here to Bellosguardo and trying to imagine what I was doing.

When Anna got back I was in tears, I still had the thing in front of me. She took one look at it and said, 'This is Kevin again,' then picked up the letter and screwed it into a ball. She put her arm around my shoulder. She said, 'You were foolish to have opened it. But now you will write *him* a letter that will stop him from troubling you again.' And together we worked this letter out, we were a long time over it, some of the things she wanted me to put I wasn't that happy about at first, like how long it was since I'd been satisfied by him, but she was right I guess, the thing had to be settled once and for all, there was no use holding anything back. In the end it ran to around eight pages.

When I'd sealed the envelope, Anna grabbed it and said, 'Now I shall post it,' and was out of the door lickety-spit; I suppose she was afraid I'd change my mind. And now I guess that's it, which is a strange feeling. I don't mean that when I threw him out this last time I ever thought I'd have him back again, any more than I did the time before. But this is like locking a door on someone after you've slammed it. You don't want them to come back, but there was always a chance they'd try. Now, he won't even try.

In a day or two, I guess I'll feel freer than I've felt for years. Anna thinks so.

## 22

KEVIN's *room at the Pensione Oltrarno. Night. The room is dark and empty.*

*Suddenly and brutally the door bursts open, banging hard against the wall, and* KEVIN *appears. Snapping on the light, he stands rocking in the doorway, his hair awry. The collar of his tweed jacket, turned up, rides high on his neck, the knot of his Guards tie is wildly askew, the collar of his white shirt has burst open, and the shirt itself is spattered with what might be blood or wine. The expression in his eyes is that of a desperate animal, bent on destruction. He slams the door viciously and, when it at once bounces open, slams it again, then turns and locks it with an exasperated gesture. Looking balefully around the room as if for victims, targets, his eye rests at last on the washstand, as if upon an enemy and, striding across the little room, he picks up the full water jug, raises it in the air, and smashes it to the floor, where it flies into pieces, in a cascade of water. Next, he picks up and smashes the empty basin. Whirling round, he pulls the bedside lamp from its socket and flings it against the wall beside the door. An empty whisky bottle – it, too, standing on the bedside table – flies after it. Like a fire feeding on itself, his rage seems to grow as he gives vent to it. He picks up the wooden chair which stands by the table and bangs it repeatedly against the floor till one leg, then a second, then a third falls off. Then, tilting the table itself to send a cataract of books and papers to the floor, he picks this up in turn, raises it high in the air like a weight-lifter, and dashes it against the tiled floor.*

*Now he goes to the wardrobe and, with a kick, shatters the mirror on its door, following this by seizing it at either corner and wrestling with it frantically, his face purple, eyes dilated, his breath coming harsh and staccato, till at last it totters towards him and he stands back, letting it topple and crash. At this, still panting, but evidently sated, he is still at last. His eyes have lost their ferocity and are remote, unfocused, almost entranced. After a few moments he goes, like a somnambulist, to the bedside table, picks up and unscrews the cap of a small, brown bottle of pills, pours a stream of yellow tablets into his hand, and gulps them. This done, he crosses to the chest of drawers, pulls out the middle drawer, takes from this a full bottle of whisky, opens it, tilts the neck to his mouth, and takes a long pull, swallowing about a quarter of it before he bangs it down on top of the chest of drawers. Then he staggers over to the bed, lies down, closes his eyes, and is at once stertorously asleep.*

*A few minutes pass, then there is a shuffling of feet, a cautious whispering, in the corridor; finally a timid knock on the door. When this is not answered, there's a second knock, the voices rise, are joined by other voices, other, shuffling feet, till at last the door handle is tried.*

The Voices: *È chiuso* . . . Closed . . . *Ma deve essere pazzo* . . . *Matto* . . . *Hai sentito che chiasso?* . . . Knock it down . . . *Poverino, deve essere la moglie.*

## 23

He tried to kill himself, Anna! They called me from the *pensione*.

*Figurati.*

Aren't you surprised? Doesn't it bother you?

It is for you I am worried, *carissima*. I myself was expecting it.

You were *expecting* it?

*Qualcosa del genere*. After what he had told that girl to come and say, I thought that he would *try* to kill himself.

He swallowed half a bottle of sleeping pills and a whole lot of whisky on top of that. They only just got to him in time. And there's a note for me, Anna!

Of course there is a note for you. *Era da prevedere.*

I don't understand you. If he didn't mean to kill himself, why did he leave a note?

I think he meant almost to kill himself.

But if they hadn't knocked that door down. If they hadn't heard him bust up his room.

He bust up his room? *Allora, tutto spiegato.*

I don't follow you, Anna. What is it that's explained? He's back from the hospital now. He's asking for me!

But you must not go.

## 24

KEVIN's *room at the Pensione Oltrarno. Four o'clock in the afternoon. The room has been set to rights again. There is a new jug, a new basin, another table lamp, another chair, but no mirror on the wardrobe, from which the splinters of glass have been removed.*

KEVIN *lies in bed, reading the* 'Observer.' *He wears a brown checked woollen shirt. His face is very pale and has an expression of listless resignation. After a while, he drops the newspaper, takes up a packet of Nazionali cigarettes from the bedside table, lights one with a silver lighter, and lies smoking passively, now and then dotting ash on the floor.*

OUTSIDE, *the tapping, high-heeled footsteps of a woman.*

*At this,* KEVIN *becomes galvanized with a sudden hope, his body remaining stiff as though he were magically trying to control events.*

*There's a knock at the door, so tentative as to be nearly inaudible.*

KEVIN, *almost in a whisper*: Come in.

*The door slowly opens, and* LUCY *diffidently appears.*

KEVIN: *Lucy!* Oh, God! (*He bursts into tears.*)

LUCY *stands regarding him with the same uncertainty. She does not move. She seems less concerned with his reaction to her presence than with that presence itself, the question whether she should stay or go.*

KEVIN *sits up and stretches out his arms to her.*

KEVIN : Oh, darling, you don't *know* how wonderful this is, you don't *know* how I've been longing for it!

LUCY *does not appear to hear him. After a hiatus, in which* KEVIN *still sits, his arms outstretched, as if petrified, the smile gradually vanishing from his face,* LUCY *begins slowly to move across the room. She takes only a few steps, as if under hypnosis, stops again, then speaks.*

LUCY : Anna didn't want me to come.

KEVIN, *after a moment's hesitant surprise* : But you *did* come.

LUCY : Yeah, I came. I don't know if I should have done.

KEVIN, *with desperate insistence* : Of course you should have come. It's *so* marvellous to see you!

*He jumps out of bed, dressed in shirt and underpants, and leaps frantically about the room, as if he fears that* LUCY *will leave unless she be distracted. Picking up the chair which stands behind the table, he whirls it across, and plants it beside her.*

KEVIN : Sit down, darling! God, this is ridiculous! I've nothing to offer you.

LUCY, *after a fractional pause, sits down.*

LUCY : I don't want anything.

KEVIN, *bending over her, almost in supplication* : Can I kiss you? *Let* me kiss you! God, it's wonderful to see you!

LUCY, *in the same, dead monotone* : I don't want to be kissed. They say you nearly died. They called me up to tell me.

KEVIN *snatches a pair of trousers from the back of her chair, and quickly wriggles into them.*

KEVIN : I have *never* been better! Seeing you has *revived* me! (*Another of his manic laughs.*) Seeing you *inspires* me!

LUCY : How do I inspire you? All you ever did at Bellosguardo was drink.

KEVIN, *from behind her, puts his hands on her shoulders.*

KEVIN : You have *always* inspired me.

LUCY *rises from her chair, escaping his hands.*

LUCY : Maybe at the beginning. Before we got to know each other. Anna thinks you planned all this.

KEVIN, *with sudden sharpness* : All what?
LUCY, *walking to the window between bed and washstand* : This trying to kill yourself and not quite making it.
KEVIN, *with subdued ferocity* : Anna – I'm sorry, darling –Anna can be the most malevolent woman I know.
LUCY, *bridling* : Don't go attacking Anna, Kevin. She's given me more than you ever have.
KEVIN, *stiffly* : Given; or taken?
LUCY, *turning from the window* : It's you who've taken from me Kevin; not Anna. Anna tells the truth. She tells me things I haven't seen for myself.
KEVIN, *with enormous effort* : I see.
LUCY : They told me on the phone you wanted to see me. That's why I'm here.
KEVIN, *with renewed euphoria* : I *know* it is! (*He goes to her and grasps her hands.*) I am so grateful to you!
LUCY, *withdrawing her hands* : What did you want to say to me, Kevin? That you want me to take you back again?
KEVIN : You *know* how much I want to come back!
LUCY, *looking about the room* : Sure I do. It's a whole lot more comfortable than here.
KEVIN : It isn't that! You must know it isn't that!
LUCY : What is it, then?
KEVIN, *fortissimo* : I *happen* to love you!
LUCY : It's no use shouting at me, Kevin.
KEVIN, *momentarily closing his eyes* : I apologize. I am simply trying to tell you that if there were a choice between living here with you or in Bellosguardo without you, I would a *thousand* times rather live here.
LUCY : You just say these things. You say whatever you think's going to work for you.
KEVIN, *in abrupt anguish* : Lucy, it isn't true!

LUCY *brushes restlessly past him, moving about the room.*

LUCY : It is so, Kevin. All the things you promised me the last time. How you'd stop drinking and get down to work. How you'd try to make a proper life for me.
KEVIN : Lucy : I have been thinking down here.
LUCY : That isn't all you've been doing.

KEVIN: I *wrote* to you. I tried to explain.
LUCY: It didn't explain it to *me*.
KEVIN: It was true, darling, I swear it.
LUCY: That you love me so much you start an affair with the first girl that's available?
KEVIN: It was *not* like that.
LUCY: And what was so great about her? A big college girl, that's all.
KEVIN, *uneasily*: You saw her?
LUCY: For God's sake, Kevin, you sent her up to see me.
KEVIN, *stunned*: *I* sent her to see you?
LUCY: You know you did.
KEVIN, *with stumbling desperation*: I did *not*. I had no *idea*. She actually *visited* you?
LUCY, *regarding him*: You really didn't know?
KEVIN: Lucy, on my *honour*!
LUCY: You've told me so many lies. I can never tell.
KEVIN: I am *not* lying.
LUCY: You mean she came just like that, on her own?
KEVIN, *breathing very deeply*: Yes.
LUCY: Then why did she tell me you were going to kill yourself?
KEVIN, *appalled*: She told you *that*?
LUCY: Sure. That she was afraid you'd kill yourself.
KEVIN, *shaking his head in hopeless incredulity*: I simply don't understand.
LUCY: You must have told her that.
KEVIN: I told her nothing of the sort.
LUCY: Then how did she know?

KEVIN *wonderingly shakes his head again.*

LUCY: You've told *me* often enough.
KEVIN: I did *not* say anything like that to *her*.
LUCY: Did you love her?
KEVIN: I was grateful to her.
LUCY: Why, did *she* inspire you?
KEVIN: There's no need to be cruel, Lucy.
LUCY: I just want to know, that's all. Did she inspire you?
KEVIN, *abstractedly*: She reinvigorated me.

LUCY: Then why didn't you stay with her? If she's supposed to have loved you so much. If she understood you so well.
KEVIN, *with emotion*: You know why.
LUCY: Because you couldn't keep her? Because she saw through you in the end, like they all do, like I have?

KEVIN *wordlessly shakes his head.*

LUCY: All I'm asking you is this, Kevin. What's different between this time and the last time?
KEVIN, *looking remotely above her head*: That I have nearly died.
LUCY: Through your own fault, nobody else's.
KEVIN: Through my own fault. Nevertheless, I almost died. And I have been allowed to live. One is *not* the same, after that.
LUCY: It's too late for you to change, Kevin.
KEVIN, *with quiet deliberation*: It is not too late for me to change. I *have* changed. There is one thing, however, in which I have not changed, and that is in my love for you.

LUCY *is still moving restlessly about, as if to avoid* KEVIN.

LUCY: You talk and talk until I don't know where the hell I am. Anna was right; I should never have come, then I wouldn't have had to listen to you.
KEVIN: Thank God you did.
LUCY, *turning suddenly towards him*: And how about Anna, if you did come back? She's living with me now. You know that?
KEVIN, *flatly*: Yes. I know that.
LUCY: After how you behaved to her and Mother; the way you insulted them. I don't suppose she'd even want to stay.

KEVIN *watches her silently and anxiously; there's a faint twitch at the right-hand side of his mouth. His expression is that of an apprehensive poker player.*

LUCY: And she's more help to me than you are, Kevin. (*Still* KEVIN *doesn't answer, but continues anxiously to watch her.*) I just don't know. I'll have to think about it, I can't give you an answer right now. Don't try and kiss me.

*She has now backed across the room as far as the door*

*and, opening it, she disappears, closing it behind her as* KEVIN *springs desperately towards her. His fingers on the handle, he seems for a moment to be about to open it, then he changes his mind, turns hopelessly away, flings himself on to the bed, and lies there with his hands over his face.*

# THREE

## I

Nigel! My God, it seems such ages!

Almost exactly a year.

And you haven't changed at all! Neither of you.

Haven't I? I feel as if I have. You certainly haven't.

And *how* is Cambridge?

One's left; that's the trouble. I'm afraid I'm working in a merchant bank. Rupert's luckier. He's gone to the Bar.

A merchant bank! Is it absolute hell?

Oh, it could be worse, I suppose. Provided one can survive five years as a glorified office boy. I sometimes think of you sitting up here on the hill, looking at this sensational view while I have to look out at mine, and I simply turn green.

There are times when I would willingly change places with you.

You're *not* serious?

I am com*plete*ly serious!

You'd honestly prefer the well of a City officc block to this?

I would prefer London to Florence. I would prefer the *possible* true green of the English countryside to the actual, inadequate green of the Tuscan landscape.

Well, any time you want to swap.

How's Lucy?

Lucy is flourishing. She's in town at the moment, shopping with Anna; you remember Anna? They should be here any moment.

Super.

Have you finished your novel?

*Al*most. I showed some of it to Evelyn while he was in Florence.

Evelyn Waugh?

Yes.

What did he say?

He said he liked it enormously, but if it came out within the next five years, everybody would compare it with his own trilogy, so he'd have to protect me by writing a foreword.

How absolutely splendid.

And we are having Roland Wilkinson to stay.

Fascinating.

We have been in correspondence for months after an article he wrote about Dylan. I wrote to congratulate him, and pointed out certain things which slightly modified his thesis.

Was he pleased?

He was terribly grateful. In any case, we were both completely in agreement as far as Dylan's death-wish was concerned. *Here* come the drinks; *Grazie, Maria!*

Thanks. Aren't you drinking any more?

*Not* at the moment. In fact, not for an indefinite period; which I shall prolong as far as possible.

Total abstinence?

Except for wine at meals. And *there* is the car! *Io vado, Maria!* Lucy! *An*-na! Guess who's arrived?

It's us again.

Well, hi! History repeats itself!

The first time as tragedy, the second as farce.

Which is this, then? A tragedy or a farce?

Her laugh.

Just something Karl Marx once said.

That old fool never wrote anything intelligent.

Don't get Anna on to Karl Marx, now!

The corrupter of the twentieth century.

Kevin tells me you're expecting Roland Wilkinson.

Yes! Isn't that interesting? He's coming a week from Thursday. We're hoping he'll take a look at Kevin's novel and maybe recommend it somewhere.

I remember he came and spoke to us at Cambridge, once. About Hardy. He was really awfully good.

Lucy and Anna : a drink?

And *you* are still not drinking, Kevin?

Watching, crouching, always ready to pounce.

Nothing but wine, Anna.

How about that, Anna?

*Che bravo.*

Bitch. She looks at me with her malign scepticism. And of course will pour poison into Lucy's ear. Watching, crouching, hoping. She will never forgive me. Nor I her.

I was telling Kevin he's completely unchanged : and so are you.

I don't know whether that's good or bad. Eh, Kevin? Is it good or bad?

It's wonderful. Year by year, we shall come back, looking older and older, while *you* remain totally unaltered : like *The Picture of Dorian Gray.*

*Endlessly repeating ourselves. The first time as tragedy, and* all *the other times as farce.*

## 2

I have not been drinking for a month. I have not been drinking because I have been frightened. By the pain. And what the specialist at the hospital told me about the pain; or didn't tell me. That it was *not* my wound. That I had been drinking too much, and must cut down immediately.

Lucy knows nothing of this; in any case, she has no

belief in the pain. Or, if she believes in it at all, regards it as a weapon that I use against her, something I can induce at will.

Roland Wilkinson is our *deus ex machina*, who will change everything; or by whom we shall be changed. At the touch of his hand, these bones will live, these rambling, scattered notes I have accumulated, which I describe to Lucy as my novel, will be transmuted into gold; or into manuscript. At the sound of his precise mellifluous voice – which I have heard on the Third Programme – I shall be spurred into lasting activity. Where at the moment I am blocked – unable, again, to do that which I most want to do – I shall be liberated.

Each idea I get I discuss, immediately, with Lucy – a tribute, a hostage – who likes all of them. And each, the following day or sooner, seems banal, derivative. A hospital scene purloined from Alun Lewis or from Wilfred Owen. An attitude to combat borrowed from Siegfried Sassoon. Oh, Lucy, dear, how easy it must have been to impress you. How easy it still is: in brief parentheses. Before Anna digs her claws in you again, or your mother writes from New York, deploring my return, upbraiding your weakness. Or your kindness. Your mother, who will also soon be visiting us; against whom I so badly need to store up some defence.

Now and then, when Lucy leaves them about, I see those letters. Full of antipathy for me, incredulity that we should be together again. Like Anna, she will never give up, will never understand what I give Lucy or what Lucy gives me; which is not what she thinks it is.

How strange it was, returning this time. On a month's trial; like a domestic. To find that Anna had gone, so sure she was that she was leading from strength, that in a month she would be back.

'Anna says it wouldn't work to have both of you here. She's moved out, so we can see if we can make a go of it.'

I knew quite well why she'd moved out. As a spell might be broken. As a witch might fly away on her broomstick, routed by true love, whether she knew it or not.

That night I went to Lucy's room. She sat up in bed. 'Kevin? Is that you?'

'Yes, darling, it's me.' Very low, praying that she wouldn't tell me to go.

'What are you doing in here, Kevin?'

She was half asleep, yet I knew the tone, the tone of token protest, then I was in her bed, my hand on her breasts, so small after Ruth's, my hand between her thighs.

'What are you *doing*, Kevin?' half asleep, then coming into her, moving inside her, while she lay passive, like a happy child, at last crying, 'Kevin, Kevin!' a sound I hadn't heard for, oh, how long. And waking together, Lucy in my arms, opening her eyes, looking at me, closing them again, then wriggling against me.

How long did it last? Was it three weeks? A fortnight? And what brought it to an end? Hard to decide that, but important. Hard, struggling through a gorse bush of humiliation, half-remembered pain. Anna, surely? Somehow. Some argument, provoked by Anna. Oh, God, I do remember. One night I fell asleep and set fire to the bed. Waking in the night from a dream about the war; an exploding mortar shell, the smell of smoke, my sergeant screaming he'd been hit. And waking to find it was Lucy who was screaming; and the sheets on fire: Instant banishment; to my own room. 'And you're lucky I don't throw you right out again.'

Anna to stir the cauldron.

Creeping back next night; to find she'd locked her door. Since when, I've slept with her . . . once, twice? To be sent back immediately, to my own bed. 'I'm just not taking any risks, Kevin.'

*J'ai vécu.* This time narrowly and unintentionally. Waking in hospital, first the feelings of bafflement, disorientation, a mysteriously aching stomach; then of corrosive shame. At what one had tried to do. At what one had failed to do, so that the mere fact of living was despicable.

And, oh, God, the room. I was sure I'd smashed my room;

a vague nightmare of violence. Glass, wood, china, flying to fragments. Having to face *them* again, the family; who had probably saved me, as it was. Then, layer beneath layer of pain; her letter, and the cruelty of it. Which reeked of Anna – something she's admitted to me, since. Closing my eyes at that; opening them again to a brisk rustling, a starchy locomotion, to see – what? A ghost? An enormous seagull? No, my God, a nun, in an immense, winged wimple. Closing my eyes once more. It's all one needed. For her, I must lie here in a state of mortal sin.

Yet curiously, I planned nothing. It emerged from a mood, a total nihilism which itself came out of utter desperation, the letter having thrown a sheer, rock wall up in one's face. I have a blurred memory of drinking till I'd nothing left to drink, then out of the *pensione* to a bar, another bar, a nightclub where they wouldn't let me in, picking up a whore in still another bar, going back to her miserable room in God knows where, unable to do anything; then the *pensione* and my room again, my room that seemed intolerable, a dungeon, smashing, smashing, till there seemed nothing left to smash but me. In which I failed.

Reaching out to the nun. '*Mi scusi.*'

'*Sta buono*.'

As though to a child, which is exactly how I feel. Quite weak and totally dependent. And indifferent. One had tried to die, wanted to die, so in a sense was dead, lived by the merest chance; a revenant. And my intention was quite genuine, whatever Anna persuaded Lucy to believe. I wanted to die because there was simply no reason to live, even if it emerged as a drunken impulse. I *was* drunk, it *was* an impulse. If I had not been drunk, no doubt I'd have been strong enough to control it, which is perhaps why I did get drunk.

How good they were to me when I got back to the Oltrarno. Putting me in a different room, till mine was habitable again. Ringing Lucy for me; at their own suggestion which I accepted, as I then accepted everything. Not a word, a look of recrimination, only gentleness and pity.

And then, she came. And when she did, I knew that everything was going to be all right again, whatever she said – which I dismissed as Anna's vile ventriloquism. All that mattered was her presence, that she'd come. And, having come, would take me back with her.

My investigation continues; though now without the same harsh urgency, thank God. I think I have proved what I wanted to; events have surely proved it. My love, my need. My need that grows out of my love. So it becomes a mopping-up operation, a series of sporadic forays into various territories; some into England, most to Italy, one into New York.

I have seen the future, and it doesn't work.

Possibly the strangest month of my life. After six months of marriage.

When I was, metaphorically, taken up to the top of the Empire State Building and offered the kingdom of this world. Which I refused.

What I can see now as my trial by fire, her mother's attempt to destroy our marriage, to show me to Lucy as something feeble and corrupt.

On our first day, there was a snowstorm. Brightness falls from the air. And beats into one's face, making the whole city still more phantasmagoric, people looming at one through a white curtain, skyscrapers appearing and disappearing like peaks in a blizzard. And Lucy all at once quite different, as her mother no doubt knew she'd be, very gay and febrile and adventurous. 'They've laid this on for us, they've laid that on for us. We're going here, we're going there.' Theatres and nightclubs and endless cocktail parties. With Lucy as determined to exhibit me as her mother was to expose me. My curiosity value. My British accent. Which she should surely have known, her ridiculous mother, would work for me rather than against me.

A wonderful time, in some ways; Lucy *so* proud of me.

'Isn't he charming?'

'He's *so* attractive.'

'I *adore* his accent.'

'Kevin, they just love you.'

Which was quite untrue. They neither love nor hate, have neither the capacity to love nor the courage to hate, though hatred is what they mostly feel, however seldom they show it, however much they cover it with a firework show or cordiality, vast generosity, the animus showing through only in flashes, then vanishing again, like all those figures in the snow.

Lucy's stepfather, for example, a broker or something. Woolly white hair and spectacles; a teddy bear, with a doll's expression of glassy bewilderment. Very kind and quite lost. Always wanting us to get together for the talk we never had, because he never really wanted it. Switching off, in the middle of a conversation, like so many of them did, because there is only so much bonhomie to go round. When it runs out, they must wait till it's replenished.

Gestures across space; hands across the stratosphere. In – for instance – a nightclub. A magnificent Negro jazz band playing. Leaning to me across the table. 'Kevin, I want to know *all* about what happened to you in the war.' Not just what happened; all of it. 'Lucy tells me you had a very fine and distinguished record. I was on Guadalcanal. I don't think I ever felt more alive. Tell me something; did you ever used to get scared?'

'Yes,' I said, 'all the time,' then Mrs Harrison, as usual, was on us like a sheepdog; and that was that. When I brought the subject up again, another time, he just said, 'Sure, we have to talk about that, Kevin,' and cut off. Gestures, reflex actions. In a context of perpetual motion, eternal escape, unreal reality.

Poor men in the prosperous streets, shambling up with their hands out: 'Got a dime?' The absolute degradation of the down-and-out, who obviously believe, by some quirk of Puritanism, that it's their fault, that to fail is to sin; and to be punished. The Negroes a reservoir of hope and humanity. Such knowing smiles, so bitterly amused by it all, so subtly mocking.

Lucy crawling into my arms, into my bed – no double

beds in that house – after we'd been there ten days, whispering, 'I'm frightened, Kevin,' and I telling her, 'They're all frightened, darling.'

Except for Mrs Harrison; I must give her her due. Unvaryingly cool, with her frigid little smile, immune from love, endlessly manipulating.

Everybody drunk, half drunk or drinking; hadn't she thought of that, either? That however much I drank in self-defence, to keep the cold out – every kind of cold – there would be others who would drink as much; and more?

Arthur, her present husband, shambling up to me one night. Half drunk, as we both were. 'Want a word with you, Kevin.'

'About Guadalcanal?'

'Just a little proposition want to put to you. Thought you'd maybe like to stay here. Good for Lucy, too.'

Up to the pinnacle of the Empire State Building, by express lift, soundless coffin. (High wire, concentration-camp wire, to discourage suicides; a bleak, broad river curved below.) And I, untempted.

'It's incredibly nice of you, Arthur.' Which it was. How nice the men are.

'Nothing, Kevin. I mean . . . you're an attractive person. Everyone likes you. Could help the firm.'

'But honestly, I don't think so.'

'Why not? Thought you didn't like it in Italy?'

But I like it less here. Where the faults are not even human faults. Where there's no landscape at all, not even a landscape to react against, but just a claustrophobia of skyscrapers, endlessly put up and torn down, dust blowing, drills thundering, generators shuddering. Where there's no comfort even in the bars, dingy and guilt-ridden, the final obscenity of solitary drinking taking place in public.

'Change your mind, you can always come back.'

'Thank you, Arthur. I *do* appreciate it.'

Her smile next morning, and her eyes; glaciers.

Lucy on the aeroplane, her head on my shoulder. 'I *never* want to go back again, Kevin.' And one's own bottomless feeling of relief. Look, we have come through. Survived, escaped. And need never – I was sure – go back again.

How we loved each other when we got to Bellosguardo; refuge. And how wonderfully ironic it seemed; that her mother's plan should so have backfired, soldering rather than sundering. Are we always going to need these crises, in order to live happily together? A violent storm before each passage of calm? Should we – I've considered this before – visit New York once a year, as her mother's often suggested we should, so we can appreciate what we've got; in ourselves, in Bellosguardo? So that Lucy can rid herself of her persisting *idée reçue* that *real* men work all day in skyscrapers? Or perhaps it's just she who should go back to New York, even though her mother would be at her night and day, so she can see the alternative.

Is that what's going to happen to all of us, the concrete world, the skyscraper world?

Things fall apart, the centre cannot hold.

No centre; only a roaring vacuum. I understand so well how Lucy, how Ruth, can draw no sustenance from it, why they turn to Europe, though God knows why anyone should turn to Florence. Which reminds me suddenly of Clovis, writing his strange apologia for the city; or is it for himself? We are still avoiding one another.

## 3

Well, damn me if he ain't back up that little old hill again. With Hiyah. Which I suppose makes him happier, *poverino;* like a mangy escaped zoo lion, that crawls back into its cage.

Cut me stone dead today at the corner of Via Cavour, walking side by side with Hiyah, who treated me the same way. I can understand it better than ever, now; I guess I've just got too much on him, I've been present at too much of the game. What a mean little face she has. And how pathetically hangdog he looks when he's with her. He seems to me to have gotten worse since I last saw him, as though something's happened, but I don't know what. Not that I ever really believed in all that histrionic leaping around, but at least he could find the energy to do it. Now he looks deflated; someone's let the air out of the balloon. I suppose the whole Ruth thing was Custer's Last Stand, and now the Indians done got him.

Florence looked exquisite today, the sky a very soft blue, though I don't suppose he noticed it. Coming down the Borgho Pinti, one suddenly, at an intersection, had the Brunelleschi *cupola* jump into view, so round and soft in that gentle light, and somehow proud – like a pregnant woman. Then *bang*! at the next intersection, like a consort, that marvellous *campanile*, the two of them side by side, masculine and feminine. What more could you ask?

Seeing Kevin and Hiyah brought me down to earth and then, just to point up the moral, crossing that ugly Repubblica, a Vespa missed me by a quarter of an inch, buzzing past right out of nowhere. One sometimes gets to think they've as much to do with Renaissance Florence as the Romans have to do with Ancient Rome. Then home to cook myself a hunk of lamb I'd bought, and to get back to my chapter on Leonardo's drawings.

Time's running against me. The longer I go on, the more I realize it's a building that can't be completed; or at least not by me. I'll be lucky if I lay the foundations and leave the plans. Which, curiously, I'm now able to accept. What else can anybody do in this era but fail, even in secondary activity? What counts is the quality of the failure. I shall just go on looking, go on writing and tearing up, while the ultimate recipe, the figure in the carpet, dances about in the distance, for ever out of reach. Is Kevin's failure any worse than mine? Or Nunberg's, whom I've seen again, quite ecstatic to be back, reacting to everything, and so to nothing.

*In fondo siamo tutti forestieri.*

## 4

A *little* man; so much smaller than one had expected, perhaps from the voice, which itself is different, much less sepulchral. And definitely a kind of rodent; a friendly, snuffling squirrel, or a pet mouse. About sixty, I suppose, so compact and self-contained, endlessly alert, squirrel eyes darting behind his spectacles. He says very little, mostly smiles. But oh, the joy of having an ambassador from Grub Street, to hear the news and the gossip and the anecdotes, to revive the world I knew and *he* knew.

The first night, Lucy went to bed at midnight, but we were out on the terrace till nearly three, talking above the cicada chorus, while old faces sprung out of the dark. He'd known Lewis and Sidney Keyes, he even remembered the poem I'd published in *Penguin New Writing*, and said he'd liked it. He'd spent the war in the Ministry of Information, 'pumping out hatred'. If he'd been younger, he sometimes thought he'd have been a conscientious objector.

'Which must have taken courage,' I said to him. 'No, no, I mean it. It was easy enough to do what everybody else did, even if it meant getting killed. Especially if you were so young that you weren't yet used to acting for yourself.'

'But does one *ever* act for oneself?' he said, and looked at me with that Pickwickian twinkle which mitigates his shrewdness, and one's own feeling that one's being catalogued, categorized, prior to appearing in his next travel book.

He drank whisky, I bore him company in watered Chianti, which also intrigued him. 'Don't you drink?' he asked.

'I've given it up,' I told him, cheerfully.

'Why?' Looking closely at my face, as though he divined from it a reformed drinker.

'Health,' I replied, and that was that.

The next of his insidious questions: 'Do you like it here?'

What should I tell him? That it's no longer a question of liking or disliking it, it is, for an infinity of reasons, but most of all Lucy, the one place left to me, the last square on the chessboard. I hesitate so long that he adds, 'It seems almost *too* ideal,' which provides me with my lead.

'It is *too* ideal! Oppressively ideal. One sometimes longs for fogs and beer and ugly pubs and tubes and traffic jams.'

'A surfeit of beauty?' he said.

'A surfeit of a certain *kind* of beauty.'

'Yes, what one acquires is never the same as what one's born to.'

'I was born to Shropshire,' I said, 'and nothing will ever replace it, let alone this hackneyed, over-stylized backcloth.'

'Yet you stay here?' he said, with his keen little squirrel-gaze.

'But I have no intention,' I said, 'of dying here.'

After which we talked for God knows how long about Dylan, then about Norman Douglas, whom he'd known, and who preferred Italian scenery to English.

'He called our "salad country".'

'But remember,' I said 'that he was half-German.'

At last, 'And what about your novel?' which Lucy had brought up at dinner, but which I had never mentioned to him in my letters.

'I don't know,' I said, 'I don't really know about it as an art form,' and we were on to the *nouveau roman*, Beckett and Burroughs, the decline of Naturalism. He talked quite brilliantly, and seemed to sense I didn't want to talk about my own work.

I told him of the literary magazine we planned here. *Bellosguardo*; he was very interested and promised he'd write for the first issue. Then we spoke about literary magazines in general, the old *Criterion* under Eliot, Jack Squire, Frank Harris, *New Writing* in the war, *Botteghe Oscure*, which had failed in the end, making him wonder, he said, if it could be done from Rome, or Florence, from anywhere outside the conflict. I told him I was sure it could, especially from Florence, with its English literary traditions.

The more we talked, the more I realized *this* was what I really wanted to do, this, if anything, was my vocation; to be not a poet, not a writer, but an editor, which in turn was the contemporary way of being a patron, of being the catalyst to bring other talents to fulfilment. The idea grew, took wing, spun high into the air. The review would have to be superbly produced, I said, to which he answered, 'But the young are your market, aren't they? How would they be able to afford it?' A problem which I solved immediately: 'A reduction for students? Like *The Times* have always done, at Oxford and Cambridge!'

The policy of the review would be catholic but discriminating, nothing would be included or excluded *per se*, not even pornography. We might devote a whole issue to a single theme, a single country, even a single writer.

He sat and listened, sat and nodded, asking a question now and then; how would we distribute it? what would be our rates of payment? how much criticism would we publish? In the end, I asked him directly, 'Do you think we can succeed?' to which he answered, after cogitation, 'Might do. Quite a lot against it. Depends how long you can afford to subsidize it, really. Heaven knows one needs somewhere like that for new writers to publish.'

When I went up to bed at last, I felt exhilarated. I longed to tell Lucy all about it, it was terribly important to me that she should know and share it with me. I actually stopped a moment outside her door, which is around the corner from my own, but then went to bed, where I couldn't sleep, the idea of the review churning and churning in my head, one notion begetting another, till all of them shone in the dark like so many fireflies.

I woke at nine. Lucy always had her breakfast in bed, but when I went round to her room there was no answer, and when I tried the door, it was locked, the very worst sign; yet how could I have possibly upset her? My stomach was water, my spirits plummeted. *Not* now, *not* today, *not* while Roland Wilkinson is here. I knocked again, hoping that she'd simply overslept, but from inside there came the sound of a cup chinking on a saucer. She was awake.

Just took off and ignored me, Anna. I might as well not even have been there.

But what did you expect, *cara*?

He gets someone like that in the house, he doesn't want to bother with me. And now it's nothing all day but this magazine he wants to start, like a kid with a toy.

Which you, of course, must buy for him.

He may think I will, he's going to be disappointed. I know just what would happen if I did give him the money.

*Questo senz'altro*. And this other one's encouraging him.

I don't like him. Those patronizing English airs of his.

Are you sure that he is what he says he is?

You mean a literary critic?

*Certo*. It seems strange to me that a literary critic should come to stay with people that he does not know; not even with a famous writer.

That's right, I never thought of that. But Kevin wrote to him. That's how it came about. Through Kevin writing to him at his newspaper.

Perhaps he's just a friend, who knows about it. Or maybe all those letters never reached the man; someone else at the newspaper could have intercepted them.

Kevin seems to have accepted him okay.

Has Kevin ever met him before?

I guess not.

*E allora*.

Kevin, are you sure this man is who he says he is?

Roland? But of course I'm sure.

Well, I'm not. I've been talking to Anna, and she's not certain, either.

What the *hell* does Anna know about this?

Now, don't go talking that way about Anna, Kevin. You've got her to thank that you're back up here at all.

Have I?

You surely have. And don't forget I can ask her to move back in again, any time I like.

What *is* the matter, Lucy?

I just want to know who this man is, that's all. How do I know he isn't some kind of confidence trickster? Using this magazine idea to get some money out of me, and that's the last we'll see of him?

This is absurd!

No more absurd than the way the two of you cut me right out when you're together. This is my villa he's staying at, Kevin.

You went to bed last night. You said you were exhausted.

Of course I went to bed. What use was there in staying up when you'd completely excluded me, talking about people I'd never even heard of?

Lucy, you've no *idea* how much I wanted to include you! I wanted so much to talk to you that honestly, I stood outside your door and almost woke you up.

Oh, sure, you wanted to get some money out of me.

Lucy: what is it you want?

You can tell him he's got to leave tomorrow.

For God's *sake*, we're giving the party for him on Saturday.

I don't care. I'm not giving any party for somebody that ignores me in my own home, someone who may not even be what he says he is.

I have seen *pic*tures of him.

Pictures prove nothing. You tell him he's got to leave tomorrow. If he's still here after noon, I'll tell him so, myself. What's the matter? What are you pulling that face for? Are you trying to kid me that you've got that pain, again?

It's all right. I shall be perfectly all right.

Because it won't work any more, Kevin. You're not going to go blackmailing me, any more.

Poor, poor Lucy. At the mercy of that evil spider. And I, sitting on the terrace where she left me, the pain very sharp and fierce, so fierce that it frightens me. I want a drink, but I'm afraid to have a drink, yet how else can I face Roland Wilkinson, and what the hell do I tell him, when I face him?

Roland, I don't know *how* to say this.

He cocks his head and looks at me, not with alarm but, so much worse, with interest, like a lepidopterist with his killing bottle.

*Ab*solutely out of the blue, we've heard from Lucy's parents. We weren't expecting them for weeks, but they've suddenly decided to come today.

He doesn't believe a word of it; why should he? Just looks at me, and smiles a little. I wish I could die. I wish I could disappear. And pity. My God, I see a definite *pity*.

If only we had one more room.
  That's all right.

Smiles again, a quick little twitching smile, nods, and walks away. I want to run after him, explain, apologize, confess, but what can I possibly say? It was all so nice, all so wonderfully promising, till that bitch Anna poisoned everything. The pain is agony; I can hardly stand up. Perhaps I should have told him I was ill and had to go into hospital; which might still even be true : I can see *one* possibility.

Roland : look *do* have a coffee. I'll get Maria to bring it to you on the terrace.

Looks at me now as if I were a little crazed, but never mind. Now up to his room. Thank God; there it is, right beside his bed. Find Lucy.

Darling; look. His passport.

What do you mean, his passport?

Here it is. Roland Wilkinson. You see the photograph? Perfectly genuine.

I still don't want him here. Have you told him to go?

I am *just* about to tell him. But darling, look at all the people we've invited. Whatever are you going to say to *them*?

I'll tell them he had to leave, that's what I'll tell them.

But you were so looking forward to the party.

That was before he came, and the two of you cut me right out.

Darling, we were *not* cutting you out. Why don't you ring Anna, and tell her we've authenticated him?

That still doesn't change the way you both behaved. The way you're trying to get money out of me for that stupid magazine.

It was only an idea, darling. If you don't like it, I'll abandon it. Half the satisfaction was to have you interested in it, too.

I'll call Anna, then I'll talk to you.

Roland, *ev*erything's all right!

Oh, is it?

We've cleared it up, we've got through to them, they're not coming till next week.

Splendid.

Not in the least surprised. Precisely the same smile.

So you will stay now, won't you?

Yes. I shall go and unpack.

The party, Lucy looking adorable and *very* young. Wearing a sleeveless blue silk dress that suits her perfectly, that makes her look so fragile and evanescent. Marvellously animated; and getting on so well with Roland, as I knew she would, once the ice was broken. She and Roland and the Consul, talking. I hear her laugh; *ha-ha-ha-ha-ha*. And see him look at her – curiously – docketing another specimen. What book will he put us in, and how shall we appear? I go towards them.

And they published the same one that they rejected! I think that's wonderful!

Her laugh, again.

He has met Robert Clyde, too, and they obviously took to one another; they know so many of the same people. We talked about the review – Robert still wants to publish sections of it in Italian, but Roland thinks this would turn it into another *Botteghe Oscure*, neither fish nor fowl. Pipe dreams, anyway; Lucy won't hear of it, now. But perhaps in six months, a year, when it has simmered down . . .

Anna over there, talking to the Marchesa Fantini, her lizard eyes flickering perpetually across the terrace. I've beaten you this time, my venomous old lizard, but I know it's just one battle in an endless campaign. Thank God at least my pain's much better, and I am still not drinking. The glass in my hand is full of *acqua minerale*. Lucy looks at it, looks at me, and smiles.

Pouring a whisky, now, for Roland Wilkinson.

Roland, *do* forgive that ridiculous misunderstanding.

Nothing to forgive.

And you *will* come again?

I should love to.

Would you really? Would you really come again? Perhaps at Christmas?

Delightful.

*So* stimulating to make contact with the real world!

If it is the real world.

Yes . . . But I suppose in a sense one must almost seem to be in hiding up here.

Not at all. Isn't is rather what you said about conscientious objectors? I'm not sure it doesn't take more courage.

Does it? Does it?

I suppose it does. The more I've thought about it since he left, the more perceptive a remark it seems. Peace has her victories. And merely a gloss, in fact, on my own theory of the simplicity of war. What courage, after all, does it require to live even in New York, the middle of the maelstrom, where the maelstrom sucks you up and whirls you round, where the ultimate luxury is the lack of time to reflect?

Here, there's too much time to reflect, and it is this which needs courage. To confront oneself, rather than escape from oneself. For if this is escaping, it's an escape from an escape. The ultimate escape, presumably, being from the self. To cease upon the midnight with no pain. The fakir staring glassily at his navel, till his soul goes soaring into space to join the infinite.

Here on the hill, I proclaim the uselessness of all activity, not least my own. Our perpetual urge to find significance in nothing. Our failure to achieve fulfilment in the things of the flesh, any more than in those of the mind or the spirit. I am a failed poet. If I were a successful poet, what more would I have attained? An appeased vanity? Over the years, perhaps, a slight alleviation here and there of the human condition; but far less than a doctor or even a priest. Which brings one to the whole phenomenon of what one looks down at in the valley, with its cloud-capped towers and mouldering palaces. Does it fructify the present or simply, as I believe, crush it? I've argued this at length with Peter Clovis, who seems to think it's the last repository of human genius, and has sacrificed his life to prove it. Whereas to me, however beautiful, it remains a mausoleum, peopled by pygmies.

Each year, the tourists pour in in their coachloads to look at things they have been told are marvellous, eternally significant.

How many of those troupes of chattering South Americans, those cohorts of intense Germans, mustered by numbers, those fish-and-chip-munching chara-born English, those blue-haired regiments of American matrons, draw anything from it at all?

I don't think I am a Philistine. I respond to green hills, green woods and the sea. To the Chapel at King's, to Durham Cathedral, soaring like a rock face over that little city. So I can understand, intellectually, why Clovis should love Florence, why Lucy should adore Florence; should love the grim Palazzo Vecchio and the sentimental Duomo, should love those disintegrating frescoes, those endless broad acres of oil paint. But they don't speak to me; not a word. And if they did, would I be entitled to elevate my response into a mystique about the city, any more than I've the right to make such claims for Durham Cathedral, Shropshire fields and trees, Cornish cliffs with all their wild intransigence?

What is art, come to that, but the imitation of nature? In what way is a cathedral superior to a mountain? A picture to its subject? Why paint a landscape or sculpt a head, when you can look at them? Why write about either, or anything, to put them only at a still further remove?

Oh, yes; it takes courage to sit up here on the hill.

## 5

He's stopped drinking for the moment, at least there's that, though I don't know how long it's going to last. I don't even know why he did it, it was so unexpected; he said he gave it up for me, but I don't believe him, I never know when to believe him, I don't know when to believe anything, what with him one side and Anna the other. If only I could say this one's always right, so the other's got to be wrong, but it won't work that easily. Like this business with the English writer who stayed here, when it looked like Anna could easily be right, only she turned out to be wrong. When I got to know him better I liked him; I guess at first he was shy, that's all, and maybe I was shy as well. I still tend to be shy with people. The thing with Anna is she means so well, she's always looking out for me, and sometimes I guess maybe she tends to be a little over-zealous.

I still don't know for sure was I right or wrong taking Kevin back, or even what made me do it. Anna says, 'That's why I told you not to go and see him. You thought I was inhuman, but all I said to myself was, once she goes, she is lost. That one knows too well how to play on her feelings.' And this is the funny thing: I didn't even mean to go. I fought it down, this wanting to see him, this feeling guilty, whenever I got to noticing it, knowing this was exactly what he wanted, like Anna said.

Then driving down the Lungarno one morning I suddenly looked up and thought that's where he is, right there in that building, maybe I'll just go in and see how he is, because even if I'd decided to go in, I was sure as hell determined that he wasn't going to talk himself back again. It was going to be five minutes with him, and *basta*.

But when I got into the *pensione* they all came crowding around me, the whole family, with these serious faces, like the whole thing was my doing, saying, '*Sta male, signora, sta molto male, chiede sempre Lei*,' how much he'd missed me, how much he'd been talking about me, so by the time I got up to that crummy little room, I was confused. And seeing him there didn't help me any, lying in the bed, I'd never seen him look so weak, like the life had drained out of him. I can tell you I really had to make an effort not to let him work on me, like Anna had said he would, and remember this was why he'd done it, anyway. Especially when he went through the whole bit about loving me and our needing each other; after ten years together, it can be pretty hard to resist.

That was what Anna saw as well; that once I got back in the inertia, it would be awful hard to get out of it. I remember her face when I walked back into the villa and said, 'I've been to see him, Anna, and he's coming back here.' It shocked her so much it wasn't true: she's always pale but this time her face looked like it was carved out of chalk. All she said was, 'Then you are crazy, quite crazy.'

I said, 'For a month, that's all. A month's trial.' She said, 'And the month will turn into six, six months will turn into a year, till you will find exactly the same thing will happen again.' I said, 'It won't turn into anything, Anna, not if he doesn't change.' She said, 'Do you seriously expect him to change?' I said, 'No, I don't, but this way, nobody can blame me. Not Kevin or anybody.' Including all the little people at the Oltrarno, who he's charmed round on to his side. Well, okay, he tried to kill himself for me, if that's the way you want to look at it, and I gave him his chance, I took him back again.

I didn't want Anna to move out, it was her own idea, and when she'd gone I really missed her, I missed her companionship, which is something that I just don't get from Kevin; only in a strange kind of way I felt freer, too, because Anna's such a strong personality, she's a lot like Mother in that way, if you don't watch it you're inclined to find everything's decided for you, where with Kevin it's just the other way around, you have to decide every little thing.

For a time after he'd got back, things weren't too bad, he was very attentive, we even slept together a while, but I just can't make love with a man I don't respect, and pretty soon Kevin had gone right back to where he was, drinking too much, shutting himself away, spending the whole day reading a book or playing music, so that we were leading two separate lives again, and then, whenever I bawled him out, pretending that he had this pain, which is one thing he just can't fool me with, though he certainly tries.

What I know I'll never forgive him is his being unfaithful to me. How he has the nerve to keep telling me he loves me, when he takes off and does a thing like that, not once, either, but twice, then giving me this stupid story about trying to kill the pain. What does he think I am?

I've never been unfaithful to Kevin, and God knows there's plenty of opportunity here, the way the Italians go after you, especially those two times when they knew I was on my own. There was one guy Anna used to bring up here, really creepy, he called himsef a *marchese* but that was for the birds. One night when he'd been here playing canasta with us and Anna had gone off early to bed for some reason, he jumped on me, and I had to dig my nails right in his face before he'd give up. I told him, 'Get out of here, or I'll telephone the police. I'll make a *denuncia*,' and I told Anna, 'Don't you ever ask him up here again.'

She looked real surprised, she said she hadn't any idea he was like that.

Kevin was only the third man I'd ever had, and what there was with him didn't last very long, not from my point of view, anyway. That kind of thing's only as important as you allow it to be, if you ask me, and one thing I despise in Kevin is he's always been that way, a girl only has to look at him. My mother had his number the first time she ever met him, she said, 'He's a Don Juan, dear, and a fading one at that. He knows he's got to make his killing soon, or he's on the scrap heap. Don't you be *it*.'

I knew that side of him was there okay, the Don Juan side, but then I used to think there was this other side that Mother hadn't seen, the artistic one, which I exaggerated so much I guess because I was still very young, I still got illusions about people.

When Mother was here last, I told her, 'He promised me everything, and he's given me nothing.' She said, 'That's how Kevin lives, on promises.'

Sometimes I lie awake and think is this all, is this all there is in life, do I have to spend the next thirty years up here watching Kevin fall apart, wondering what the hell to do with every day, seeing the same people over and over? There just has to be something more.

I'd go back to New York, only I know it's worse, you're moving all the time and getting nowhere, and I remember what it did to me before. At least here you have beauty, it's everywhere around you, you look down from the villa, you look up when you're in the city, and there it is, whether it's a church or a mountain or just a slope of olives, but Kevin can't even see *that*, which is what's so fantastic about him, the thing I've never been able to understand, and him supposed to be so goddam artistic. Maybe this ought to be enough, but it isn't. Maybe I ought to get involved with it more, go back to taking courses and such, but somehow there just doesn't seem to be the time, though I still go to a lot of exhibitions.

When I tell Anna things like this she gets on to religion, she's very religious, Greek Orthodox, she's always talking about this patriarch in Rome and that one in Paris, she says she doesn't know how she'd ever have come through all she has if it wasn't for her religion giving her the strength. I was brought up Episcopalian, but it never meant a lot. Now and then women I've known here in Florence, Italian Catholic women, have said why don't you take instruction, and I've thought about it, I've seriously thought about it, I even had a talk once with a monsignore, but somehow or other, I don't know quite why, it doesn't attract me, there's something kind of oppressive about it all, it seems to go with this whole Italian business of the men doing what the hell they like and the women being submissive, and the ones I know here, it surely doesn't seem to make *them* any better.

So here I am again, stuck with Kevin. God knows I had my chance when he went back to that first wife of his, and behaved like I didn't exist any more. I don't know what got into me then, why I behaved the way I did. Maybe because I was so young and, like I said, I had these ideas about him – after all, how long had I known him? – and on top of that, we'd never lived together. You've got to live with Kevin before you know him; even now, you'd be surprised how many people he can fool.

That's something else I find it hard to forgive him for; that whole time when he was with Joan, the way he humiliated me, the way he made me suffer. Refusing even to talk to me, making me practically go down on my knees to him. My God, if I knew the half of what I know now, there wouldn't have been any of that. I look at him today and I just can't believe it ever happened. I should have let her keep him, that's what I should have done, it would have served her right. I can still remember the way she'd look at me if we saw each other in the street, before I'd got him back and afterwards; like I was something she'd stepped on. And who the hell was she? The only reason he went back to her was because I'd gone off and left him on his own; he admitted it to me. She didn't look anything particular, she didn't dress well, and as for this painting she was meant to be doing, from what I heard from people who saw it, it was a laugh.

We never spoke a word to each other, but she wrote me a letter after Kevin came back to me which I never did forget. It said, 'I congratulate you on the success of all your devious manoeuvres, but I wonder if you've overestimated your powers?' When I read it I thought what the hell did she mean by that, apart from it being sour grapes? I showed it to Kevin and he said he didn't know either, just to tear it up. Which I did, but I still kept thinking about it, and today I guess I can see what she meant, though if it comes to that, what the hell did she do with him in all those years?

So here I am again with Kevin. Anna said to me when she knew I was having him back, 'It can surely be only out of pity; you cannot pretend that you love him,' which funnily enough is something I hadn't thought about for years; I just took having him around for granted. And when I did think about it, the strange thing is that I just didn't know.

Oh, sure, I loved him all right first off, when we were doing all those things together. Maybe part of it had to do with the romantic kind of way we met, which kind of set the pattern for everything; the way I saw him as a sort of knight errant, which now just seems too funny for words.

I guess I loved him in New York, too, that time, when he was so different from anybody else, so individual. I'd look at him at cocktail parties or at dinner parties, very handsome with that high colour of his, his eyes all alive and his voice so beautiful, and I'd think how he had something you'd just never find in an American man. I still see it now, occasionally, at parties here, any time he feels he has to put on a show and somebody throws the switch. Which has this other side to it, it means that he can do it when he wants to, and when we're alone he just doesn't want to any more;

we live here like two strangers. Sometimes I get so lonely at night when Anna isn't here and I've nowhere to go that I just go into the kitchen and talk to Maria and Sergio or play word games with them. When he first got back from the Oltrarno he had plenty to say all right; for a week or two it was too good to be true, we were like we were ten years ago, him talking about things he'd done, people he'd known, what went on in the *pensione* with the oddballs they have there, what he was going to put in his novel. His novel!

The other day I came right out with how I felt, we were having lunch and he was reading some damn paper. I said, 'Why don't you ever talk to me, Kevin?' He put down the paper and looked at me like I was crazy. He said, 'What about?' and that got me really mad, I started yelling at him. I said, 'What about? A husband hasn't got anything to talk about to his wife?' He said, 'I'll be delighted to talk about anything you like. What have you been doing this morning?' which was worse still.

I said, 'I told you last night what I was going to do this morning. I've been to the Palazzo Pitti to look at the new collections, only you don't give a damn, you don't even listen.'

He looked at me in this kind of glassy way he's gotten into, a lot of things just don't seem to get through to him. In the end what he said was, 'Did you see anything you particularly liked?' I said, 'Yes, I saw an evening gown by Pucci and I've ordered it, if that interests you at all.' He said, 'Of course it does,' with the same glassy look, like I was some child that was bothering him, then dropped his eyes and went right back to his paper.

I'd just had enough, I grabbed it away from him and I said, 'If all you want to do is read the papers, why didn't you stay right there in Florence and do it?'

As for that novel of his, it stays just where it always was, in his head. Oh, sure, he's read me little bits and pieces that he's written, and when Roland Wilikinson came he said he'd done the same to him, read stuff to him because none of it was typed yet, and how Roland had really gone for it and said he'd talk to publishers in London. It's the same old Kevin. Before long, he's going to be drinking again.

## 6

*Very* carefully rationed. And such a complex operation to get hold of any at all; waiting until Lucy's out to go gliding down the hill, furtively to the Porta Romana, then come whistling up again with the bottle under my coat, hoping to God she won't come suddenly past in the car. But how else is one going to withstand the visitation, her mother and Arthur, though Arthur will to some extent mitigate her mother. Her abominable mother.

The pain, lately, has been bad. This morning, for the first time, I actually woke up with it, horribly sharp, and lay there afraid to move, so much wanting a drink. For strictly medicinal purposes . . . It subsided very, very slowly. It was an hour before I dared sit up, another hour or so before I dared get out of bed, but it gradually ebbed away during the morning, leaving one weak and alarmed.

They are coming for ten days, during which Mrs Harrison will deploy her forces. We shall circle each other with great respect, like two boxers fighting for the umpteenth time. What new surprise can she have been preparing, what feint, what trap, what treachery? Last time it was the bribe, the attempt to pay me off. Sometimes, during those months in the Oltrarno, I wondered if I should have taken it. Assuming, that is to say, I'd known what would happen – that Lucy would get rid of me again. Wouldn't life in England, amply subsidized, have been a thousand times better than exile in one squalid room in Florence? But each time, I knew that I'd been right, I could have done nothing else, that it was Lucy I needed, not a haven; or rather, that my haven was in Lucy.

Though wouldn't the best thing of all be England with Lucy – who will never, never move (my guarantee, my ultimate defence against the forces of Mother).

If Arthur is coming too, she must have some specific use for him, as buttress or battering ram, poor devil. Lucy likes him, but I think he irritates her, she smells out the weakness in him, or what she would consider the weakness in him and I, perhaps, would call his humanity; just as I suppose she does in me. These poor American women, trained from birth, like hounds or ferrets, to pursue fallibility, to gnaw and gnaw away until they find, to their amazement, that there's nothing left. Mrs Harrison – I can never call her Barbara, or whatever it is – has done it to two husbands, is doing it to a third, and will no doubt do it to a fourth. Moreover, she's indoctrinated Lucy with her own attitude to her father, of whom she speaks so very scornfully, whom she's scarcely seen since she was a child. Now and then he writes to her, pathetic, pleading letters, as though he'd quite readily accepted guilt, and taken himself at their valuation.

Arthur and I. War veterans, survivors. We have this bond; that we might both be dead, but we are still alive. Perhaps she's seen this, perhaps that's why she's bringing him, knowing that she and I can only meet head on, while he, even if it didn't work the last time, might possibly prevail on me.

## 7

Silent upon a peak in Bellosguardo. Both drinking. I, with a bottle of *acqua minerale* for camouflage. Arthur pledged to complicity.

'I know how it is, Kevin. Now and then I have to do just that with Barbara. She can smell the rum in a Coca-Cola.'

And is now in Florence with Lucy. Shopping.

We overlook the detested panorama.

'So you really like it here, Kevin.'

'Not really.'

But he hasn't listened.

'It's certainly one hell of a view.'

Quite remote. More even than in New York, now he's free from that marionette jerking, the conditioned responses, the telegrams and anger. Though not from phone calls, when he changes, becoming suddenly very brusque and brisk. We'd another one this morning. 'It's up four points? Well, just go right along with it.' I think I like him better, here.

'Do you ever look down, Kevin, and wonder how you'd take this hill? Or how you'd defend it? What kind of a field of fire you'd have? That fighting you did out here. Or maybe it seems kind of blasphemous to you.'

'No, no, I've sometimes thought about it. I honestly wouldn't care if they dropped a land mine on it all.'

'You wouldn't care? Why's that, Kevin? Oh, sure, that's right, Barbara told me. I guess I'd feel the same if I was up here too long.'

I've been up here far too long. St Simeon Stylites. Though he was celibate by choice.

'Maybe one needs a little of this and a little of New York. We have a crazy kind of life at home.'

The endless, untouched youth of American faces. He must be at least as old as I am, but his cheeks are pink, his eyes so blue and guileless. Even those grey curls can't age him. Whereas his wife will never be old, and has never been young.

He behaves to me as if he knows nothing of what's happened, though she must surely have told him. Her own, distorted version. He listens yet doesn't listen; so protects himself. Water over the rock.

'How are the Italian women?'

A trap? I can't believe it.

'Devious.'

'Is that right? I've chased one or two in New York. They certainly took some catching.'

What *are* her plans? My own plan: silence, exile and cunning. While hers, I suspect, is that of provocation, which God knows worked the last time. How foolish I was. Now, I simply bite the bullet, smile and smile, respond to her digs and jabs with offers of tea, wine, coffee, whisky. The first time we found ourselves alone together, she shook me warmly and treacherously by the hand and said, 'Kevin,

I want you to know that so far as I'm concerned, what's happened happened. I hope this time we're going to get along.'

To which I responded, I hope, with properly synthetic enthusiasm, assuring her that I'd forgotten it all long ago.

There'll be no offer to me this time; she obviously won't try that again. Nor one from him to take a job in New York. Perhaps she'll try to work indirectly, through Lucy. Already the poor girl's showing her usual signs of being pulled both ways.

Anna, I notice, has kept well out of the way. How strange that she and I for once should almost be allies.

'You ever used to go to the whorehouses here, Kevin?'

'Now and then, when I first arrived.'

'How were they?'

'Rather antiseptic.'

A last resort in winter, out of the tourist season. Or in those long periods when Lucy was rejecting one.

'I tell you where I liked them : Tokyo. They really knew how to make a man happy.'

Not here, where they always let one know one was paying for it. So quick and sceptical. Those bland, anonymous rooms with their low beds, their basins and bidets, and their cloying smell of powdered flesh. Directly after the orgasm, a feeling of utter defeat, total isolation.

'How many times you been married, Kevin? This the second?'

'Yes.'

'The second time around, huh? Mine's the first. Any kids?'

'None.'

'I've got three. One at Harvard, one at Annapolis, one married. You ever want children?'

'I should have liked a son.'

'I don't see mine too often. They live with their mother. Lucy upset she can't have children?'

'I think she's come to terms with it.'

'That's a restless girl; it could have made a difference to her.'

I have drunk a lot, but I say nothing.

'She's got her mother's energy, but I guess there's only so much you can do with it, here. Where would you rather live, Kevin? England?'

'Yes.'

'I understand that. I don't see why the hell Lucy sticks out here; neither does her mother.'

And, shaking his head, cuts out again. I, too, have nothing more to say.

The car.

Drain the glass, fill it to the brim with *acqua minerale*. A little mineral water clears us of this deed. Arthur snaps out of his trance at the first sound of her voice, a conditioned reflex. 'Hi! How did it go?'

'We saw the most *lovely* exhibition. Piranesi. Have you seen it, Kevin?'

'Kevin never sees anything, Mother.'

'Oh, yes, I was forgetting.'

She lets him make love to her, I imagine, as a reward. And makes it well, too, probably, with a passionless expertise. Leaving him grateful. There are time when I have been aware of her eye on me. Predatory. I have looked away.

## 8

I know there's no use asking you to move.

Then don't ask me, Mother.

I'm not going to live for ever, dear. You can't blame me for wanting to see a little more of my only child.

Mother, we've been through all this before.

Kevin hadn't tried to kill himself, before.

What do you mean by that?

Just that he knows he's got you where he wants you, now. And as long as you stay here, you'll never be rid of him.

Kevin has *not* got me where he wants me.

Are you sure?

I am perfectly sure. If I wanted, I could get rid of him tomorrow.

Then why don't you?

Because at the moment I don't happen to want to.

Don't tell me you're still hanging on in hope?

You wouldn't understand, Mother.

Do *you* understand, dear? Are you keeping him here like a beat-up old dog you just can't get around to having put away? Is that it?

Mother, I'd prefer not to talk about it.

Is he writing that novel? Has he really given up drinking?

Kevin has not been drinking for two months.

Are you sure? Look into his face. Take a look at his eyes.

I don't have to look at his eyes. There's nothing in the house except wine.

Nothing he's told you about.

Mother, will you stop? You're just confusing me.

## 9

On our way to Sant' Andrea. Arthur driving the Lancia they have hired. Rather well, very competent, looking strong-jawed and square-shouldered in the tight blue short-sleeved shirt he's wearing. One can see he must have made a good soldier. Always at his best in action; driving, barking into telephones.

Beside him, Lucy. In the back of the car, myself and Mrs Harrison. All is jollity; with undercurrents. We shall drink wine and eat garlic toast and be merry. Tomorrow they go back, and it has all been bloodless, mere manoeuvres, not a real shot fired. Mrs Harrison, though her responses are impeccably in tune, seems tight and tense. Next to her, I am Ghandi, passively impregnable.

'Who was it got exiled there, Lucy? Savonarola?'

'I've told you, Arthur, Machiavelli.'

'I guess there must have been worse places.'

Places of exile are neither better nor worse. They are mply, and this is the pain of them, different. How keen they were here on banishing people: Dante, Machiavelli. Some of that, at least, is left to them in residue, though now they can't make exiles. Instead, they receive them – and ignore them.

'You ever read *The Prince*, Kevin?'

'No.'

'I had to read it in college.'

'That's wild! Arthur read *The Prince* in college! I thought all you ever did was go out for the football team and date the co-eds!'

'Well, I have news for you Lucy. I read *The Prince*.'

'And how was it, Arthur?'

'Pretty goddam dull.'

'Did *you* ever read it, Mrs Harrison?'

'No, Kevin. I never did.'

Unwise, but irresistible. Prepare for counter-attack.

We sit rustically in the open, at a rustic wooden table, eating the odorous hot hunks of toast. It is dark, the cicada chorus drowns everything. The air is cool, but still benign. Lucy bubbles like a happy child. *Not* laughing.

'And right here is where Machiavelli used to drink, Mother. Isn't that wild?'

Sombrely, I suppose. Forgetting-drinking. How odd that somebody should feel nostalgia for Florence. I should never miss it. But there we are again; the otherness of other places.

Lucy's face, so young and eager in the dark; ecstatic that we're all getting on so well together. I take her hand beneath the table and she squeezes my fingers, then gives me such an open, beautiful smile.

'Do *you* like it here, Kevin?'

'Yes, enormously.'

'You think you'd prefer it to Bellosguardo?'

What is the old bitch after? Does she want to exile *me* here?

'I should prefer anywhere where I have my dear Lucy, wouldn't I, darling?'

'Yes, I've heard about that.'

'*Here's* the spaghetti.' Which should quieten her a while. Lucy tense now, poor dear. All her effervescence gone.

'I've certainly enjoyed this trip. Enjoyed the party, too.'

'Yes, it was nice to see those same old faces. I think it's wonderful how you never get tired of them, but maybe that just comes of living in New York.'

'We get plenty of people passing through, don't we, Kevin-wevin?'

Ah, the look on her mother's face at that; not even the dark can mollify it.

'Yes, of course we do, darling.'

'I guess I just never get to meet them.'

'I believe she's drunk.

'Do let's have some more of this marvellous garlic bread.'

'How do they make it, Kevin?'

'They rub it with garlic, heat it, then pour on a little oil.'

'Sure tastes good.'

'Then of course you have Kevin coming in and out, as well.'

Ignore that.

'Why don't you just stop it, Mother?'

'Darling, I'm not even starting anything. I'm concerned with your happiness, you know that's all that I'm concerned with.'

'Okay, cool it, Barbara.'

'Arthur, I do *not* need advice from you.'

'Not giving you advice, honey. Just don't see why we have to spoil a pleasant evening.'

God, how I begin to like that man.

'You tend to forget, Arthur, that Lucy is *my* daughter.'

'I don't forget that, Barbara. You don't let me forget that.'

'Mother, will you have some more wine?'

'Yes, dear, I will.'

'How about you, Kevin?'

'Kevin will probably refuse, dear. He's being *very* cautious.

Though when he gets home, he might *just* have the tiniest sip of whisky.'

'My *dear* Barbara –'

'I'm not your dear Barbara. And you are certainly not my dear Kevin.'

'I *think* I shall be able to survive that.'

'Oh, you'll survive, okay. You survive drink, sleeping pills, everything.'

'Mother!'

'Now listen, Barbara –'

'It's Lucy I'm worried about. How long will *she* survive?'

'I'm okay, Mother.'

'I don't think so, dear. Not the way you look right now. I haven't seen you for a year, remember, and Arthur hadn't seen you for a whole lot longer.'

'Don't bring me into this, Barbara.'

'I'm not bringing you into anything, dear. You know as well as I do how shocked you were by the change in Lucy.'

'Not shocked.'

'Well, whatever you like to call it.'

He looks, with melancholy embarrassment, down at the table. My friend, my comrade-in-arms. Lucy, beside me, is a-quiver. I try to take her hand, but she's possessed and snatches it away; though not from me as me. For the moment, she sees only her mother.

'Are you saying I can't manage my own life? Is that what you're trying to say?'

'I don't want to say anything to you while you're in this state, darling; it's just impossible to get through to you.'

'You mean to dominate me.'

'I know what I mean, dear.'

'I've built myself some kind of a life here, Mother. It may be a long way from perfect, but it's a damn sight more than I ever had in New York.'

'I don't know that I'd call it a *life*, dear.'

'Then what *do* you call a life? Running your ass off in that crazy city?'

'That's vulgar, Lucy.'

'How would you know what's vulgar and was isn't? Have *you* any appreciation of beauty? You walk around Florence with your eyes closed. All you ever look at is the shop windows.'

Lucy, I admire you. I have never been so intensely proud of you.

'Maybe you owe just a *little* of what you have to your mother, dear.'

'Oh, sure, I'm not denying that. But do I have to go on paying interest on it the rest of my life?'

'*Shall* we have coffee?'

'Yeah, that's a good idea of Kevin's; let's have coffee.'

I was wrong. She has never read *The Prince*.

## 10

Of all things, Joan is here. On a vacation. Five years or so older than when I saw her last, married again, and remarkably little changed.

This morning, there was a double ring at my front door bell, I pushed the button to open it, stood at the top of the stairs expecting some sister of mercy, when who should turn the corner but she. Smiling all *over* her face, that apple-cheeked face, the apples just a little bit less rosy, but still right there on the tree.

'How *are* you, Peter?'

'Well, how are *you*?'

'Absolutely fine,' she said, and we kissed each other. 'I'm married again.'

'*Complimenti*,' I said. 'When and who?'

'Two years ago; to William Paine. He's a lawyer. Didn't you get the card?'

And then, God damn it, I had a horrible thought that I did get the card, meant to do something about it, and never did. We'd kept writing to each other for a few years after she'd left Florence, but then it just seemed to fall away, it was probably my fault.

I showed her into the apartment, and she looked round it in that brisk way of hers which is always just this side of the presumptuous and sometimes falls right over, the way some English have. She said, 'Still got the little Beccafumi. Still got that gorgeous mirror I always wanted to steal from you. Still living in the same Stygian gloom.'

'If I'd known you were coming,' I said, 'I'd have lit the chandelier,' and she laughed, which is the great, redeeming thing about Joan; she can laugh at herself.

While we talked, we were weighing each other up like a couple of old *duchesse* at Doney's; I knew she was at it and she knew I was at it. She'd gotten just a little plumper and certainly a little grey, or she wouldn't have her hair that blonde. As for me, she seemed to approve of what she saw, because she suddenly came out with, 'I think it's absolutely unfair. You're not a scrap older. It must be something in the atmosphere of Florence.'

'It is,' I said, 'we're all embalmed,' at which we both laughed, again.

'And how is your painting?' I asked, to which she came back very quick and bright, 'Splendid' – like a good English amateur – 'how's your treatise?'

'Oh, coming along,' I said.

'Have you found the elixir of art yet?'

'No,' I said, 'but I'm still pursuing it. Now tell me, what exactly brings you here?'

'Just touring,' she said, with that same brightness of hers, which I must say rather tends to wear me down. I guess it may have come from being a nurse and having to keep up the patients' spirits. 'Bill had to go to the States and I told him, "Very well, if you're going to have a trip on your own, I'm going to have a trip on my own. It's years since I've been to Florence, and I'm jolly well going!"'

'Good for you,' I said, and wondered how soon she'd start asking about Kevin. Last time she'd come, as I remembered, he'd been safely up the hill and they hadn't clapped eyes on each other; he hadn't started the now-you-see-me-now-you-don't act. She showed me a photograph of her new one, who looked like a handsome English horse, very fancy; I'd say he was a good five years older than she is. She said they lived outside London, but she came up a lot, that she was taking classes at some art school or other, and that maybe next year she'd have an exhibition; a friend of Bill's apparently owns a gallery. Then we left the subject. She knows what I thought of her painting – she never did like to be advised – and I know what she thinks of my opinions on painting.

She said, 'I've come to replenish myself. One should never stay away from Florence more than a couple of years.'

'I can't stay away more than a few weeks, I'm afraid,' I said. She said she thought that could be awfully dangerous, and I asked her, 'Do you think I've succumbed to the danger?'

'I think perhaps you're immune from it by now,' she said.

'Or maybe I'm part of it!' I told her, which was another laugh.

Her attitude to Florence is a strange one, somewhere between Kevin's and the Nunbergs'. She speaks the language well, her taste is fairly good, but there's a residual obtuseness that simply won't disappear, this Anglo-Saxon thing that art just isn't for gentlemen and you can't quite take it seriously, even though she wants to be a painter herself – provided she can be a lady at the same time.

In the end, out it came, *very* carefully thrown away, with her eye fixed firmly on the chandelier. 'Do you ever see anything of Kevin?'

'Oh, occasionally,' I said. 'He walks right by me.'

'What's been happening to him?'

'Quite a lot,' I said. 'He's been a real little Dante, these last few years. Thrown into the Inferno twice, and climbed right back into Paradise. Or maybe the other way around.'

'You mean she chucked him out?' she asked, looking very, very angry. 'The vindictive little bitch.'

'Well, that's how she's always seemed to me,' I said, 'but Kevin appears to see something more in her.'

'The only thing Kevin's ever seen in her,' she said, 'is her money.'

'Well, is there anything else to see?' I asked her.

'*I've* never thought so,' she said. 'The nasty, scheming, spoiled little brat. I knew exactly what would happen, and it has. I wrote her a letter after she'd inveigled him back to her. She simply wanted him on the mantelpiece to show her friends and spite her mother. She must have made his life hell.'

'And yet he goes back,' I said.

'Kevin's frightened to do anything else. He'd rather crawl back and be bullied day and night than come out and face the world, after twenty years.'

'The world?' I said.

'*His* world. Or what used to be his world. *You* might be strong enough to withstand Florence, but Kevin's certainly not. It's like putting something in a tank of acid; it simply dissolves without trace.'

'I have a little sympathy with him there,' I said. 'I don't know whether I could face *my* own world. I can't even imagine what it would look like.'

She asked me had I seen Kevin when he was down in Florence, and I told her yes I had, the second time. I said he'd had Ruth around, who seemed like a pretty nice girl, then Ruth had gone home, and he'd started cutting me again. I also told her how Ruth had come to see me and said she was afraid Kevin would kill himself, and I'd told her there was nothing she or anybody else could do.

Joan thought quite a while about that, she seemed pretty shaken up, but at the end she said, 'No, I suppose there's not,' and she shook her head; I was afraid for a moment she might even be about to cry. She said, 'I can't bear to think of him alone, here, in the winter.'

'Nor could Ruth,' I said.

She was quiet again and then she said, 'She sounds as if she would have been just right for Kevin, even to the youth. He needs youth.'

'Oh, perfect,' I said. 'But he'd just have pulled her down with him.'

'You've never liked him, have you?' she asked me.

'Not really, no,' I said.

'Of course not,' she said. 'The two of you are oil and water,' then she got up and began wandering about the room, touching things, picking things up and putting them down in a disturbing kind of way.

'Shall you try to see him?' I asked.

'No,' she said, 'there wouldn't be much point. It would only make me miserable and angry.'

She had her back to me, but I could see her face in the mirror above the mantelpiece, all crumbled up with grief, that girlish buoyancy quite gone, so that you saw it now for what it really was, a middle-aged face, lines appearing like cracks in an earthquake.

Suddenly she flung up her hands and gave this cry, 'Oh, if he weren't so *weak*!'

## 11

The pain is back. For the first time since her mother left. Not as bad as it has been – I'm a connoisseur of it, now. Less sharp, more resistible, but there.

Lucy knows I am drinking again. Last night, when she was out with Anna at some bloody party, I sat with a bottle of whisky in the living-room, listening to Bach; and fell asleep. She woke me, shouting, 'Kevin, Kevin!' and, opening my eyes, there she was, towering like a temperance angel, the bottle held aloft.

'So you've been drinking all this time. You've been lying to me.'

My explanations; all quite useless.

'It was this *morning*. I simply bought *one* bottle this morning.'

'Yeah, and how about all the other bottles?'

'This was the *first*.'

'And me standing up for you against Mother. She was right all along; so was Anna.'

'I have been in *pain.*'

'Don't let's have that again; that pain. You use it as an excuse for every little thing.'

All, in retrospect, so utterly absurd. Defending oneself as if from a charge of infidelity. And yet disastrous, too.

'Why didn't you level with me, Kevin?'

Losing all the ground I'd gained, and more; she's sure now that I never stopped at all. And I, I am sure of nothing. Not even why I stopped; or why I began again. What's true and what is false.

Why *now*, when things had gone so well? Her mother routed. One more rebirth out of one more crisis. Going, that night when we got back, to her room, *knowing* she'd be waiting for me. Making love with her was like a celebration, almost a covenant.

'Darling, you stood up to her so well, you were magnificent.'

'She just has to learn she can't run me any more.'

'She can't. You showed her that she can't.'

'And you were so controlled. The way you wouldn't let her rile you.'

'And wasn't Arthur splendid?'

'The first time I've ever seen it.'

We saw them off to Pisa in triumph; it was like escorting a defeated army to the border. Lucy wonderfully cheerful and affectionate, Arthur cheerful, too, babbling about how much he'd enjoyed it all; her mother full of sour solicitude, pretending to be concerned about her, which meant about me, telling her, 'Now be sure and write every week, tell me ex*act*ly what's happening, and call us once a month. I like to hear your voice, then I can tell how you are.'

At the airport she said, 'Goodbye, Kevin,' and offered me her cheek like the side of an iceberg.

Afterwards we stayed in Pisa for a magnificent lunch, then I insisted we both go up the Leaning Tower. At the top, I pretended to be afraid of falling off, and Lucy laughed so much she had to lean against the parapet to recover. Real laughter, not The Laugh.

Now, I suppose she'll exclude me again. 'I don't want you tonight, Kevin.' With Anna heaping fuel on the flames.

## 12

He tried to kill himself. Kevin tried to kill himself. *That* is what she reduced him to. This evening, I went round to the Oltrarno and they told me. I cried when I heard, and they were incredibly sweet, taking me up to that vast old-fashioned kitchen, pouring me cups of coffee, giving me cognac.

It was where he'd lived for a while when I first came out to him in Florence and he was terribly poor, though afterwards he'd moved into my own *pensione*. They still like him, though apparently he never paid his bills, and he smashed his room to matchwood. '*Tanto simpatico*,' they say, with that wonderful ability of simple Italians for getting to the root of people, judging them by their essence, rather than their actions.

'*Ma* lei, *signora*,' they said, and shook their heads. They'd obviously taken Lucy's measure, too. I asked them about the American girl, this Ruth, and they were a little embarrassed at first, it was charming, then they said, '*Però, era simpatica*,' and the lovely old Falstaffian father, with his white head, rumbled from the stove, '*Una gran bella ragazza*.'

They took me up to the room he'd had, though I didn't really want to go, up the treacherous staircases and along the gloomy corridors, pursued by the thick, sweet cooking smell wafting from the kitchen; the same room he'd been in at the beginning. The little *padrona* bounced over to the window and said, 'There you are. Look; he could see their villa,' and sure enough one could, up there in Bellosguardo, among all the pines and cypresses.

There was one of those glorious, rosy Florentine sunsets,

bands of pink across the sky, everything pink and deep blue and dark green, and my heart ached for it all; I knew so well why people stayed here, why Peter slogged on year after year on his impossible thesis, which even he must know by now is never going to come to the boil. Now I'm back, I wonder why I ever went away, though I know why I went away, quite apart from what happened with Kevin; the impossibility of ever getting anything done here, ever striking root here, the risk of simply being swallowed alive, like Kevin, or fossilizing, like Peter.

I should like to see Kevin just once, I think. For half an hour, not more. Just to see how he is. Except I know how he is. How he must be. Cut down, diminished by that little scorpion he's married. I look around this tiny, dismal room and I feel glad he had at least some happiness here.

Leaving the *pensione*, I set off on a nostalgic, terribly hackneyed *giro*. Past the Ponte Santa Trinità, all spick and span and new, now, down to the Ponte Vecchio, which I turn and cross. They've closed it to traffic and it's full of a Babel of tourists, English and French and German, clustered outside the little silver shops. To get away from them, I turn and lean on the parapet, looking downriver, where the sunset is dying out now into thick, blue bars above the pencilled treetops of the Cascine.

We used often to come here at night, when the lights were bobbing in the water, and Kevin would recite the poetry that he'd written in the war. When I'd first heard it, on little boats sailing in and out of the grottoes on Capri, lying in the sun on beaches there or at Ischia or Amalfi, wandering around the stones at Pompeii, it had sounded wonderful. Now, I was older and I found myself thinking, yes, that's Dylan Thomas, that's pure Wilfred Owen, that was Yeats, though his voice was so beautiful that I still loved him for reciting them, for *wanting* to recite them; I found myself saying, 'Lovely! Splendid! I *do* like that!' I wonder if he reads poetry to her. I'm quite sure he did; in the beginning.

Sometimes, he used to make up parodies.

*The river glideth at his own sour will.*

I'd tell him, 'You're a barbarian, Kevin.' Though in fact he was more like a frustrated child; if he couldn't have the thing he liked, he was jolly well not going to like anything else.

On the left bank, there are the two perfect *cupole*, Santo Spirito and the Carmine; so perfectly serene. I turn back across the Ponte Vecchio, through the chattering tourists, cross the Lungarno, and stroll through rabbit-warren streets to the Piazza Santo Spirito itself, so long and broad and dusty. Rough and casual, even to the great, red walls of the church, against which an urchin is kicking a football; like some peasant girl, quite unaware of her own beauty, or ready to take it for granted. It doesn't say, 'Look at me!' like the Signoria.

Somewhere in the square, by one of the scruffy pavement cafés, a motor-bike explodes and dies away, explodes and dies away. When it's quiet, one hears those harsh, undulating Florentine voices, and when *they're* quiet, only the dirge of some poor little cricket, dug out of the Cascine and hung in a cage. Typical of Florence, that *festa*, cruel and sentimental and imaginative.

In the last light, the *cupola* looks full and impregnable. Every shape here is so perfectly, sublimely human. Couldn't Kevin get anything from it all?

## 13

Joan's in town, Kevin.

*Joan!*

My heart thunders, my stomach's in turmoil; why? There's nothing to expect, or fear.

Anna says she saw her in Piazza Signoria.

Of course, Anna. The eternal spy and informer.

I wonder what on earth she's doing here.

I don't know. I thought maybe *you'd* know.

I've *ab*solutely no idea. Was her husband with her?

That wedding card; thrown at one like a revenge.

Anna says she was on her own. She says she'd got fat.

Dear Anna.

It's a funny place for her to come to, after all that happened.

She paints. She loves Florence. I'm sure she's come to terms with things by now.

*I'm* not that sure. I never trusted her. She took you away from me once.

Darling, that's all so terribly remote.

I don't know about remote. What reason do I have to trust you, those two times you were in Florence?

I assure you I don't want to see her any more than you do. I couldn't imagine anything more embarrassing.

Or more disturbing.

Well, I don't like it. And she'd better keep away from here.

I don't think you need worry about that.

If she is here, she has a reason to be here.

You mean Kevin?

What other reason?

But he looked so startled when I told him.

Kevin is not stupid.

You mean you think Kevin sent for her?

*È ben probabile.*

Why would he want to do a thing like that?

He has done it before.

Anna, I'm worried.

*Non c'è motivo*. Either it may not be true, in which case there is nothing to be worried about. Or it is true, in which case you are better rid of him.

That's right. And anyway, she's married, herself, now.

*Certo*. There could be nothing of permanence.

I know why you're going into Florence. You want to see her.

Darling, that's just nonsensical. I'm simply going in to the Reading Room.

How come it's the first time you've been this year?

It's not the *first* time.

It is so.

Well, if you don't believe me, why don't you come with me?

If I came with you, of course you'd go to the Reading Room.

Very well, then I shan't go into Florence at all. Will that satisfy you?

Ever since you heard she was here, there's been this change in you.

There has; an almost chemical change. The city drawing me, uncannily, like a lodestone. I have been there twice now in four days, courting and avoiding the fearful joy of seeing her, never turning a corner without feeling the frisson of a possible encounter – rising, fluttering, dying. And when I have been down the Via Romana and across the Ponte Vecchio, through the Signoria and the Repubblica, past the Duomo, round and back again, up the Tornabuoni – the most perilous of all – across the Ponte Santa Trinità, along the Lungarno and the Borgo San Jacopo, buzzed by a dozen wretched motor-scooters, till at last I've reached the safety of the Porta Romana, I feel a vast relief and a tugging disappointment.

I think I should just like to see her, *not* to talk to her. To follow her, perhaps, invisibly, for five or ten minutes. I wonder how long she means to stay?

# 14

I should have gone last Wednesday, but I am *not* staying on for Kevin. Or certainly not primarily for Kevin. I'm a prey to the whole place, I roam about the galleries and the churches, looking endlessly at gilded primitives, clouds and olive trees, and those implacable Florentine profiles.

Peter comes with me sometimes, and he's awfully good; on who really influenced whom, or didn't, what materials they used, the development of perspective, the use of colour, the growth of spatial relations. We spent hours and hours one morning in the Uffizi, an afternoon in the Accademia, another in San Marco, and yesterday he was fascinating about the doors of the Baptistery, when you could see them for the crowd; whether the Biblical scenes should strictly be classified as painting or sculpture. So long as we don't venture beyond the Renaissance, our relations are idyllic.

I'm sure I shall start painting again myself, soon, which is one of the reasons I had in the back of my mind for coming. The light's so clear, and yet so subtle. At the moment I feel I want to paint mountains; the mountains that hide Vallombrosa, on a day when you can see it and on a day when you can't. Or go out to the coast, somewhere below Carrara, and paint the Alpe Apuane; the lovely tranquillity that I remember, deeper still when you saw it from a beach shrieking with radios and children, the gradations of light from that sombre undulation in the foreground, never quite defined, back, back, back to the shining white marble that looks just like snow. And, on the best days, when the sky's a lovely, limpid blue, the great, fleecy puffs of cloud, hanging over the summits like smoke.

I should like to paint them, not as the old Florentines would have done, but as Turner might have painted them, exciting, full of throbbing power and violence. I asked Peter what he thought of Turner, and he said rather grudgingly yes, he was an important painter, he'd stayed just the right side of Abstractionism, which is anathema, along with Expressionism. He's looking for the philosopher's stone, and of course he can never find it, because it isn't to be found; here or anywhere else. Still, at least it gives him an excuse for burying himself away here; he can tell himself he isn't just living in the past but *using* the past.

One drowns in beauty here, suffocates in beauty. I realize, coming back, more clearly than ever that I would have been mad to try to settle here with Kevin, it could *never* have worked, it would have been the end of my painting. How can one work, surrounded by perfection? Yet this isn't all, there are still things to be done, and I'm determined to do them.

The life here, the real life, is in the backstreets – it's all that's left – the cool little caverns where the artisans work, chipping and shaping and carving – the working-class life. You find it down the Borgo San Frediano, and in the streets round Santa Croce, throbbing and caustic, full of humour. They're quite aware of their tradition, but it doesn't seem to inhibit them, it breaks through in their self-confidence and in the splendidly elaborate way they speak. I'd have them *any* day in preference to the stuck-up, shut-off, selfish middle classes, and as for the aristocracy – or what's left of it!

This week, Peter gave one of his famous dinners. I helped him prepare it, he cooks simply but awfully well, with lots of lovely herbs and masses of garlic. Armando, who runs the gallery, came with his wife, who's sweet and charming, and Gianni Roghi, the picture restorer, came with *his* wife, who smiled and never says anything. Candlelight and gorgeous wine, and the whole evening very funny and malicious and destructive, everyone and everything torn to little bits, till it left you at the end with a feeling of absolute emptiness, of how much clever Florentines despise themselves.

What they seem to be saying all the time is, we're nothing, but look at everybody else. Nothing spared or sacred; what was being painted here, what was being exhibited here, publishing, politics, the last Maggio Musicale, till one longed for just a single positive remark. It all seems so narrow and incestuous and gossipy, though if you read Cellini or Vasari, you see that Florence was always full of feuds and backbiting; except that in those days they stabbed each other in the back with real knives, and at least the gossip was about heroes.

Peter, of course, was in his element; he really seems to hate the present. A few sharp digs at Kevin, abetted by Armando – *'Ah, sì, quello lì di Bellosguardo'* – that one from Bellosguardo. '*And* every now and then from Florence itself,' Peter said, and they all laughed, though I couldn't laugh, I could only think of the poor thing in his room, desperate and lonely. I wondered if Peter knew that he'd tried to kill himself; I somehow don't think he does.

Kevin. So weak and such a failure. And William. So well organized and such a success.

## 15

It's ridiculous. We are Dante and Beatrice, re-enacting that sugary little fable. Except that I saw her, not crossing the Ponte Vecchio, but, so much more banal, the Piazza della Repubblica. Where I sat at a café table, outside the Giubbe Rosse, having decided it was better to be static than peripatetic, to let things come, rather than pursue them.

And she came; past the corner by Gilli's, where the louts who lean there on their motor-scooters all turned their heads to watch her in unison, and let out their usual cheap babble of effrontery; which she magnificently ignored. Wearing a sleeveless summer dress, fine and sturdy. Not much plumper – that, of course, was a libel. Walking the same brisk walk, purposeful but feminine, none of that a-sexual arm-swinging and seven-league striding one gets in certain English women. My stomach, my heart, my solar plexus, all oscillating with the shock of it all; shock of recognition. Unable to move, even to raise an arm and wave, capable only of willing her to come across the square, see me, greet me. Did I want to to see her? Passive and motionless as instead she swung straight on, crossing the square indeed, but only straight to the opposite pavement, at which I opened my mouth to cry, 'Joan!' – she was only a café-length away from me – but brought out nothing.

Get up and follow her, get up and *follow* her. Throw down some money on the table, and run after her. No movement. Becalmed. As if caught in the finest equilibrium of doubt, unable to move, unwilling to stay.

You wanted to see her, and you've seen her. But not for long enough. And seeing her, besides, has worked a change, has made me want to see her a second time and, yes, quite definitely, to talk to her. As if in some way – however absurd it seems – she could assuage the pain. She's always been so good with pain. Oh, God, I wish I hadn't seen her, now. I wish I'd stayed up on the hill.

If he keeps on going down to Florence, there can be only one reason.

That he's looking for her?

That he is seeing her.

Maybe I ought to have him followed. You think so, Anna?

*Figlia mia,* it depends how much you really want to know.

My dear Lucy, I assure you I have *not* seen her, and I have *not* been looking for her.

Which is true. To see her by chance for a matter of seconds is surely not to *see* her. To wander round unthinkingly, making no effect to discover where she stays, isn't looking for her.

I don't believe you, Kevin. For months and months you hardly leave the villa, now suddenly you're in Florence every day.

*Not* every day. Once this week. Twice last week.

Well, if you haven't seen her, you're sure as hell looking for her.

Very well; I shall not go into Florence at all. I shall not venture beyond Bellosguardo.

That means she's probably left; you've got no more reason for going.

Lucy!

Don't act so goddam innocent, Kevin! You've betrayed me before, you'll betray me again. Only the next time I find out, there won't be another time.

I saw him the other day, just for a second; I knew it must happen, sooner or later. From a taxi, driving down the Borgo Pinti. There he was, bouncing along in a white suit, with that absurd actor's walk of his – he *should* have been an actor – great, long strides, arms swinging like a soldier's, looking sternly up into the sky with what I used to call his Imperial look. He was, oh, how ridiculous, and oh, how sweet.

It all happened so quickly that I didn't do a thing. I had this instinct to roll down the window and shout at him, but I was too slow; then to tell the driver to stop, but I was somehow too confused, we turned the corner into Via Ricasoli, and that was that.

Yet now I'm determined to see him. He makes me feel as I felt the very first time I saw him, lying on his back, asleep under the mosquito net, his face so fine and young and calm, his forehead pearled with sweat. Protective. Which is his secret with women, though he'd hate to hear me say so. Not his looks, though he's still handsome. Not his firework displays of wit and name-dropping and the Golden Treasury, but simply that; the mothering instinct. And now I want to mother him again.

## 16

*Piazza Goldoni, on the Lungarno. Mid-afternoon.*

*The day is hot and clear, the sky a rich blue, thick with stately white cloud. Outlines have a sharp immediacy; the green and white façade of San Miniato, high above the river, has perfect, triangular symmetry, but no depth, as if pasted on to the sky. Below it, the balustrade of the Piazzale Michelangelo is black with the anonymous faces of tourists.*

*Marching down the smooth white pavement of the Ponte alla Carraia, opposite the little* piazza, *comes* KEVIN. *His walk, in the heat, is unnecessarily brisk, verging on bravado. He wears a lightweight suit of narrow blue and white stripes, and his expression is one of almost defiant indifference. The red traffic light stops him on the kerb of the Lungarno, where he maintains his air of extreme detachment, staring disdainfully above the cacophony of cars and snorting motor-scooters.*

*Across the* piazza, *from the Via della Vigna Nuova,* JOAN *appears. She is a well-built, pretty woman of indeterminate middle age, crisply self-contained. Her hair is short, curly and dark blonde, her nose is straight and short, giving her the aspect of an agreeable Pekinese. She wears dark glasses.*

*As the lights go green, both* KEVIN *and* JOAN *set off across the Lungarno.* JOAN *has scarcely left the pavement when she sees* KEVIN. *Momentarily she stops, her lips parted, then walks on, making straight towards him, smiling slightly, watching him as he advances, unheeding, till he is almost upon her. Only then does he stop, begin to sidestep, look down at last, and see her.*

KEVIN, *flinging wide his arms*: Joan! My God! Joan!

JOAN, *more softly, with a loving smile*: Kevin!

*They embrace in the middle of the road, oblivious to protesting traffic.*

KEVIN: *God*, how wonderful!

JOAN: Isn't it?

KEVIN: Look here, we can*not* go on standing in the middle of the road.

JOAN: Can't we? *Why* not?

KEVIN: Because we shall be *killed*, that's why!

*Taking her hand, he hurries her back across the street, whence she has come.*

KEVIN: I knew you were here.

Joan, *tightly hugging his arm*: Did you? How did you know?

KEVIN : I have my informers.

JOAN : And I knew *you* were here. I saw you!

*They are walking briskly up the Via della Vigna Nuova.*

KEVIN : Then why on earth didn't you speak to me?

JOAN : Couldn't. I was in a taxi.

KEVIN : Then I shall admit it. I saw *you*!

JOAN : And where were you?

KEVIN : At a café in the Piazza Repubblica.

JOAN, *looking up at him, smiling*: Why on earth didn't you speak to me?

KEVIN : You were there and gone. Dante and Beatrice.

JOAN : But they never married. (*Squeezing his arm.*) Kevin, it's *so* nice to see you.

KEVIN : *And* you.

JOAN : Where shall we go? The old Tabby Cat?

KEVIN : It's gone. They moved to the Lungarno.

*All at once, as they approach the Via Tornabuoni, he grows anxious and circumspect; he seems to be thinking frantically.*

KEVIN, *abruptly* : I know.

*Still more hastily, he escorts* JOAN *across the Via Tornabuoni.*

KEVIN, *tense and low* : Enemy territory.

*They go across the Piazza Santa Trinità, down the narrow Via delle Terme, across the brash, rebuilt Por Santa Maria, finally emerging on the Piazza della Signoria, opposite the vast, chrome elegance of the Palazzo Vecchio.* JOAN *regards it with loving admiration,* KEVIN *ignores it. He rushes her on, left, diagonally, across the* piazza, *through drifting, staring groups of tourists, to a small* bottiglieria. *Inside, at the wooden tables, a few thick-fingered, pot-hatted farmers and men in caps are drinking; they look up with some surprise.*

JOAN, *laughing as they sit down* : Come here often?

KEVIN, *unsmiling* : Very infrequently.

*The proprietor serves them with a litre of red wine.*

JOAN : Just like a spy film!

KEVIN : Florence is *not* London.

JOAN, *putting her hand on his, and looking at him affectionately* : *How* are you, Kevin?
KEVIN, *looking away from her* : I'm dying.

JOAN *takes away her hand, tilts back her head, and, to* KEVIN*'s annoyance, bursts out laughing.*

JOAN : Oh, darling! Just as melodramatic as ever!
KEVIN, *with heavy pique* : I was not joking.
JOAN, *gradually mastering her laughter, till it dies down to the occasional brief, involuntary giggle* : I know, darling, I'm sure you weren't.
KEVIN : If you find death a joke, and pain a matter for amusement.
JOAN, *taking his hand again, speaking tenderly, as if to soothe a child* : What's the matter?
KEVIN : I have this dreadful, intermittent pain.
JOAN : The wound?
KEVIN : No. Not the wound. Here.

*He touches the left-hand side of his stomach.*

JOAN, *gravely* : How long have you had it?
KEVIN : For about the last eighteen months.
JOAN : Have you been looked at?
KEVIN : Yes. They didn't know. Or rather, I think they did know, but wouldn't tell me.
JOAN : And what does Lucy say?
KEVIN, *gazing into space* : She doesn't believe me.
JOAN, *appalled* : Doesn't *believe* you? *Why* doesn't she believe you?
KEVIN, *rigidly* : I have no idea.
JOAN : You mean when you're in pain, she just ignores it?
KEVIN : She accuses me of lying.
JOAN, *outraged* : *What* a poisonous little creature!
KEVIN, *uneasily* : There are perhaps . . . extenuations.
JOAN : Such as *what*?
KEVIN : Certain misunderstandings in the past.
JOAN, *shrewdly* : When you *were* shamming?
KEVIN : When I may have *appeared* to be.
JOAN, *quietly* : I see.

*There's a hiatus, in which both seem to withdraw to inner*

*worlds,* JOAN *as if to reflect on what she's heard,* KEVIN *on the implications of what he's told her.*

JOAN, *at last, looking at him* : Do you really think you're dying, Kevin?

KEVIN, *without looking back at her* : Yes.

*There is another pause.*

JOAN, *glancing away* : You tried to kill yourself, didn't you?

KEVIN, *sharply reacting* : Who told you?

JOAN : I found out.

KEVIN : I demand to know who told you.

JOAN, *wearily* : What does it matter?

KEVIN, *with bitter resignation* : I suppose if that bitch Anna's been spreading the story all round Florence . . .

JOAN : It doesn't take much to spread a story round Florence. Is that Anna Krutkova, who used to spend all her time waiting to pounce in the American Bar?

KEVIN : She eventually pounced.

JOAN : On Lucy?

KEVIN : Yes.

JOAN : I imagine it wasn't very difficult.

KEVIN, *again avoiding her eye* : Lucy has always been too trusting.

JOAN : Tell me about the pain. Is it short or sharp, or steady and dull?

KEVIN : It varies. Sometimes it's so sharp it's unbearable. At others, it simply throbs; one can reach a *modus vivendi* with it.

JOAN : It's not the eternal *fegato*?

KEVIN, *shaking his head* : I have had tests.

JOAN : Does it come at any special time? After you've eaten anything particular? After you've been drinking? After exercise?

KEVIN, *distantly* : It seems to come on . . . when things are worst.

JOAN : When there's tension.

KEVIN, *with reluctance* : Yes.

JOAN *nods to herself.*

KEVIN, *urgently* : What could it be? Have you any idea?

JOAN : It could be anything or nothing.

KEVIN : Such as *what?*

JOAN : You're miserable, aren't you, Kevin?

KEVIN *turns his head and doesn't answer.*

JOAN : She's given you ten years of misery.

*There's a heavy, melancholy silence.* KEVIN *dully brooding,* JOAN *gloomily reflective.*

KEVIN, *addressing the table* : It hasn't *all* been miserable. JOAN *remaining silent, he gathers momentum and resistance.* There have been moments. Days. Whole months.

JOAN : And then she chucks you out.

KEVIN, *stiffly* : That is *not* how I would phrase it.

JOAN, *gently* : Why do you stay there, Kevin?

KEVIN : Because, *strangely* enough, I still happen to love her.

JOAN, *neutrally* : I see.

KEVIN : You do *not* see. You are determined not to see.

JOAN, *coaxingly* : Don't let's argue. Not now. Not this time.

KEVIN, *instantly subsiding* : Very well.

JOAN : Are you writing at all?

KEVIN, *uneasily* : At the moment, no. But I have an idea for a literary magazine.

*On* JOAN*'s face there appears the shadow of a smile, instantly suppressed, as* KEVIN*'s eyes dart to her suspiciously.*

KEVIN : *Bellosguardo.* Robert Clyde and I would edit it from here. Roland Wilkinson came to stay with us and was ex*tremely* impressed.

JOAN, *with mechanical brightness* : Good!

KEVIN, *after giving her a wary glance* : It may or may not be bilingual.

*Having said this, he subsides into further, silent melancholy. Once again,* JOAN *takes his hand, till at last he looks up at her, with eyes full of fear.*

KEVIN : Joan, do you think I'm going to die?

JOAN : Why should you? Why *should* you?

## 17

How *can* I leave now, knowing what I do? He *will* die if I leave him here; he may be dying as it is. And so furtive, so frightened; which he never was before. There's a hollowness about him now. Thinking of her, I think of those ichneumon flies one learned about in Natural History, whose grubs hatch inside a chrysalis, then gnaw away until there's nothing left.

It's no good saying it's his own fault, that it was all predictable, that he's deserved whatever's happened to him. The point is simply that it's happened, and unless someone does something, rescues him, there's no hope left.

In a sense, indeed he's dying, so that what he's dying of, what the pain means – if it means anything at all – becomes irrelevant. Or, if one's going to be crueller still about it, perhaps – in the same sense – he's dead already. So resigned, so apathetic. He can scarcely be bothered to justify himself. It's horribly easy to imagine the kind of existence he and she must lead, if only from the names he mentions; all that dreary sub-world one used to avoid here, so drab and parasitic, hanging on by its fingernails; a kind of pseudo-society that they've put together like those sculptures fashioned out of *objets trouvés*.

Is it love I feel for him, or just pity? And does it even matter, when whatever it is is so very real and intense, tugging and tormenting me? But I know Kevin. He'll never leave unless he's somewhere else to go, which means someone else to go to; and what can I offer him now? I have a marriage. Not passionate, but happy and good, to someone who loves me and who'd be hurt. Besides, we've tried twice, failed twice, and what earthly reason is there to believe we'd do better, now?

Peter Clovis, of course, would say that Kevin would just drag me down with him. He probably would. But when you see someone drowning, does that mean you simply let him drown? I can't let Kevin drown.

# 18

To meet so much kindness again. Something one hadn't encountered for so long. Since Ruth, who was just as kind, and who has vanished, who's been swallowed alive. But then, I never answered her letters.

Joan digs at me, of course. Determined to prove to herself that I *am* unhappy, I *have* been punished for rejecting her. She's older; as we both are. Seeing her close, one's aware of wrinkles, lines, a thickening of the body, something indefinably forced about her vivacity. I wonder how she found me, if it comes to that? Still attractive, I know; I can see it in her eyes. When that goes, everything goes; the possibility of change, if one wants change, of succour, if one needs succour. Not that I should ever, voluntarily, leave Lucy, but it's frightening to be defenceless, terrifying to grow old.

But oh that I were young again, and held her in my arms.

I am still young; young enough, at least, to hold her in my arms. Young enough for the possibility of choice, the illusion of freedom. 'If you want to see me again,' she said, 'I'm at the Pensione Volterra,' and off she went, without looking back. A habit of hers; she never looks back. And I shall ring her. I should like to see her again. She reassures me so much, and it's so good to know she has no bitterness. Why should she? I'm married, she is married, though she's oddly reticent about her husband, talks of him in generalities. A lawyer. *His* first marriage. I have the impression of something tall and bland and slightly desiccated. I wanted to ask her if she loves him; I still want to. Though if I do, she'll know what I really mean: does she love *me*? I think she does. It would be marvellous if she stayed here.

# 19

Joan's seeing Kevin again, which I think is very foolish, and I've told her so. Which was perfectly futile, as always. Joan can never be told anything. She simply shrugged it off. 'We met by *sheer* accident, and we'll have the odd coffee together, that's all.' But I know that look in her eye; I've seen it there before, just as I saw it in Ruth's. The redeeming glint. The 'Raising of Lazarus' look. And if she doesn't know by now that Kevin will never be redeemed, by anybody, she's just beyond hope.

I don't know what this new marriage of hers is like, I've an idea from the way she talks it may not be too exciting, but it's certainly not worth risking it for Kevin, who trades on being resurrected; always has and always will. Ruth thought he'd try to kill himself, and here he is, high as a kite. Joan thinks he may be seriously ill, and somebody ought to get him away from Hiyah; I think he's as ill as it suits him to be. Maybe it's the nurse in her coming out; I wouldn't know. She's certainly a better nurse than she is a painter.

Yesterday she brought around a canvas she's done of the mountains downriver, before Vallombrosa. Technically she's improved, there's no doubt about that; her drawing's a lot better than it was, and she has more of an idea of perspective. But to do anything new with that kind of subject requires a vision she'll just never have; there was nothing in the picture that couldn't have been a lot better done in a good colour photograph, in fact there was less, because the photograph would have gotten much closer to the subtleties of the light. I congratulated her, I told her she'd obviously made progress, and left it at that. But when she started dragging in Turner, I simply let her go on talking. To experience that kind of a personal vision, you have to be prepared to let your feet leave the ground.

I told her, if she was meeting Kevin, to be careful; Hiyah

could easily turn vicious, and in Florence, everyone's nose is up everyone else's crotch. She asked me could she bring him round to see me. 'Now why in the world would you want to do that?' I said, to which she replied that he badly needed friends; she didn't want to leave him hanging high and dry when she went, with no one to turn to but those dreadful people from the American Bar. It was Ruth all over again; would I keep an eye on him? I told her she'd be wasting her time getting us together, that Kevin and I were like a couple of tied saplings; cut the rope, and we just sprung apart. 'But if ever you want to meet him here,' I said, 'where you won't have half Florence looking at you, I'll give you the key, and I'll go out. Just let me know when I can come back.'

'You're so kind, Peter,' she said, 'and such a bitch.' Then she kissed me.

## 20

They have been seen together.

Where were they seen? Who saw them?

Outside a café near the Ponte Vecchio. At five o'clock yesterday afternoon.

He was meant to be at the Consulate! He said he was visiting with the Consul!

He was with her.

I've had enough of it, Anna. I'm going to call him on it.

He will deny it.

But this time, I have proof.

And he will have some very good excuses, *sta sicura.*

Well, they won't be good enough. I'll tell him if he wants her, he can get the hell out of *here.*

You can be perfectly sure which he will choose; or pretend to choose.

Meaning he'll keep right on cheating on me.

If you permit it.

## 21

Anna was right. I put it to him, and he just denied it. Even when I told him he'd been seen. Jumped like a jack-rabbit, then told me it wasn't true. He said he'd caught sight of her once, that was all, but he'd let her go right on by.

I said, 'Look, Kevin, if you want to go back to her, you go back to her. Sometimes I think it was the dumbest thing I ever did, not letting her keep you that first time.'

He just got very tense, the way he does, clenching his teeth, and repeating over and over, 'I do *not* want to go back to her, I do *not* want to go back to her,' then, wouldn't you know it, this look came over his face. I was meant to know he was in agony, he had his pain, but I simply ignored it, I went right on talking. I said, 'If you want to meet her, meet her. If you want to sleep with her, sleep with her. If you want to go off with her, go off with her. But don't think you can keep right on living in my villa and having me support you.'

So then we had the whole performance; his hands over his stomach, his eyes closed. Falling back into a basket chair. I said, 'You've done it too often, Kevin. Why don't you try it on her for a change?' Then I walked away and left him.

But the whole thing's on my mind, disturbing me. I keep wondering what the hell she's up to, down there, what schemes she's working on, because she surely is, she wouldn't come back here for nothing, and Kevin's so weak, he'd fall right in with them, just like he did the last time.

Maybe she's found this new marriage of hers doesn't work, and she thought to herself, okay, I'll get Kevin back, or maybe she just thought, while I'm in Florence, I might just as well bust up *her* marriage, I'll humiliate her, I'll show her I can take him away from her any time I want. Well, the worst thing I could do to her is just say, take him, just land her with him, and see how she likes it. He's no husband to me, he could go tomorrow, the one thing that gets me down is this not knowing, all this waiting. Anna says, 'You can resolve it any time you like,' and I know that, but that could be just what Joan wants.

When I'm in Florence now, I find I'm looking out for her myself, that's the effect she's having on me. I'm all tensed up, I'm back on sleeping pills at night, any moment I think I'll see her, or *him* and her, I can't walk in the streets with an easy mind. Sometimes I think I'd *like* to run across her, then at least I could ask her what are you doing here, what is it you want? Except I know all I'd get would be one of those frozen British looks, like I'd been fresh to the Queen.

There *is* something going on. I damn well know it, or he wouldn't keep sneaking into Florence, on top of which there's his attitude when he's here, keeping out of my way all he can, even more than usual and, when he doesn't know I'm around, sometimes whistling to himself. I'm not going to take much more of it.

## 22

Peter Clovis' flat. An assignation. Perfectly absurd, yet curiously exciting. Like a charade, a mere ceremonial, a symbolic repetition; what else could it logically be? And yet, as I climb those vertiginous stone stairs, stumbling in the dark, I feel the inward flutter of a hundred past encounters. A conditioned reflex, nothing more. At the top of the staircase, there are tea and compassion, nothing more; friendly reminiscence. *If she's there.*

The flutter again; the eternal *frisson* of every assignation. Will she come? Is she there? The quiver of uncertainty which is an essential part of it all.

At the top of the stairs I stop, breathing hard, looking at the front door. Breathing *much* too hard; I must start swimming again. Go to the coast or to an island, and swim. Lucy doesn't swim. Joan adores swimming.

Peter Clovis' flat. What if he's there? Swallow disappointment; *how* nice to see you! An empty, three-cornered conversation, precious time killed stone dead, Clovis' malignantly smiling eye observing us, enjoying it, for ever looking on from outside, no obvious liaisons, no involvements. How one envies him, in some ways; so much anguish avoided. But if we are all of us outside, in Florence, he is on the perimeter's perimeter.

I press the bell. Infinite hiatus, running true to ritual; the moment of truth. Footsteps. They sound like hers. Click! The knob turning. Joan? Yes. Thank God.

'Darling!'

'Darling!'

Into his elegant, prim, exquisite bachelor's flat, full of sumptuous sterility, pictures that I know are good, but don't respond to, *objets* that I know are beautiful, but don't live for me.

'Wasn't it kind of Peter?'

'Yes, *extremely* kind.' It was. To lend us his shrine, his hermit's case, his immaculate bunker. Double mirrors? Walls wired for sound? A rat behind the arras? Celibacy of angels, drapes and candelabra. He knows that it is quite, quite safe to leave us here together, that not a winged cherub will be disturbed, let alone the bed with, if I remember right, its glorious antique velvet counterpane.

We sit like strangers on a hard Venetian sofa. 'Tea?' she says, at which I spring to my feet; this is simply too much. 'God!' I cry. 'It's just like some Victorian suburban brothel! Everything genteel and ladylike, tea and gentility, until you just *happen* to find yourself in the bedroom.'

'Well, we're not going to find ourselves in the bedroom this afternoon!' she said, and out she went to make the tea. But at least the ghost had been laid, and we could laugh, now. And how splendid it was to laugh, how little one had laughed, for so long.

I followed her to the kitchen, where she behaved as though she *were* a terribly genteel prostitute, who'd picked up an Army officer: 'I hope you don't think I invite *everyone* home who speaks to me in the street. *Please* don't do that with your hand, Captain, it's not very nice,' so by the time she brought the tea into the sitting-room, we were both practically helpless, we'd open our mouths to say something, and simply start laughing again.

Then suddenly I kissed her, she looked so delectable sitting there, laughing, and once I'd done it, even on that damnable hard sofa, it was as if we'd set a complete process in motion, something which just went irresistibly on, whether you wanted it to or not, yet something quite natural, rather than mechanical. I kissing her, she kissing me. My hand on those fine, full breasts of hers. Her tongue in my ear. My hand on her thigh. Her hand between my legs. I could hear her saying, 'Kevin, we can't, we can't,' but I knew it meant nothing; just a formal protest.

And we *did* go into the bedroom, we *did* strip off that priceless red coverlet, and there on the bed, beneath God knows how old and venerable a carved Madonna, who'd seen nothing like it for Heaven knows how long, we made love. Not once but twice.

Lying side by side, looking at the painting that hangs on the opposite wall, all fleshy, floating graces and goddesses; Joan said, 'This must *not* go on. It is thoroughly ridiculous.'

'But extraordinarily pleasant,' I said.

'Yes,' she had to admit, 'extremely pleasant,' and she ran her fingers across my chest. 'But none the less absurd. It was simply an aberration on both sides. Now you must go back to Bellosguardo, and I must go back to London.'

'Not yet,' I told her, 'you can't possibly go yet.'

'Oh, yes, I can,' she said. 'I shall go back tomorrow!'

I put my leg over hers and said, 'And what if I won't let you?'

'You've no alternative,' she said. 'To start with, what would happen if Peter Clovis came back and found us lying here like this on his beautiful *settecento* bed?'

'He would be delighted to see it put to such good use.'

'Oh, no, he wouldn't,' she said. 'He'd never forgive either of us, and you know it.'

'Then we must replace everything *very* carefully,' I said, 'or he won't allow us here again.'

She said, 'I've told you, Kevin, there isn't going to *be* an again.'

But I didn't believe her, I felt too euphoric; I was perfectly sure she wanted there to be another time, then another and another, and I couldn't see beyond that, I'd no wish to.

Suddenly she asked me, 'How's the pain?'

'The pain?' I honestly couldn't focus for a moment; the pain belonged to a completely different state of being. 'Oh, yes,' I said, 'the pain. I don't think of it when I'm with you; I don't remember it,' and she bent over me and began kissing my face.

'Stay here, Joan,' I said, 'stay with me.'

'Can't,' she said, 'I'm a married woman, strange as it may seem at this moment.'

'Please,' I said. '*Please* don't go, yet. Stay with me.'

'Oh, Kevin,' she said. 'You're such an insoluble problem.'

## 23

Heavens, how careful one has to be, how strongly that charm of his still works. I'd quite underestimated it. There was no *arrière-pensée* at all; I simply wanted to be able to talk to him in peace and private, and I can see now that it's quite impossible; for me just as much as Kevin. It's as though whatever there is between us never completed its full course. Physically, anyhow.

And now I'm in absolute turmoil. After I'd left him, I went straight back to my *pensione* and packed my cases; it seemed the only thing to do, if I were so incapable of behaving rationally as soon as I came back into his orbit. I'd catch a train that evening down to Rome, and that would be that.

Except it *wasn't* simply that. And when I'd packed my cases and locked them, I just left them where they were and went out for a walk. It was quite dark, the air cool but clinging. Across the river, black and rippled in the night, there hung a high moon, plump and almost full, marbled with shadowy blue. I looked up towards Bellosguardo, where one could just make out a silhouette of trees, strange and minatory, like trees in a haunted forest. I thought of him there and wondered what he was doing, what he was thinking. Away to the left, there was a curve of big white bubbles round the parapet of the Piazzale Michelangelo. Here and there, towers and *cupole* were picked out of the night by artificial light so pale, so delicate, that it seemed they themselves were phosphorescent; the *campanile* of Santo Spirito, with its fine, solid arrogance, the Carmine and its *cupola*, exquisite but somehow comfortable, like a Rubens nude.

I walked away from the Lungarno; I couldn't look at Bellosguardo any more. I went into the Piazza Signoria which was very quiet, just a few people sitting out at café tables. Under the marvellous *loggia*, all that noiseless, petrified violence, going on eternally. Poor Centaur. Poor Medusa, too; her eyes closed in a kind of rapturous relief. So peaceful, after so much blood and fire. Savonarola burning. The Pazzi and their followers swinging from those rough majestic walls.

Stone. Bronze. Marble. Paint. Like a giant preserved for pygmies to look at. Kevin and I are pygmies. So is Peter. Lucy too. Performing our useless pirouettes on the giant's belly.

Walking on, through the Piazza del Duomo, under the tremendous, earthy bulk of San Lorenzo. Half hearing all the silly badinage behind me: *'Vuole andare? Viene con me, bella!'* no more than a background noise by this time, like the Lambrettas buzzing. They'd be scared out of their wits if one turned round and answered, 'All right: where?'

Round the great walls of Santa Maria Novella, confronting that immaculate *loggia* in the square, then up again, towards the Arno. I can't go back to Kevin. Yet if I don't, he'll die. And if I do? Down, down, down to the bottom with him, I suppose. The eternal nurse, for ever saving him from himself. Except that now there's William, too. Who's strong. Who'd suffer, but survive. Who's given me so much that Kevin couldn't begin to give me; peace and comfort.

Life with Kevin again. The infinite, daily frustration of it. Living God knows where, working – for I'd have to – at God knows what. And so much harder when one's ten years older. Oh, Kevin, Kevin, that's your talent, to make other people sorry for you, to make women feel guilty when they're perfectly innocent.

Strolling and strolling. Back to the Arno again. Back, and back and back; just as I come back to Kevin. Couldn't we live *here*, down below, while she lived *there*, up on her hill? No, of course we couldn't, there'd soon be the bombardment of notes again. And he won't go back to England, even if they agreed to it; for all the nostalgia and the Nature poetry. It would all be too real, and he's frightened of change. He's been back, and he knows his England doesn't exist any more; it's an England of the mind.

If only one could set up a *ménage à trois*. Totally unfair to William, perfectly acceptable, I'm sure to Kevin. Or if one could come here once or twice a year, to rejuvenate him. Equally impossible.

Why didn't I catch that train? But I can catch it tomorrow. I *shall* catch it tomorrow.

## 24

In my *pensione* room, the telephone ringing, wrenching me from sleep, and instantly I think, *Kevin*! Who else but Kevin? Jangling with weariness and panic, panic feeding on weariness. But not Kevin's voice; a girl's. American. Cautious.

'Joan?'

'Yes?'

Fumbling for the light, pressing the switch. Blinded.

'This is Lucy.'

Lucy? *Her!* Waiting for recriminations, hysterics.

'Can you come up to Bellosguardo for a crisis?'

'For *what*?'

I'm quite lost, bobbing on a sea of sheer confusion.

'A crisis. Kevin's collapsed.'

Now I'm not confused, just frightened.

'How? When? What's wrong with him?'

And this little, flat voice, that I've never heard before, this flat little lost, inadequate, childish voice, tells me, 'I don't know. Just collapsed and fainted. Earlier on, he'd said he had this pain.'

'How bad is he? Is he still unconscious?'

'We've put him up on the sofa. Now and then he comes around for a while, then he goes off again.'

'Have you phoned a doctor?'

'Kevin doesn't want our doctor, he doesn't like him. He says would *you* get him a doctor?'

*'I?'*

One was beyond anger; beyond anything but shock.

*'I?'*

And the clipped, little, bankrupt voice, 'He thought if *you* don't know one, you could ask Peter Clovis.'

'All right,' I said, 'I'll ask him,' and I hung up. Then, thank God, the discipline took over, the hospital conditioning, acting not thinking, because to think was to risk disintegrating.

Peter was incredibly cool and composed; it was wonderful to hear his calm voice, I'd forgotten how good he is in an emergency, even if he thrives on accident and illness, like some old woman on a park bench.

'Well, if Hiyah can't cope, I guess we'll just have to take over,' he said. 'I'll call my own doctor, and I'll pick you up in a taxi.'

I struggled into my clothes, all clumsy with sleep, then went downstairs and stood waiting for Peter in the doorway of the *pensione*, trying to tell myself it couldn't be anything serious, that she'd obviously panicked and Kevin always exaggerated. I despised her and I was furious with him; for getting ill, and for still being able to make me care so much.

After a quarter of an hour the taxi came, Peter sitting there very alert and poised, while I was still shivering with exhaustion and worry.

'The doctor said he'd come right away,' Peter said. He himself reminded me terribly of doctors I'd worked with in the war, very grave, his lips slightly pursed, as if deliberately assuming what he took to be the proper manner. He asked me, 'Have you any idea what it could be?'

'No,' I said. 'He's been complaining of pains, but they could just as well be psychosomatic.'

He laughed suddenly and said, 'You mean they're Hiyah-pains?' but I couldn't laugh with him.

We were crossing the Ponte Santa Trinità, but this time I was scarcely conscious of the view along the Arno. I was half aware of a *cupola*, a lamp, a tower, the great, squat bulk of the Pitti, but it was just an irrelevant montage. My thoughts were all of Kevin, lying in pain, perhaps dying.

We took the road to Bellosguardo, and began climbing, under lowering ranks of trees. The sky was breaking up into pale, sick, leprous patches. I took Peter's hand and gripped it with all my force; there was a slight stiffening, but he didn't take it away. He was perfect; immensely kind, yet not a scrap over-solicitous.

We turned, turned again, then we were at the gate, and I just couldn't wait, I leaped out of the car, rushed up to it, and tugged the bell. For a few moments, I heard nothing. I was praying, let him be alive, please let him be alive. Peter came up very silently and stood beside me; he put his hand gently on my arm. At last there was the sound of a bolt being pulled, a door opening, a crunching on the gravel, till finally the gate was unlocked, pulled back; and there was Kevin.

'My *dear* Joan! *Peter!*'

Large as life and jolly as could be, with that maddening,

histrionic jollity I knew so well. '*How* very nice of you to come all the way up here! My God; come in!'

I suppose we must have looked at him with stupefaction. For a while we were motionless and speechless, and Kevin, seeing this, grew all the gayer, capering about, beckoning us in, till at last Peter said, quite flatly, 'We thought you were ill.'

'Bless you, no!' he said, and I could have hit him. 'I'm *per*fectly all right.'

'But you collapsed,' I said. 'Lucy telephoned me. We've sent for the doctor.' And exactly at that moment there was the sound of another car climbing the hill. It stopped, a door slammed, and a thin, blond man appeared out of the night, saying in a very taut voice, '*Sono il Dottor Eliani.*'

Kevin greeted him with the same mad cheerfulness, the doctor looked at him in sheer amazement and said, '*Ma Lei è quello che è malatto?*'

'*Non malatto, non malatto,*' Kevin said, in his awful Italian, then shepherded us into the villa as if it were some kind of a party. The three of us looked at one another, the doctor with his eyebrows raised and his eyes wide, Peter with an expression of complete exasperation. It was all so strange that the strangeness of coming to the villa itself, the place where she'd virtually carried him off and incarcerated him, just didn't affect me; any more than the prospect of meeting *her* for the first time in my life.

When we came into the *salotto*, rather a gloomy room with some very good antique tables and chests and chairs – *seicento* and *settecento* by the look of them – there she was, standing there to meet us. What struck me most was her quite extraordinary insignificance. We'd seen each other before, of course, walking past one another in the street, ten years ago, and she'd looked commonplace enough to me then, but at the same time at least there'd seemed to be a kind of shiny malevolence about her. Now there wasn't even that; it was inconceivable that she could dominate him as she did, make him suffer as she did, this little, pale, plain, insubstantial thing. I saw her suddenly as a leech or a vampire, who grew fat and strong only by sucking life out of other people.

She said, 'Hallo, hallo,' in her closed, flat voice, and stuck out her hand which the doctor took, but Peter and I didn't. 'Kevin seems a lot better, now', she said, still quite without expression; no effort to apologize for dragging us all out of bed and up to Bellosguardo in the dead of night. I suddenly got terribly angry and I yelled, 'For Heaven's sake go to bed, Kevin!'

At least that put a stop to his capering; he looked at me, then from me to Lucy, who didn't react in any way but stayed perfectly expressionless, then he obediently turned away and lay down on the sofa. Once he was there, he tried to make a joke of it again, looking up at me and saying, 'Is *this* all right, Staff Nurse?' then laughing. I said, 'If you bring us all here at an hour like this, you might at least have the grace to appear to be ill.'

The doctor asked in Italian what had happened, and Lucy answered, in an Italian that surprised me, because by now I expected absolutely nothing from her, that he'd complained of stomach pains earlier in the evening, then during dinner he'd suddenly collapsed at the table, and they'd had to carry him on to the sofa. The doctor then asked Kevin if he was still in pain, and Kevin answered with a great roar that made the doctor wince, '*Heavens*, no, I'm *completely* better!' with this same absurd boisterousness. The doctor began to question him in English, but it was quite hopeless. Kevin was determined to be bright and breezy, whatever it might cost, and I could feel the doctor getting angrier and angrier.

'How long you have had these pains?'

'Oh, *on* and off for a year or so, but this was something quite exceptional, wasn't it, Lucy? It had *never* happened before.'

'How can you describe these pains? They are gradual or sudden?'

'Sometimes one, sometimes the other. But I am *not* in any

*real* sense ill. I am *still* capable of swimming more than a mile. I could go out and swim a mile, tomorrow.'

I motioned to Peter and Lucy that we should leave them; Kevin was hopeless as long as he had an audience, and the three of us tiptoed out of the room, I the last, raising my hand to him and trying to make a reassuring face, because he started up on the sofa and suddenly one saw all his fear; like a child in hospital whose parents suddenly go out and leave him.

Outside the door, we all three waited for each other to speak. Lucy looked from Peter to me with a curious kind of appeal, almost as if she were in our house, not we in hers. Her behaviour was so odd that I didn't even dislike her for the moment; I was simply puzzled. At last she said, in a very quick monotone, 'Do you want to sit down?' then instantly turned her back and walked quickly down the passage, as if she were desperate to get away from us, if only for a moment.

She led the way into a rather dim little sitting-room, with a few drably covered armchairs. I had the idea that for all the time they'd been there she'd never really bothered with the place; there was nothing you could solidly put your finger on and say, that must be hers. Or, for that matter, *his*; but this was no more than I would have expected.

Once we'd all sat down, there was another silence. I couldn't think of anything but Kevin, down the passage, and Lucy was just an irrelevance; she seemed almost to accept as much, herself, by the way she was behaving. Peter was looking up at the ceiling with his what-fools-these-mortals-be look. In the end it was Lucy who spoke, in this sudden, abrupt, *enfant terrible* way she had, as if every now and again one were tuned in to a conversation she was having in her head: 'If he was that ill, he wouldn't have got up again.'

Peter gave a sceptical sort of laugh and said, 'If it were anyone else but Kevin, I might agree with you.'

'It's happened before,' she said. 'One minute he's meant

to be in agony, the next he'll be jumping around, just like tonight.'

'*Meant* to be?' I said, looking at her hard, and her eyes fell away.

'You saw how he is now,' she said. 'An hour ago, he was flat out on that sofa.'

'Well, what exactly happened?' Peter asked her, with just an edge of exasperation showing through, though she obviously didn't notice it. She spoke in this perfectly expressionless tone, looking blankly at me, 'I was asking him had he seen you in Florence, and right away he starts all this making faces and holding his stomach. Then halfway through dinner, he drops his knife and fork and he collapses, the way I told you; slides right on down to the floor.'

'Usually he doesn't slide that far,' said Peter, but he got no reaction to that, either. She just said, 'Not before he hasn't.' She reminded me of shellshock cases I'd known in the war.

'So then you put him on the sofa,' Peter said, with a little feline smile. 'And you called Joan.'

'Kevin asked me to call Joan.'

He was still wasting his time. Half of her just didn't seem to be there at all, almost as if she were hypnotized. Even after her telephone call, or *because* of her telephone call, I'd expected to find enormous hostility, but instead here she was, quite calmly accepting me, and even admitting they'd been quarrelling about me, as if she took it for granted that I'd take it for granted too. I couldn't understand her and I didn't want to; I was just more and more appalled that Kevin should have spent ten years of his life with someone like this.

All at once, there was the sound of the door of the *salotto* being opened very noisily, footsteps coming towards us, then the doctor stalked into the room. He was terribly angry, quite vibrant with rage; a pulse was twitching away in his cheek. He said in Italian, 'I've told him if he wants to make a fool of himself, that's his own affair, but not to make one of me, especially in the middle of the night.'

Then he turned and strode out again, followed very quickly by Peter, who came fussing after him like a mother hen. I heard their voices fading away towards the front entrance, then there were Lucy and I : alone.

I suppose it should have been one of those great Bernhardt-Duse moments, but the fact was that we sat there saying nothing. There was too much to say and too little, and *I* certainly wasn't going to begin. Besides, in her present state, anything one said seemed to be distorted or deflected in some way. She just looked straight into space, as though she were all alone in the room; completely without initiative, like a child: which was exactly what she was, I thought, looking at her pinched little petulant face, a perpetually spoiled child, which had no idea how to cope with trouble, because there'd always been someone there to cope for her.

In the end I just stood up and walked out without a word to her, and went into the *salotto*. Kevin was sitting on the sofa, very woebegone; another child. As I came in, he looked up at me with a relieved kind of smile and said, 'Our doctor was *not* amused.'

'Well, did you expect him to be?' I asked. 'Getting him out of bed at this hour to attend somebody he's never seen and who's meant to be at death's door, then telling him there's nothing the matter with you.'

'But there isn't!' he said, and tried to spring up from the sofa with his arms stretched wide, but this time it wouldn't quite work, he hadn't the strength, and he immediately sank back on to the sofa. He gave me a weak little smile and said, 'I simply collapsed. Just like that. There was this sudden, shooting pain. And I collapsed.'

'Lucy said you and she had been quarrelling about me,' I said, and he looked very sheepish.

'I remember *some*thing of the sort.'

'Oh, come on, Kevin,' I said, 'you remember perfectly well, don't pretend you don't.'

'I told her I *had* seen you,' he said, 'there had *been* meetings.'

Suddenly I found myself asking, 'What on earth keeps you here, Kevin?' though I knew it was a hopelessly rhetorical question, the moment I'd asked it.

'There are *things*,' he said with his hands together, looking at the floor, a tableau, Blessed Are The Meek. 'Certain obligations. Certain . . . affections.'

'And what did the doctor say to you?'

'He wanted to put me into hospital, which of course was absolutely out of the question.' He raised his head, looked sternly into space, so that I knew we were going to hear another of his dramatized, imaginary conversations, and he said, 'I told him, I am *not* going into an Italian hospital. If I go into any hospital, it will be in England, and it will be a hospital for Army officers.'

I shook my head and turned towards the door, but he called me back, '*Joan!*' with such desperation that I had to look round. 'Joan, don't be angry with me! *Please* don't go!'

'I'm not angry,' I said. 'I'm going to look for Peter.'

I found him in the garden, coming back from the front gate. 'I did what I could to pacify him,' he said. 'I told him a little bit of the background. Apparently Kevin just dug his heels in from sheer fright and refused to go for any examination.'

'I know,' I said. I hate talking to Peter about Kevin. I know just what he thinks about him and I can't really blame him, but his view of Kevin is from the outside – his view of almost everything is from the outside – while mine's from the inside, and there's no reconciling them. Kevin's not a coward, this is something that goes beyond mere physical pain, because he bore enough of that in the hospital at Naples. But it was all just too complicated to explain, especially at this hour of the night, when the not sleeping and the worry were beginning to catch up with me again, and all I wanted to do was to go home to bed and sleep and sleep and forget about everything, until I could find the strength to cope with it.

'And Hiyah?' Peter asked.

She was exactly where I'd left her. Sitting quite still, like a sad little waxwork. From the doorway, Peter looked at her, then looked at me, and smiled one of his smiles, but I didn't smile back. She was either pathetic or despicable. God knows she wasn't funny.

# FOUR

## 1

Anna, can you come on over right away? Kevin's gone. I don't *know* where the hell he's gone. He's just not here. Last night he wasn't home for dinner, I went out again myself, and I just naturally assumed he'd be back before me. Sure, that's what I think, he's gone off with *her*, that's exactly what he's done. No note, nothing at all, only his suitcase isn't there; the one he keeps on the top of his wardrobe. Maria says she saw him come downstairs with it, like it was heavy. I don't know how I *should* feel, Anna, I only know how I *do* feel. Coming like this, right out of nothing, no warning, nothing at all. He's taken a couple of suits with him, I guess, a few shirts. You know what I'm going to do with the rest? I'll give the whole darn lot away. Sure I'll never let him back again, but that isn't it; it's the way it's all happened. Not even a note.

## 2

The extraordinary magic of trains. Especially at night. The dark and the movement and the intermittent light, the syncopation of the wheels. The illusion, always, of being carried to the better from the worse, of an ecstatic escape. Never more than now, with Joan's dear face smiling opposite me. If only it could be prolonged for ever, one endless moment of travelling hopefully. Because at either end of the journey, there is Lucy. Whom I have left without explanation. *Not* out of cowardice, but out of pity.

One could have told her to her face, one could have left a letter. Or rather, one could *not* tell her to her face, it would have ended in tears, abuse, incomprehension. And I might have stayed; only, at the last, to leave. For I had to leave, simply to live. Joan convinced me of it. As for a letter, that has always seemed the ultimate cowardice, or unkindness. Her letter to me when she left Florence that time. Wounding, cruel, unnecessary. Letters. A suicide note, propped on the mantelpiece. A valedictory, left in the middle of the double bed, with open drawers and cupboards all around. Or falling like lead on to the mat, to lie there, like an unexploded bomb.

No. I said to myself, I shall leave it; I shall wait: I shall go back, and *then* I shall explain to her. Or I shall telephone, although I hate the telephone. But at least, with all its disembodied horrors, it transmits the voice; one can say, on a telephone, I am leaving you but I still love you. Then, perhaps, I should write; after we had spoken. When a letter would no longer come as the first intimation.

Joan asked me, 'What did you tell her?' She is slightly, just perceptibly, unsubtle in such things, going by rules of fair play and forthrightness which simply don't apply in such cases, tending to bring more hurt than healing. What Lucy and I had between us – *have* between us – is something very deep and very real, but we are mutually destructive. Where Joan and I are mutually creative.

I said to Joan, 'I have told her in my own way.'

We shall go to Rome, we shall stay in Rome, we shall head south; and then we shall decide where to live. Not, oh God, *not*, in Italy. Perhaps in England, in the green. Even in Ireland.

Smiling at me. I smiled back at her. It's like an elopement, or another honeymoon. I feel so painfully sorry for Lucy, I'm sorry for Joan's husband, but there are things which are written, relationships which seem to be indestructible. It's something Joan and I both know.

I look across the second-class compartment at him, and I

think, I must be mad, I must be mad. Yet at the same time, I feel terribly excited and happy. And guilty. Because I'm quite sure he hasn't told Lucy. He was so evasive. I shall have to find out, but not yet, not now, destroying the moment. Yet I've no hatred for her, no feelings of gratified revenge. If I'm taking him away, it's for his sake, not mine; to save what's left of him. After that abominable night, I knew I couldn't leave him up there in Bellosguardo. At the same time I knew – oh, how well I knew – that there was only one way to get him away. Perhaps he sensed this, perhaps this was even why the whole thing happened. God knows. Kevin's always been astonishingly quick to smell out any kind of sympathy.

But the next afternoon, there he was at my *pensione*, carrying a suitcase, and melodramatically telling me, 'I've left. I have decided you are right. And now, you and I must leave together.'

I was utterly stunned. I asked, 'Leave for where?' and he pranced about crying, 'Anywhere!' in that devil-may-care way which was once so Byronic and irresistible, but now seems so pathetic and contrived. Except that there seemed to be some obsolete chord in me which it could still strike, however inappropriately, however strange the music. I knew I wasn't going with him, there was just no question of going, yet part of me *wanted* to go, to get away, to be with him. It was that old charm of his, that unquenchable irresponsibility, which made *me* feel irresponsible, like the woman who went off with the raggle-taggle gypsies.

He knew it, too, and off he went on a great, rambling, romantic tangent about what we'd do and where we'd go, so that it was terribly hard not to be swept away. And even now, sitting in the train, it's difficult for me to say exactly what did decide me, whether it was Kevin's propaganda or my knowing that to leave him in Bellosguardo was to leave him to die. Perhaps it was a little of one and a little of the other, his rhetoric tipping the balance, providing the fuse that lit the keg, after all the smouldering and the brooding that I'd done; worse than ever since last night.

God knows what I shall say to William. Thank goodness he's still in New York. 'We shall go south!' Kevin said, 'south to the sun!' which is wonderful as long as the sun shines and the money lasts; after all, how many middle-aged couples can elope south, to the sun?

Dear Kevin; eternally living in the phrase, the gesture and the moment. I look into his face and see it changed yet unchanged, so much older, yet just as young, disintegrating, yet not disillusioned. He was beautiful when I saw him first; now one would look at him and say, he must have been very handsome. It *was* a poet's face, and now, I suppose, it's a drinker's face. Would I have stopped him becoming such a drinker? Could I have turned him into a poet? It must be the measure of his spell on me that I should ask myself such questions at all.

I must make him write to Lucy. And then, some time or other, I shall write to William.

## 3

I open the door, and whoever should it be but Hiyah. Looking exactly the way we'd left her at Bellosguardo; like someone had just carved her out of soap.

'Hi,' she said, 'have you seen Kevin?'

'No,' I said.

'I thought maybe he'd been staying overnight with you,' she said.

'Now, why ever would he want to do that?' I asked.

'Well, he could have done,' she said, quite snappily. 'You two and Joan seem to have gotten pretty thick.'

'I'm afraid I scarcely see him,' I said. 'The other night was the first time in a long while.'

'How about Joan?' she said. 'Have you seen *her*?'

'No,' I said, 'not since that night. Why, can't you get hold of her?'

'She's checked out of her *pensione*,' she said. 'They don't know where she's gone,' and suddenly it began to grow clear to me. She was afraid they'd gone together. 'You'd better come in,' I told her.

'I can't stay long,' she said, 'I can't stay more than just a minute.'

She was moving around as though she were on wires; even when I put her on a chair, she still kept jerking about like a puppet. I called Joan's *pensione* and she *had* checked out, the only address she'd left was the one in London, and this seemed very strange to me, because although there were times when she could be pretty toffee-nosed, I certainly wouldn't have expected her to leave, after that night, without even calling me to tell me.

I asked her, 'Doesn't Kevin ever do this, normally; take off for a day or so?'

'He's never done anything like this before,' she said, 'not without telling me. If he's ever out of the villa, it's just for like a few hours at a time.

'Apart from one or two longer absences,' I couldn't resist saying, 'which of course you knew all about.'

'You mean the times he stayed down here in Florence?' she said. 'Yeah, I knew all about those.' There was simply no shaming her. 'Do *you* think they've taken off?' she asked me.

'I don't know,' I said, though it was beginning to look alarmingly as though they had. 'I hope not.'

'Why do you hope not?'

'Because I don't think it would be a particularly good idea for either of them,' I said.

'Do you think it would be a good idea for me?'

'I meant,' I said, 'that they're both a little old for that kind of thing.'

'That wouldn't stop Kevin,' she said. 'Kevin doesn't think that way. Kevin's clock stopped at thirty-five.'

And yours, I thought, at seventeen. I asked her had he left any message. 'No,' she said, 'he didn't leave a thing, he just sneaked off like a thief. But if they get in touch with you, you can tell him this. Not to bother coming back when the whole thing falls apart, because this time, the door's going to stay locked.'

'All right,' I promised. 'I'll tell him, if I ever hear from him,' and I saw her to the door. A wasp with nothing left to sting.

## 4

I've got Anna staying with me at the villa, again. I just can't face being here on my own, right now. Everything happened so fast, I'm still in a spin. Kevin collapsing that way, Joan and Peter Clovis and the doctor all coming, then Kevin and her disappearing. Anna says, '*Meno male,*' but she doesn't understand. First off, it just *has* to come as a shock, there's no way round it; what else could it be?

I've been doing crazy things. I even called Mother in New York, how about that, and of course she came through with the same stuff as Anna, what was I worrying about, I should be delighted. I guess maybe I should, but this isn't the way you want to lose anybody, having them just disappear like this, vanish right off into space, thinking you know what they've done, you know who they've gone with, but never being sure. Except that now I *am* sure; at least that he's gone off with *her*. I've been round to her *pensione* and asked them did she leave alone. They said no, she had a man with her, and when I asked them what he looked like, was he English, was he carrying a suitcase, it turned out to be Kevin, okay.

When he asked me to call her that night, *her,* that was when I should have started looking out. It was just an excuse to get her up here, to make his sneaky plans with her, right under my nose, and to show me up in front of her. Walking round the villa like she owned it. Patronizing me the way she did. And that Peter Clovis, with his nose stuck in the air; the two of them taking over.

Okay, I thought, now they've seen for themselves just how ill he is. He's meant to be dying, and when they get up here, he's at the gate to meet them, doing handsprings.

Yet they *still* look at me like I've been doing something wrong, I haven't taken proper care of him. You wouldn't believe it.

When he collapsed at the table, I just knew it wasn't real. I told him, 'Get up, Kevin! You know damn well there's nothing the matter with you; you can't fool anyone this way!' And when he didn't get up, I got madder and madder, I was sure he was doing it just to annoy me, because he surely couldn't believe I was going to fall for it.

In the end I went across and stood over him; I was so mad I even prodded him with my toe. I took the water jug off the table and threw it all in his face, but he just gave a kind of groan and moved his head a little, which was what started me wondering; he'd never carried anything this far, before. That was when I called Maria and Sergio, and Sergio said, 'Let's put him on the sofa.'

When we started to move him, he groaned again, and his head rolled in a creepy kind of way. By now I didn't know what to be, angry or scared, and not knowing made me even angrier. I thought, if he hadn't tried to fool me so often, there wouldn't be this problem. When we'd got him on the sofa, I said, 'Kevin, wake up,' and I slapped his cheek a little, though Maria and Sergio were saying no, don't do that, call a doctor. But it worked, he did wake up, his eyes opened, moved around, then finally focused on me. It was then he went through this thing of getting a doctor, only not our doctor, getting one through Joan, and I thought sure, why not, let *her* take some of the responsibility if she's still so crazy about him, why should I take it all and get nothing; let *her* see what he's really like; which I can see now was a mistake. Or maybe it wasn't a mistake. I still don't know, and like I said, it's no use Anna telling me I've been lucky.

Right now, I'm extremely restless. I don't like being in the villa too much, I have to get out and get around, I'm happiest when I'm in the car, driving about. When I'm up here, all I can think of is Kevin, her, and this thing they've done to me. I'm doing crazy things. Like calling in on Peter

Clovis, who probably helped them fix it, anyway. He didn't do anything for me, just said he thought it was a bad idea, because they were too old for that kind of thing. Not a word about me, you'd have thought I hadn't any feelings.

What I mean to do is find them. I don't know how, but I'll do it. I want to be able to tell Kevin to his face just how I despise him for running out on me, and then to tell her, okay, you've taken him, now keep him, but don't think you've gone off with anything I wanted. I haven't told any of this to Anna, because I know she'd try and stop me. Anna's happy with things the way they are, I'm aware of that. I know she's quite content living here with me in the villa, though I'm not going to say she hasn't been a good friend, my only friend. 'Don't distress yourself,' she says, 'especially about someone as negligible as he is.'

'Just don't let him think he can get away with it,' I tell her. '*That's* all.'

I'll find him, okay. Kevin doesn't run that fast any more.

## 5

Rome. Looking even more beautiful than Florence, lovely enough to make one cry, with all those perfect harmonies of sun and shapes and colours and trees, everything rich, deep and warm, art and nature so exquisitely counterpointed. Tangible thick green of leaves against those throbbing reds of tiles and walls. Lush, like a hot-house flower on the very brink of going to seed. It hasn't any of Florence's *signorilità*: it succeeds through sheer excess, overwhelms you with its superabundance. Kevin hates it, inevitably; but let him. He shan't spoil Rome for me. The trouble is, of course, that it's too much for him. He wants his nice, safe, grey English cathedrals, his water-colour tints and his Gothic gloom. He wants his oaks and elms and willows, but *I* want my cypresses and pines. Pines like the ones which bend vertiginously on Monte Mario, inclining like a line of courteous, listening giants. I know what Kevin means when he says Rome nauseates him, that it's a marzipan city, yet I can adore it for a while, for all its overblown corruption, even if it has grandeur without dignity, even if I'll never be subtly and totally enslaved by it, as I am by Florence. I want to stay here and paint and paint and paint until this lovely late summer light has gone – and the petals fall.

We're staying in a nice, neat, musty little hotel I know, just above the Spanish Steps, so calm and quiet inside, though the scooter-noise bounces off the walls, in the street, like tennis balls. There's a lift like a coffin it's so narrow, with elaborate glass doors that take an age to slide shut, and rattle when it moves; which is incredibly slowly, shuddering like an old, old man. Downstairs in the foyer, which is like a dark cool cavern, the old white-haired *padrona* sits smiling to herself all day. I introduced Kevin to her as my ex-husband – I couldn't bear to shock her – and we live next door to one another, in separate rooms, sleeping in mine.

In those long, hot, hovering hours of the *siesta*, we make love; just as though we'd never been apart. Each of us remembering what the other wants. His body's stouter, of course, its old tautness has gone, but it's still surprisingly strong and good. It's like him; it seems to be able to resist anything; bullets, drink, idleness.

We stroll the streets a lot, and talk about Rome in the war, where we once spent a glorious leave. The city was ours then; nothing but uniforms, the raucous Roman life subdued. As it is, now, in the summer heat, when they've all fled to the hills or the sea.

I *know* this is just an interlude, but Kevin has always lived from one interlude to the next, treating each as though it were real; what happens in between is a sort of no-man's-land, a hibernation. Perhaps that's why he's never lost that boyish bubbling of his, that ridiculous optimism.

It was all, 'Look how this has changed,' and 'Do you remember that?' A hotel where he and I had stayed for a few shillings a night, which had now gone terribly grand and expensive. We'd stand outside and watch all the fat, rich tourists going in and out, and giggle. It was curious how we both seemed to be regressing, laughing at all the things we would have laughed at then, feeling gorgeously irresponsible and subversive, young and poor and happy. I said to him one night, while we were sitting at a café table in the Via Veneto, watching the extraordinary passing show, 'How can you say you aren't enjoying Rome?' to which he answered, 'I enjoy remembering Rome.' Which is perfectly true. He seems to like places as far as they have memories for him, as far as he can use them to rejuvenate himself, whether they're Rome or Capri or Calabria or Cambridge. So sad, in a way, as if he were quite resigned to his life being over, completely committed to the past, just like a very old man.

He reads the papers a great deal; our room is snowed under with English newspapers and magazines, great drifts of them over the bed, piles of them on the chest of drawers, avalanching on to the floor. He lies on the bed and reads for hours, or he'll sit on a bench he's discovered under the wall of the Pincio, where it's shady. If I want to paint or to look at a church or gallery, I can safely leave him there, knowing that if I come back in an hour or two or three he'll still be there, placidly reading.

I'm sure those ten years have had a lot to do with it; it's a routine he's been forced into devising, an attitude he's had to adopt. I get little hints of the sort of life he must have led; from certain grimaces when he's deep in a paper and I speak to him, from the way he sometimes starts when I come into the room, the way he holds up a paper when he reads; like a barricade. I sometimes think I could kill her for what she's done to him; and yet he consented to it, he dropped me quite callously and ran to her.

When he's asleep, there's such a look of relief on his face, a kind of half-smile. And the pain has disappeared, as I'd hoped it would. He never complains of it, and if I ask about it, he shrugs it away, very irascibly – 'Not a thing, nothing' as if it were something he's ashamed of.

He wants to turn this whole thing into a sentimental

journey; Naples, Capri, Ischia, then that little seaside village in Calabria, where we went for our 'reunion'. I think he'd like it to go on indefinitely; as far and as far back as Shropshire, Cambridge, even his public school, anywhere that he's been happy, with or without me, until he's no memories left. After which – what? Nothing else, I suppose, but to confront the present, which he just can't bear to do.

The other day, walking down the little, narrow Via della Croce, over the cobbles to the Via del Corso at the bottom, a car driving up between the parked cars forced us into single file, and I fell behind him, watching how he was walking now, quite differently, swaggering like a subaltern, just the way he'd walked twenty years ago, when he came here as a conqueror.

It made me start to cry.

## 6

We have left the Scarlet Woman, the randy old courtesan with her obscenely painted face, her black flocks of priests and her lurking putrescence. Different from Florence but, in its way, just as oppressive, just as odious. At least Florence doesn't seriously pretend to be anything but a graveyard, where in Rome the corpses insist on getting up and dancing, trying to convince you they're alive.

In Naples, though, things *are* alive, far too *much* alive, like an ant-heap, seething and pullulating; not as predatory as they were in the war, when the poor devils were mostly half starved, but still enormously insistent and obstrusive, so that after we'd looked at the building which was once the military hospital, which is now a block of flats, and after we'd sat in the Galleria and drunk cognac and coffee and held hands and felt incredibly nostalgic, we decided to take off for Capri.

The boat was full of tourists, festooned with cameras and comic hats, with the usual over-organized phalanx of Germans, doing what they were told. So utterly different from the first time we'd crossed together, when everyone had been in uniform, English and Americans and Free French, and Joan, in *her* uniform, had looked so pretty. She had this defiant way of wearing her cap, the most masculine thing imaginable, as if she challenged it to make her look anything but feminine. I remembered her, and the cap, with shattering clarity; standing in the bows, her back to the rails, smiling at me with such affection. I knew we'd been right to come back; it had worked, just as I was sure it would. The beauty of it has been that it's not a parody of the original thing, a sort of George Grosz caricature, it's exactly the thing itself, quite intact after those twenty years.

Approaching the island was as marvellous as it had been then, that dark bulk looming out of the water, gradually taking on definition, assuming contour, colours, detail by the moment, as though one were watching a statue emerge from a block of stone.

When we landed, we got away at once from the Marina Piccola and the cafés and the souvenirs. We climbed, climbed, climbed into the hinterland, looking for the Norman Douglas Capri, the Tiberius Capri; we both knew that this was where we were going. Up lanes and paths, hot and sweating in the sun, but laughing too, making a joke and an adventure out of it, Joan matching me stride for stride, saying, 'God, you're such a fool!' yet never complaining. We spurred ourselves on by imagining we were being followed by cohorts of tourists.

'Quick!' I'd tell her. 'I hear the tread of jackboots! Flee the Teutonic hordes to come, or we'll be beaten to death with Baedekers!' Or Joan would say, 'Hurry, I smell fish and chips! It's the British; can't you hear their twanging braces?' And we'd build up this picture of dozens of little men with knotted handkerchiefs on their heads and fat women in print dresses surging up the hill.

By the time we reached Tiberius' villa, we were both exhausted, we flopped on to the grass and lay there panting and laughing, we were so close to one another, as if we were sharing a marvellous joke.

'Staff Nurse Coleman,' I said, 'may one ask *why* you were to be seen at a *notorious* villa, out of uniform?'

'Please, Matron,' she said, 'it was that Lieutenant Darnley, again. Dragged me up the hill, he did, and before I knew what was happening, I was part of the orgy.'

'The orgy,' I said, 'is about to be con*tin*ued!' and I got up, taking her hand, pulling her to her feet, then down the slope, until we were among the ruins. She was laughing and saying, 'I don't *want* to come down here, Kevin! Kevin, this is perfectly *absurd*! Let me *go*!'

It had been dark when we came here, before. Now, as we lay together, the broken stones rose all about us like a jagged landscape, like the New York skyline.

'They'll see us, they'll see us,' she kept saying.

'No, they won't,' I said, but in fact I didn't care, the very chance they might made it all the more exhilarating. It brought back that whole sub-stratum of one's life when one made love adventurously, impulsively, in fields and cars, on beaches, anywhere, because one was young, and one lived in the feelings. And I think Joan felt something of this as well, because she suddenly relaxed, and when I penetrated her, she gave this ecstatic sigh, arching her back in a great curve, and at the end we came together, it was all quite perfect, just as it had been perfect the first time. I felt potent and young and incredibly vigorous, ready to achieve so much.

I said to her, 'God, I do love you,' and she smiled, her eyes still closed, but didn't speak.

Afterwards, we climbed down again. We hired a boat and sailed into the Blue Grotto, just as we'd done, then, and not even all the chattering trippers could spoil it; the phantasmagoria of rock and light and moving water, the strange, thick, submarine twilight. Then down to the rocks above the sea, where we swam, and lay in the fierce sun, till it was time to take the boat back again. Tomorrow, we shall go to Ischia.

# 7

Sitting in this man's office. This big, fat, ugly guy behind a desk, with his little, dark pig eyes in his fat, cop's face; having to *tell* him things and wondering all the time why the hell am I doing this? Is it even worth it? Questions like, had I any idea how long the thing had been going on? Did I think I knew where they might have gone? Had my husband done anything like this before? Why did I think he'd done it? Was I sure they were still in Italy? How long was I ready to go on having them looked for?

It was Anna told me Joan had been planning on going to Rome; she'd heard it from a friend who knew someone who'd been at dinner with Joan in Florence. And it was Flavia Bertini who put me on to this man, she said he's good at finding people, though I didn't tell Anna this was what I was going to Rome for, because she can be pretty dominating, she'd probably have opposed it. As it was, she'd said, 'It's very hot. You will exhaust yourself running about in the sun, looking for something that is not worth even finding. And if you find it, that will probably be the worst of all.'

I said, 'I've got to get out of Florence, that's all, it's depressing me here.'

She said. 'Then let me at least come with you, so we can share the discomforts between two of us.'

'No,' I told her, 'I want to go on my own, I just want to be by myself a little,' and I drove there down the *autrostrada*. The heat was just terrible, the car was like an oven, with people the whole time cutting in on you and hooting you, so there were times I'd grip the wheel so tight, the blood ran out of my fingers, or I'd yell right back at them, *'Cretini! Ignoranti!'* Having a woman stand up to them on the road, that's something new to them. I can tell you, it was just like driving through hell, and by the time I got to Rome, I was in no state to see anybody, let alone this big gorilla in his crummy little office, looking me over like he wanted to eat me, asking all these nosy questions.

He wanted half a million lire in advance, as well. Next morning, though, he called me at my hotel and said he'd found out that they *had* been in Rome and the hotel they'd stayed in; he said he reckoned they'd gone to Naples. So I'll stay here till there's any more news, though it's pretty strange after so long in Florence, only a small city, really, but when you're used to that kind of claustrophobic thing, it doesn't seem small, it seems big, everything rushing at you. And the terrible remarks in the streets, men following you everywhere you go.

I'll maybe buy a dress or two, I'll go to the opera, I've got friends here I can see. One thing for sure is that right now I can't face going back to Florence; not till I've found them, or I know they've gone for ever.

## 8

In Calabria, we had our first setback. Our idyllic village has been discovered and 'developed'; the beach has been tamed and combed and planted with umbrellas like flamboyant coloured mushrooms. Cars roar up and down the narrow roads, forcing one into the side, a great white modern hotel has gone up in the bay, and there are three or four *pensioni* with gaudy coloured sunblinds. We couldn't even find the family we stayed with. Kevin was terribly upset: 'I would like to drop bombs on them all, I would like to *raze* that hotel to the ground and make a funeral pyre of those bloody beach-umbrellas.'

For my own part, I wasn't really sorry; nostalgia's all very well, but I hadn't been looking forward to roughing it again in that uncomfortable little farmhouse, and sitting in its outside privy with those strips of newspaper, praying the door wouldn't burst open when someone came and started rattling it. I suggested we went to Elba or up to the lakes, but Kevin had the bit between his teeth now and he wouldn't hear of it; we must go on up the coast until we found somewhere like the original place, as it used to be. I didn't argue too hard, even if the idea depressed me, because the last thing I wanted at the moment was to face realities; I simply wasn't ready. As long as we were here in the sun, so far away from London, everything was blissfully unreal, there were no such things as great looming moral decisions. In two days' time, William would be back from the States, and I'd sent him a cowardly postcard from Rome saying that I might stay on a little.

I'd tried once or twice to pin Kevin down to what he eventually wants to do, where he wants to go, but it's quite hopeless, he just goes drifting off into the stratosphere like a runaway balloon. One moment, he's going to make his peace with the family and they'll give us a cottage on the estate, the next, we're emigrating to Australia, where he's going to become a sort of Dr Johnson to the natives.

The only trouble is that he's gradually dragging *me* into his cloud-cuckoo land, I'm becoming just as mercurial and Micawberish as he is, and I'm afraid I'm enjoying it; it's like some marvellous surprise present; Suddenly you're given back your youthful insouciance in middle age. Except that I know it can't last, and Kevin behaves as if it will last for ever.

So off we went along the coast, and we did find somewhere in the end; a rather sad little village, but with a fine long strip of sand and a sea that I could watch and paint all day, a lovely, solid, Della Robbia blue, full of movement and modulations of the light. This was something else Kevin had done; by pulling me into this make-believe world, he really had me painting again; where for years now, as I realized, I'd just been dabbling, using it as a sort of status symbol. But he'd given me back my belief : I *wanted* to paint, and in the back of my mind there was a hope that one day we'd be able to live on my painting.

I didn't dare mention it to Kevin, because I knew so well how he'd grab hold of it and build it up until I was exhibiting in the Royal Academy and selling to the Museum of

Modern Art and Heaven knows where else; but it was one more spur to me.

We were living in romantic squalor, just as we had ten years ago; above a little bar-cum-café, where they'd given us the matrimonial bed; the walls were plastered with wedding groups and dingy family photos in thick black wooden frames and plaster crucifixions and plaster Madonnas. Kevin loved it, he was being Norman Douglas, but I found it terribly oppressive, and I tried to stay out in the sun as much as I could.

Sometimes we'd go inland, where I'd make sketches of those vast, bare, brutal mountains. They impressed me but I didn't like them; they had some quality that made me shiver, a sort of arid malevolence. You felt nothing grew on them because they wouldn't allow it to grow. Kevin would stand waving the stick he'd bought himself – because Norman Douglas had one – crying, 'The goat! The goat has wreaked this devastation! The goat has destroyed Calabria!'

He was very keen on talking to peasants, who'd usually stand looking at him as if they thought he were touched, with their mouths hanging open, and if they did answer it was in a dialect which he couldn't understand, and nor could I. Still, he was terribly happy, and he started making plans about writing a book to be called *Calabria Revisited*; he'd follow all Norman Douglas' trails in *Old Calabria* and describe the changes that had taken place. I told him I thought it was a marvellous idea, though the prospect of tramping through Calabria with him indefinitely wasn't very comforting, and at least he began make notes; he was very excited. I was going to paint, he was going to write, and we'd stay down here in Calabria till further notice. It was all decided.

So the sun shone and the days trailed by and we went on living in our Lotus Land.

## 9

*A beach in Calabria. Mid-afternoon. The sun is very bright and strong, the sky a lambent blue, thickly whorled with cumulus. The sand is dark and undulating, in places grown with pale green thistles. The sea, today, is rowdy and disturbed; waves swell sudden and grandiose, ten yards offshore. Far off, behind the beach, a bleak, grey, undulating range of mountains can be seen, sullen and immense, without dramatic peaks or spurs.*

*In the sea, a man is bathing but not swimming, leaping in the waves, shouting, spreading out his arms in joyful defiance as each new wave surges in front of him, disappearing a moment beneath it, then coming up again, shaking his soaked head like a dog, to await the next wave. It is* KEVIN.

JOAN *lies on the beach, watching him, occasionally shouting encouragement. She wears a pale blue bathing suit, and her skin has been burned a rich brown.*

*On the bank which leads down to the beach, a woman appears. Incongruously in so primitive a setting, she is dressed with elegant sophistication, in a sleeveless blue silk dress, with a motif of abstract white shapes, white high-heeled shoes, even a white straw hat, and she is carrying a crocodile handbag. It is* LUCY. *She looks silently from* KEVIN *to* JOAN, *without expression. She seems quite detached from what she sees, merely recording it, without surprise or passion. She makes no attempt to indicate her presence; there is a quality of stillness about her which suggests that she prefers that she should ultimately be seen as an apparition might be seen. And at last it is* KEVIN *who sees her, emerging from the sea, he, too, strikingly tanned, throwing back his head, extending his arms in the parody of some Triton. Till, seeing* LUCY, *he freezes, his pose becoming the parody of a parody.* JOAN *looking at him puzzled, turns towards the bank herself, and she, too, grows instantly rigid. For perhaps ten or fifteen seconds, this curious tableau is maintained;* LUCY *might be a goddess, suddenly confronting two astonished votaries.* KEVIN *is the first to break it, transforming his pose plastically from one of exultation to one of welcome, racing across the beach to the foot of the bank, with a cry of joy.*

KEVIN: *Lucy!*

*He pauses, just below her, in a second variation of his previous attitude, his arms now outstretched from his sides. But as* LUCY *says or does nothing to encourage him, he simply allows them to fall. Behind him,* JOAN *slowly rises to her feet and slowly begins to walk across the beach, towards the other two.*

LUCY, *at last*: Is this what you do all day? Swim?

KEVIN, *gradually regaining his momentum*: Lucy, for *Heaven's* sake! *Come* down and join us! Now, look – *God!* – Joan's got another swimming costume back at the café; we'll get that for you.

LUCY: I didn't come down here to swim, Kevin.

JOAN *has now reached them. She stands a little behind* KEVIN, *and her eyes gravely meet* LUCY's, *which become hostile and opaque.*

JOAN, *quietly and guardedly*: Hallo, Lucy.

LUCY: Hallo? Is that all? Hallo?

JOAN: Just for the moment.

KEVIN: *Why* don't we go up and have a drink?

LUCY: I don't want any drink.

KEVIN, *waving his arms*: Then lunch, a coffee, anything!

LUCY: Nothing.

JOAN: You can't have come here for nothing.

LUCY: That's right I haven't. I've come to get a few things straightened out. (*To* KEVIN) Things you ran off without explaining.

KEVIN *looks sheepishly away from her.*

LUCY, *to* JOAN: Did he tell you that? That he left without a word? After ten years. Without a letter. Nothing.

JOAN, *in a low, charged voice*: I see.

LUCY: Maybe you didn't tell your husband, either. Just

left him there guessing, like Kevin did me. Till one day he'll get around to thinking maybe you aren't coming back.

JOAN : I don't think that's a subject I particularly want to discuss with you.

LUCY, *with a high, wild laugh* : No, I guess it isn't! But just don't try pulling these snotty attitudes on me any more, because you've got nothing to get snotty about; cheating on your own husband and running off with somebody else's.

JOAN : And you? What did *you* once do?

LUCY, *irately* : He wasn't your husband then, and you'd taken him away from me, as it was.

KEVIN, *despairingly* : Please, *must* we?

JOAN, *ignoring* KEVIN : I don't propose to argue with you about that.

LUCY : No, of course not, you've got nothing to say, that's why. And now you've done it again, only this time it's going to be different, because this time you're going to have to keep him, you're welcome to him; *I'm* not taking him back any more.

JOAN : I'm not asking you to.

KEVIN *looks helplessly from one woman to the other; from* LUCY, *slender and pale, to* JOAN, *full-bodied and tanned, each throwing the other into relief,* JOAN *the embodiment of a robust, outdoor,* LUCY *of a protected, indoor, life.* JOAN *herself looks troubled and anxious, but her passions seem under control, where* LUCY'S *possess her.*

LUCY : That's fine, only don't go sending him back to me afterwards, when you're through with him and you can't take any more of him. When he's driven you crazy the way he's driven *me* crazy, with his lies and his promises and his loafing around!

JOAN, *vehemently* : The last thing I'd *ever* do is send him back to you!

LUCY : Is that how you're fooling yourself? That you've done something great by taking him away from me? That you're saving him, or something?

JOAN : You make everything cheap.

LUCY: No, I don't, I don't make anything cheap. I just call things the way they are.

KEVIN, *with a sudden bellow, head raised to the sky, like an anguished bull*: My *God*, you make me feel like Paris! On *whom* shall I bestow the golden apple?

LUCY *glances at him vaguely, unfocused;* JOAN *with exasperation.*

JOAN: Oh, really, Kevin!

KEVIN, *his tone unchanged*: But I'm in love with both of you! *Which* shall I choose? Both! Neither! We should all three live together, happily ever after!

*In unison, the two* WOMEN *turn away from him, resuming their own discussion.*

JOAN: I'm sorry you weren't told.

LUCY, *with another laugh*: That's just great! You're sorry I wasn't told! Like if I'd been told, everything would have been okay. I love the way you English can square things with your consciences.

JOAN: Do you remember how *I* was told?

LUCY: And this is how you've had your revenge. You've waited ten years, and now you've got back at me.

JOAN: Lucy: I am *not* getting back at you. I am not even *in*terested in you!

LUCY: No, but you're interested in hurting me!

JOAN, *in mordant amazement*: Hurting *you*?

LUCY: Yeah, hurting me. Don't you think I can be hurt? Is that what Kevin told you, that I couldn't be hurt?

JOAN: What *is* it that you want?

LUCY: I want to talk to Kevin.

KEVIN, *looking at* JOAN *with frightened appeal*: We must *all* talk, but not like this. In a human, civilized way, over a meal.

LUCY: Are you afraid to talk to me, Kevin?

KEVIN, *slowly, after a pause*: No. I am not afraid to talk to you.

LUCY: You were afraid to tell me you were going.

KEVIN, *in the same, remote voice*: I was *not* afraid to tell you I was going. I simply did not want to hurt you.

LUCY, *laughing*: That's wonderful! That's the greatest thing I've ever heard! He doesn't want to hurt me, so he walks out on me!

KEVIN: I did not want to hurt you with anything that was said or written.

JOAN: Lucy: what is it you want?

LUCY: Right now, I want to talk to Kevin.

JOAN: Kevin: talk to her.

KEVIN, *in alarm*: But I still think we should –

JOAN: You at least owe her that. Talk to her. I shall go back to change.

*Pushing her feet into wooden sandals, picking up her towel, she strolls off the beach and up the little hill, her movements crisp rather than elegant, passes* LUCY *without a word, then disappears down the bank.* LUCY *and* KEVIN, *left to confront each other, do not speak.* KEVIN'S *head is bowed;* LUCY *regards him with a look of sardonic expectation.*

KEVIN: I *am* sorry.

LUCY: That's a lot of consolation. Sorry. Why did you do it? That's what I've got to know. That's what I came here to find out.

KEVIN, *still avoiding her eye, shakes his head.*

LUCY: You're not going to tell me you love her, are you?

KEVIN, *almost inaudibly*: I do love her.

LUCY: How did you find *that* out?

KEVIN, *looking up, but not at her*: I told you; I love both of you.

LUCY: For once in your goddam life, Kevin, tell me the truth!

KEVIN: I am *telling* you the truth!

LUCY: You know something? I don't think you even know what the truth *is*, any more. You do whatever you want to do, then afterwards you make up reasons for it. I know why you married me; I want to know why you left me.

*A hiatus.* KEVIN'S *expression is one of obdurate reticence.*

LUCY: Why did you leave me, Kevin?

KEVIN *draws a profound breath, which emerges as a sigh, but still he does not speak.*

LUCY: What did that woman tell you, to make you leave?

KEVIN: Nothing. She told me nothing.

LUCY: She must have told you something. You wouldn't have done anything like this on your own.

KEVIN: She told me nothing.

LUCY: I want to know, Kevin. I'm not leaving here until I do.

KEVIN, *after a further pause; he still does not meet her gaze*: It was *precisely* to avoid something as painful as this that I left as I did.

LUCY: Oh, sure, you've always been pretty good at avoiding anything that bothers you.

KEVIN: That is *not* what I meant.

LUCY: Kevin: tell me.

KEVIN *behaves now, as if he were giving infinitely reluctant birth to a painful confession. His body writhes, his eyes dart in search of refuge. Finally he speaks; to the sand.*

KEVIN: I am afraid of dying.

LUCY, *in contemptuous outrage*: Dying?

KEVIN, *still addressing the sand*: Yes.

LUCY: And *I'm* killing you? It's because of me you're dying?

KEVIN, *almost whispering*: I didn't say that.

LUCY: But you meant it! So that's what she told you; that I'm killing you.

KEVIN, *shaking his head*: No, she didn't.

LUCY: And you believed her! After you'd made her believe you! The goddam *lies* you tell about yourself! Those *pains* you get when things don't go the way you want them.

*Over* KEVIN's *face there slowly spreads the old look of agony. Seeing it,* LUCY *goes into a paroxysm of fury.*

LUCY: For once in your life, *face* something. *I'm* not killing you, Kevin: you're killing yourself! Going to *her* won't make any difference! You'll still die, Kevin, because that's what you've got inside you! That's what you carry around with you! So let *her* have a dose of it, because I don't need it any more!

KEVIN *totters an instant, clutches his bronzed stomach with his left hand, then, with the slow, half-comic inevitability of a falling tree, pitches over on to the sand. He lies on his back, his eyes closed, his mouth open.* LUCY *bends forward from the bank towards him, shouting at him, as though if she can get near enough to him, shout loud enough, she can make him hear.*

LUCY: *I* didn't do this, Kevin; *you* did this! Do you hear me? You and no one else!

*She turns violently away, her whole movement one of denial, then rushes down the bank, stumbling, swaying, very nearly falling, her high heels, when she has disappeared, drumming a soft, frantic rhythm on the beaten path.* KEVIN, *sprawled like flotsam on the beach, does not move.*

## 10

And that was how I found him, my poor Kevin, prostrate on the sand, like a great brown starfish, so that for a horrible long moment I thought he might be dead.

I shouted, '*Kevin!*' and rushed down the beach to him, but he was breathing, thank God, very fast and light. I felt his pulse, which was weak. I brought some seawater in my cupped hands, to spill on his face, and with that, he opened his eyes. They moved, to look at me, then turned up to the sky, again. I said, 'She's gone, Kevin, don't worry; I heard her car go,' furious with myself for leaving them alone, giving that awful little reptile just the opportunty she'd wanted. I asked, 'Are you in pain?' but he shook his head, as if he'd reached a stage where it didn't matter any more. I took his head in my arms and rested it on my lap, I stroked his forehead, and after a time he reached up and squeezed my forearm.

'You'll never see her again,' I said. 'She's achieved what she came for.'

Then he spoke, so low that he seemed almost to be breathing the words, rather than speaking them.

'No, no,' he said, 'that isn't why she came.'

'Why did she come, then?' I asked, but he shook his head and wouldn't answer that. We sat there quite silently then for what must have been a good quarter of an hour. He sat up and looked out towards the sea. She was like one of those insects which inject their prey with a paralysing fluid. Until it wore off, there was nothing he could say or do.

At last he got to his feet, very heavily and shakily, I taking his arm, where an hour before he'd been skipping about like a child. He walked very slowly up the beach; he didn't draw his arm away from me, he simply behaved as if he hadn't noticed. Outside the café, he sat down, ordered a double whisky, and drank it without any joy, as though it were medicine. I asked him how he felt, and he said, 'Quite all right,' in a flat, dull voice, without looking at me. I knew now that the whole fairy-tale of these last few weeks was over, all the daydreams and the fantasies punctured. Whatever he said, I was sure this was why she'd followed us so implacably; she wanted to smash what he'd found. In her negative, destructive way, she knew him well enough, and where to hurt him.

'Let's leave tomorrow,' he said. 'Let's go to Sicily.'

Heaven knows I didn't blame him for not wanting to stay here another minute, now that she'd poisoned the place with her malignity, but I knew, and I was sure he knew, that it would be no use. One can't manufacture an Eden.

I asked him, 'What about your book?'

'I shall return to it,' he said. 'For the moment, Calabria oppresses me.'

So we went to Sicily. We got the boat from dull Reggio Calabria, where the men look at you as if you're in a cage, to horrible, ugly Messina, and from there we made our way down to a little village south of Taormina, where we found another cheap and squalid lodging, this time above a bakery, and the sun struck as hot as an inferno. Kevin bucked up a little, now, but he'd lost his spontaneity, he had to work at being madly gay. It may not have been a normal condition in the first place, but at least he'd achieved it without trying.

Now, when he thought he wasn't being watched, he looked wretched and brooding. At night, where before he'd been sleeping so peacefully, he was restless, turning about in the bed, sometimes giving strange little inaudible cries. I said to him one day, 'Kevin, you're *away* from her. She won't catch up with us again. She won't even try. She's had her pound of flesh, and that's the end of it.'

'I wish it were,' he said, then shook his head and wouldn't explain.

## II

It is not the end; it is merely the beginning. Or the continuation.

*I fled her down the days and down the years.*

Joan will never understand Lucy. Lucy will never understand Joan. Lucy will never understand herself. That terrible need which she can never acknowledge, so that it transforms itself into all kinds of irrelevant spite which is *not* Lucy, simply a denial of Lucy, because she has been brought up to fear the consequences of any show of vulnerability. Lucy speaks in code, her actions are metaphors. When I saw her standing there alone on the beach, I could have wept for her. To have been driven to such lengths, to have followed us so far, knowing that, at the end, there could only be distress and humiliation.

When I looked from one to the other, I saw Lucy so fragile and exposed, her very smartness so pathetic in that context, so incongruous, as if she daren't drop her defences for a moment. And Joan, by contrast, so sturdy and resilient. Oh, yes, she can be hurt, and *I* have hurt her, but she has strength, she's in command, where Lucy bobs about like a cork, for ever acted upon, driven, whatever her façade of toughness. When I said I loved them both, I meant it. In a sense, I suppose I am protected by Joan, while I protect

Lucy. Which means that Joan doesn't really need me, but Lucy does, though it's something she could never confess. The solution, perhaps, the impossible solution, would be for me to go off a few ecstatic months with Joan, each year. I have *never* known such happiness as I've had with Joan, which is perhaps what has always been wrong between us; one just can't live indefinitely at such a pitch. I think I've reached the stage, now, where I could write to Lucy. If only I thought it would help.

## 12

Driving back was a lot worse even than driving down. The state I'd been left in; trembling so much I don't know how I held the wheel straight. Because he's always known just how to upset me. When he collapses like that, it's directed right at me, I'm meant to think it's *my* fault, when all it means is he hasn't got any answer, it's just his way of escaping. Only this time, he actually came out with it, he was afraid of dying, he left because I was killing him. The filthy things that woman puts into his head.

He lay there a while, I guess, like he's done before, then as soon as he saw there was no percentage in it, he'll have jumped up again like nothing happened.

I won't forget the way the two of them were when I got there; like a couple of kids horsing around the beach, like there was nobody on earth except themselves, the most irresponsible thing I've ever seen. And the act he put on when he saw me; like it was such a wonderful surprise. And her, the incredible nerve she has, that goddam *superiority*, whatever she does has always got to be right, because *she's* done it. Well, I certainly told him, this time. What the hell does she think she looks like, anyway, with that fat body of hers, middle-aged, flopping around the beach like a seventeen-year-old? Telling me I don't even interest her, handing me this great line she's saving Kevin from me, when every time I tried to get rid of him he'd come crawling right on back. There's no one like the English for believing what they want to believe; they're the only people who can take a hand-out and treat you like they're doing you a favour. Well, this is the biggest favour Kevin's ever done me. Leaving. As for that stuff about loving me, it makes me so mad. He could actually stand there on that beach and tell me he loves me, with her right there beside him. To me, that's really sick.

How long do they think they can fool around in the sun? Sooner or later they'll have to start facing things, like what are they going to live on, or rather, she'll have to face them, because Kevin's never faced anything in his life.

Anna's been really good about it, though, she put it into its right proportion. She said, 'But it is quite grotesque, mutton behaving like lamb. You should feel sorry for the poor things; it is their last, pathetic caper, before the menopause sets in. This is not a summer, it is an Indian summer.' She said, 'I should have loved to see his face when he saw you. He must have felt quite ridiculous.'

'He certainly looked ridiculous,' I said, 'strutting around the beach like he was Hercules, or something,' and I began seeing it from this point of view; as something funny. At times when the whole thing started getting on top of me, I'd think of Kevin and the way he just froze when he saw me.

The one thing I'm sure of is that sooner or later, he'll be climbing up this hill again, and Anna thinks so, too. 'Oh, yes,' she says, 'he will come to Canossa. Barefoot, this time, like the Emperor.' I can't wait for that day. I can't wait for what I'll tell him, then. And if he wants to collapse, okay, let him collapse. That won't bother me.

## 13

In Rome again. Our idyll at an end. Kevin quite glum and grumpy now, like a tired child after a party. We're in the same hotel, and he's retired behind the papers again. It's still hot in the streets, the colours are still miraculous. I've been painting some of the Roman walls on that hill above the Colosseum; poignancy of dark brick and deep green leaves and mellow sunlight.

Kevin worries me dreadfully. *He wants to go back.* He never says so in so many words, but I know it, I can feel it. There's a strange, sinister force, pulling, pulling him back to that appalling woman and her villa, almost as though he wants to sacrifice himself. And it's too strong for me, that's the worst thing of all; I know I can't fight it. I feel him slipping out of my grasp, and there's nothing I can do. At the same time, I'm aware of something in me that disgusts me; a lurking relief. That I shan't have to carry him through the years. That I can go back to William and my comfortable, mediocre life – he still thinks I'm just staying on to paint – as if nothing ever happened.

This evening, I walked into our hotel room and he was packing his suitcase; he looked up as guiltily as if he were a burglar.

'You're going back to her,' I said, God knows it was no surprise, and he said, 'Yes.'

I said, 'You're mad.'

'I must,' he said, 'there's no alternative. You'd never understand, but there isn't.'

'You know what it means,' I said.

'Not *ne*cessarily,' he said, taking up that pitiful, defiant stance which always makes me want to hug him. 'I am *immensely* grateful to you. You've been *marvellous* to me. You have done so much for me; you've given me such hope.'

'Not enough,' I said. 'Not enough to save you,' and he shook his head. '*Why*, Kevin?' I said. 'Can't you *see* what will happen? She's got nothing for you, nothing to give anybody.'

'But that's precisely why,' he said, 'that's *why* I must go back,' with a little, dramatic lift of the head, acting to the last, right up to the scaffold. 'It's *because* she has nothing, because she has never really had anything. That matters.

No love, no security, no culture, no guidance. That's why she needs me, you see.'

And then I cried. I took him in my arms and said, 'Oh, Kevin, you're so sweet and so weak and so adorable.' Then I helped him pack his case again. He could never pack a case.

## 14

I've seen it, so I guess I just have to believe it. He's actually gone back to her, put his head right into the lion's mouth again. There they were, the two of them, large as life and arm in arm, coming straight towards me down the Via Calzaiuoli. And cut me dead. But who the hell cares?

# *John Braine*

STAY WITH ME TILL MORNING 35p

'His best work since Room at the Top' – THE OBSERVER

'John Braine's attitude to his mixed-up men and women is totally uncompromising. He strips their emotions as naked as he does their bodies' – ILLUSTRATED LONDON NEWS

'Marriage in the raw with all the romantic edges knocked off' – DAILY EXPRESS

'A damn good novel, no nonsense Braine' – QUEEN MAGAZINE

'. . . dealing with the swerves and switches of lust with sexual chicanery, and its devious relationship with affection' – THE OBSERVER